Praise for *D*

T0023264

"Imagine a noir *Friday Night Lights* written by a cross between Megan Abbott and Harry Crews . . . It's propulsive, twisty, and unputdownable . . . This is a book that shocks us into a new way of seeing. It's lean, muscled up, no-holds-barred noir."

—William Boyle, author of *Gravesend* and *The Lonely Witness*

"Eli Cranor knows the underbelly of Friday night lights in this stunning debut that bleeds authenticity and raw emotion. This young author is a new voice of the South to watch."

—Ace Atkins, *New York Times* bestselling author of *The Fallen* and *The Sinners*

"Eli Cranor is that rare writer who can make you gasp, cry and cheer often in the same paragraph."

—S.A. Cosby, *New York Times* bestselling author of *Razorblade Tears*

"A powerful and moving debut. Eli Cranor's writing is honest and unflinching. But what ultimately elevates this novel is its surprising tenderness. I read it in one sitting, and it'll stay with me."

—James Kestrel, author of *Five Decembers*, Edgar Award Finalist for Best Novel

"Gripping . . . Cranor's characters bristle with desperation and frustrated masculinity, a volatile cauldron of emotion that brings tension to every page."

—Steph Cha, author of *Your House Will Pay*

"Eli Cranor rockets to the top of the writer-to-watch lists with this debut. Gritty, emotional writing and a deep knowledge of the pain and pride that play out beneath Friday night lights make *Don't Know Tough* a gripping, memorable read." **—Michael Koryta, *New York Times* bestselling author of *Never Far Away***

"*Don't Know Tough* really packs a punch. I enjoyed reading between the lines, dreading the trouble Billy was bringing on himself and his fragile life-chances. At the heart of the book is the pull of loyalties—the football team, the family and religion. The characters involved in all the stresses and strains are well drawn and convincing. It's tough reading, but the humanity shines through."

—Peter Lovesey, author of the Peter Diamond mysteries, in his adjudication of the Peter Lovesey First Crime Novel Contest

"The comparison to *Friday Night Lights* will jump out at readers of this hard-as-nails debut thriller, but, in fact, beyond the thematic link to high-school football, the two stories live in very different worlds. In the celebrated TV show, there is a sense of possibility; in Cranor's novel, as in the best genuine noirs, there is only inevitability."

—*Booklist*, Starred Review

"At once a crime novel packed with violence and desperation, a modern Southern Gothic tale drenched in darkness, and a touching, brutally honest take on football as religion." **—Gabino Iglesias, *Southwest Review***

DON'T KNOW TOUGH

Also by Eli Cranor

Ozark Dogs

DON'T KNOW TOUGH

ELI CRANOR

SOHO CRIME

Copyright © 2022 Eli Cranor
All rights reserved.

This is a work of fiction. Names, characters, places, and incidents either are the product of the author's imagination or are used fictitiously, and any resemblance to actual persons, living or dead, businesses, companies, events, or locales is entirely coincidental.

Published by
Soho Press, Inc.
227 W 17th Street
New York, NY 10011

Library of Congress Cataloging-in-Publication Data

Names: Cranor, Eli, author.
Title: Don't know tough / Eli Cranor.
Description: New York, NY : Soho Crime, [2022]
Identifiers: LCCN 2021035665

ISBN 978-1-64129-456-0
eISBN 978-1-64129-346-4

Subjects: LCGFT: Sports fiction. | Detective and mystery fiction. | Novels.
Classification: LCC PS3603.R38565 D66 2022 | DDC 813'.6—dc23
LC record available at https://lccn.loc.gov/2021035665

Interior design by Janine Agro

Printed in the United States of America

10 9 8 7 6 5 4 3 2 1

for Mal, the toughest woman I know

There is no knowing what is in a man's heart.

—Charles Portis, *True Grit*

DON'T KNOW TOUGH

1.

Still feel the burn on my neck. Told Coach it was a ringworm this morning when he pick me up, but it ain't. It a cigarette, or at least what a lit cigarette do when it stuck in your neck. Just stared at Him when He did it. No way I's gonna let Him see me hurt. No way. Bit a hole through the side of my cheek, swallowed blood, and just stared at Him. Tasted blood all day.

Tasted it while I sat in Ms. Miller's class. Woke up in Algebra tasting it. Drank milk from a cardboard box at lunch and still, I tasted it. But now it eighth period football. Coach already got the boys lined up on either side of the fifty, a crease in between, a small space for running and tackling, for pain.

This my favorite drill.

I just been standing back here, watching the other boys go at it. The sound of pads popping like sheet metal flapping in a storm.

"Who want next?" holler Bull. Bull ain't the head coach. Bull coach the defense. He as mean as they come.

I tongue the hole in my cheek, finger the cigarette burn on my neck, and step into the crease. Coach hand me the ball and smile. He know what kind a power I got. Senior year, too. They got that sophomore linebacker lined up across from me. The one with the rich daddy that always paying for everything.

Coach blow his whistle.

I can see Him smiling as He stuck the hot tip in my neck, smiling when He put Little Brother out in the pen. I grip the ball tight, duck my head, and run at sophomore linebacker, hoping to kill him.

When we hit, there real lightning, thunder explode across the field. The back of sophomore linebacker head the first thing to hit the ground, arms out like Jesus on the cross. I step on his neck and run past him.

The other boys cheer.

Coach blow his whistle and already the linebacker getting up like I ain't nothing. He shaking his head, laughing, and standing again. Disrespecting me?

Disrespecting *me*?

This time I spear him with the top my helmet. Dive and go head to head. There's a cracking sound—not thunder, not lightning, and damn sure not sheet metal—this the sound of my heart breaking, the sound of violence pouring out.

Coach blow his whistle like somebody drowning. Sophomore linebacker scream cause he don't know what's on him. This boy a poser. He don't know tough. Don't know nothing. Bet his momma woke him up this morning with some milk and cookies. I try to bite his cheek off, but the facemask, the mouthpiece. I see only red, then black—a cigarette, a dog pen.

Sitting outside Principal office after practice when Coach call me in. Principal a big man, soft in places used to be hard. He look like a football coach, got a black mustache and everything. Coach look like he from California cause he is, hair all slick and parted. And skinny. Too damn skinny.

"Bill," say Coach. "What happened out there?"

Bill my daddy's name. Nobody call me Bill except Coach and my brother Jesse.

"You realize the kind a shit you in?" Principal say, cussing for me, trying to make me feel at home. "That boy you stomped? His daddy liable to sue the whole damn school."

Feel my jaw flexing, like if I could, I just grind my teeth down to the gums.

"You hear us talking, boy?" say Principal.

I raise one eyebrow, slow.

"Swear to God," say Principal. "Tell you what I ought to do. What I ought to do is call Sheriff Timmons. How about that? Let him charge your little ass with battery."

I nod. Know bullshit when I hear it. Then Coach say, "But he's not going to do that."

Principal grunt.

"Listen, Bill," say Coach. "I'm going to sit you for the game tomorrow night. Principal Bradshaw thinks that's best. Okay?"

I hear Coach but I don't. My ears ringing. That burn on my neck turn to fire.

"Call the cops then."

Principal laugh. Coach don't.

"We've already qualified for the playoffs," say Coach. "You'll be back next week, and then we'll be going for the real goal—the state championship."

"Senior Night," I say.

Coach breathe in deep through his nose. He ain't got no idea what it mean to my momma to walk across that field on Senior Night. What it mean to me. Have them call out my name, my momma name, and everybody in Denton ring them cowbells, stand and cheer? Something like that outside Momma's mind. And now they trying to take that from her, from me?

Coach look to Principal, but he already turned away, looking at something on his computer. "Bill," say Coach, "I think this is fair. It's as good as I can do."

I nod, waiting for Principal to say something, at least look up from that computer and see what he just took from me, but he don't. Whatever on that screen bigger than Billy Lowe. I'm out the door before he ever turn back, running with blood in my mouth.

"Aw, *hell* nah," say Momma.

Little Brother dangle from her arm like a monkey. Tiny fingers, white at the knuckles, holding on to her shirt like he know how it feel to be dropped. And Coach wonder why I ain't never fumbled, not once.

"Senior Night? And Coach Powers sitting you? For what, Billy? What'd you do?"

"Nothing."

"Don't lie."

"Just a drill, at practice. Hit a boy hard, real hard. Just kept hitting him."

"*Football* practice?"

"Yeah."

"Nah, hell nah," say Momma.

Momma already got the phone out, already dialing Coach when He walk in, smelling like beer-sweat and gouch.

"Who she calling?" He say to me.

I just stare at Him. Don't say nothing.

"*Boy.*"

"Coach."

He make a jab for the phone. Momma jerk away. Little Brother hold strong.

"Calling Coach," say Momma. "Done kicked Billy off the team."

"He ain't kicked me off. Just—"

"*Naw*," He say, grabbing Momma by the shirt now, pawing for the phone. "No fucking way—"

"Yes, hello? Coach Powers?" Momma say, but it ain't her voice. It the voice she use when she talk to the water company, DHS, teachers, and Coach. She talking fancy and slow. Don't sound nothing like her. "This is Billy's momma."

The man who live in our trailer but ain't my daddy start pacing. He got a bottle of NyQuil in His hand. Drink NyQuil most the time, save His whiskey up. He pull from the bottle and wipe His mouth with the back a His sleeve.

"Billy say he ain't gonna play? On Senior Night?" Momma stop rocking Little Brother. Look at me. "Austin Murphy got a concussion? Was out cold for five minutes?"

He start to laugh. "Shit yeah. That's my boy."

"Alright," say Momma. "I understand, Coach."

She still got the phone to her ear when He take it. "Billy the only fucking chance you got. You hear me? Either let him play or we take his ass down the road to Taggard. How about that?"

He chug the NyQuil some more. Don't even know how stupid He is. Cain't change schools this late in the season.

"Yeah. That right, *Coach*. See you at the game, and if Billy don't play—Billy don't *play*." He jab the phone screen three time with His thumb then throw it at Momma. She try to get out the way. Little Brother hold tight, but the phone corner hit him in the back, a sad, hollow sound. Little Brother look like he about to cry, but he don't.

Kept my mouth shut when I left the trailer the next morning. Didn't say nothing to Him on my way out. Didn't have to. The NyQuil bottle empty. Everything empty when I left Shady Grove.

Now it game time, and Coach still letting me run through the tunnel and the paper the cheerleaders spent all day coloring. Even say he gonna let me walk out on the field at halftime for Senior Night. But I ain't told Momma. He'd wanna walk too, and I'll be damned if He get to walk out there like He my daddy. I stay in the back. The band blow they horns, but they ain't blowing them for me. Used to blow them loud and sing the fight song when Billy Lowe run across the goal line.

Sophomore linebacker here. In a wheelchair, God, a fucking *wheelchair*. Ain't nothing wrong with his legs. Wearing sunglasses too. I walk up behind that wheelchair, just stand there, while our team getting beat by Lutherville. Lutherville sorry as hell, but the Pirates ain't got shit without Billy Lowe. Still standing there behind that wheelchair, smelling sophomore linebacker hair—smell like girl hair—when I hear Him start hollering from the stands.

"Ain't got shit without Billy Lowe!"

I go to gnawing my cheek.

"Bes play ma Billy!"

Now Momma too, and I can tell by her slur, she gone. I look back quick to the bleachers, time enough to see Little Brother dangling from her arms with his Billy Lowe jersey on: number thirty-five.

"Fuck this shit."

"Yeah. Fuuuuck this shit."

Ain't no telling them apart now.

Coach a true believer, though. He out near the twenty, fighting for a holding call. Don't see Principal wading through the stands like a linebacker on a backside blitz.

"Nah, hell nah. Don't touch me."

That's Momma. She see Principal coming for her.

"Swear to God," He say, like He the kind a man do something about it. He ain't. He all talk and shit and empty bottles. "Swear to God, you touch her and—"

"Boy, you listen," yell Principal at Him. "You touch me and I'll have the sheriff up here faster than greased lightning. You hear me?"

Sophomore linebacker stand and push them sunglasses up in his shampoo hair. Probably thinking they about to fight, but I know He won't do shit. Principal ain't a kid like Little Brother. And He know Principal would get the sheriff up there, and the sheriff got Tasers and clubs, and He don't want no part of that.

"We going, alright?" He say. "We gone."

Lutherville got to punt. Coach turn to the sideline to holler for the offense, and he finally see. I still got my back to them, but I know it ugly, embarrassing too. Feel them hot on my neck. I look to Coach to save me. Just put me in the game, send me to the locker room, take me by the facemask and beat the hell out me, anything, but don't leave me standing here on this sideline.

"Come on, Billy!"

It Momma.

"Take my boy down the road!" she holler. "Take Billy Lowe to run the ball at Taggard!"

Roll my neck. The burn cracks. Hot blood on my back. My mouth a open wound. I think about spitting on sophomore linebacker, covering his face with my crazy. But I'm watching him watch my people in the stands. Watching Momma and Little Brother just holding on. I look one more time to Coach, but it third and six and he got to call a play. Sophomore linebacker still watching Momma holler for me. Watching Him too. Everybody know they drunk now, and it embarrassing, fucking embarrassing.

Then sophomore linebacker save me. He elbow another sophomore in the ribs, kinda point up in the stands, point right over me like I ain't nothing. And now he laughing and pointing at my momma, at Little Brother.

"Come on, *son*, fuck this place," He yell, but He ain't my daddy, and that does it.

This time there more blood. My blood. His blood. Little Brother blood. The blood that connect us. I feel Bull tugging at my jersey. I seen a cop try and pull a pit bull off a Lab once. Had to pry the jaws loose with a billy club. I'm head-buttin the boy now. Got his arms nailed down, head-buttin him when Bull finally pull me loose.

As he dragging me away, I see Coach over there, kneeling beside sophomore linebacker. Look like he whispering something in his ear. Bet he saying, "Billy didn't mean it. Billy a good kid, heck of a running back too. Billy just got it tough. And his momma crazy and won't stop fucking. And the other day he got a cigarette stuck in his neck, and he took it like a man, and that was after his momma boyfriend put his little brother out in a dog pen, and he had to take that baby boy scraps for lunch and dinner, then breakfast the next day. Billy didn't mean nothing by it. He was just embarrassed, stuck on that sideline, right there close to them, close enough to feel the heat. Can you imagine? You imagine that, sophomore linebacker?"

No. You cain't.

2.

Arkansas happened quickly, like a tornado. In just under twenty-four hours Trent Powers drove his family the sixteen hundred miles from California, interstates leading to highways, highways revealing the occasional town, the countryside, and eventually their journey ended at a single hanging traffic light. Beyond the light was Denton, Arkansas. When Trent arrived, the football field—a hundred yards, lined and marked with white paint—was the only thing he recognized.

That's how Trent had explained the trip to his only assistant coach, Butch Kennedy. Butch can still remember the starry look in the young coach's eyes his first day on the job, like Trent couldn't believe where he'd landed. Denton was a long-ass way from California.

Seventy-some-odd days later and the two coaches are lining the field, heat rising up from the grass, remnants of an Indian summer burning on through November. Butch has been an assistant for nearly his entire thirty-year career with the Denton Pirates, a man the boys refer to as Bull. He's short and wiry, bent from the grind of the gridiron, sunspots and moles marring his thin, pale skin. Bull helps Trent with the paint, the laundry, the defense. Everything. Bull knows football. Bull knows Denton.

Trent admitted he'd never painted a field before Arkansas, only artificial green turf in California. It's tedious work, each line a representation of his patience, each line either crooked or straight.

"Young ball coaches always in a hurry."

This is Bull's only advice.

"Right," says Trent, hustling the paint carriage across the fifty-yard line.

"Going too fast, Hollywood."

"Please, don't call me that."

"Gonna have to get the green paint out."

Trent swings wide of the fifty, jerking like a distracted driver hitting a rumble strip. Bull shakes his head. He knows what—or better yet—*who* is troubling the young coach.

With an older brother who holds most of the school records for touchdowns and tackles, Billy Lowe has Pirate blood in his veins. He's a sawed-off white boy with tree-trunk thighs, built hard and low to the ground, trapezius muscles bulging up from his shoulders to his earlobes. No neck. A pit bull.

Bull knew there weren't kids like Billy in California. Bull doubted there were kids like Billy anywhere else in the world. Arkansas hills produce crazy like the Earth's mantle produces diamonds: enough heat and pressure to make all things hard.

Bull already has the green paint out, spraying over the crooked fifty-yard line, when Trent makes it across the field and turns to him.

"What are you doing?" says Trent.

"Crooked line."

"We have bigger concerns than this field."

"Ain't that the truth." Bull grunts, shaking his head. "Everything was fine until Blood Alley."

The Blood Alley drill is outlawed in most states. It's actually illegal in Arkansas, but in a place like Denton, a small town nestled in the foothills of the Ozark Mountains where poultry farms and trailers outnumber any other signs of civilization, the law is bendy like a chicken's neck. Blood Alley is football at its most primitive: one boy with a ball, one boy without, the rest of the team lined up on either side, any hope of escape afforded only through violence. It's something you do early, back in August when the players don the pads for the first time. But Trent had pushed for it on a Thursday in November, the last practice before Senior Night. And though Bull liked the crack of a solid hit as much as the next man—probably more—he knew the drill was not a good idea, not that close to game time, not this late in the season. High school boys are quick to blow their load.

The drill was fine until Billy got involved. Bull could see it in his eyes. See it before the boy ever took the ball and flattened their sophomore linebacker, Austin Murphy.

"I'm not painting that line again," says Trent. "I can barely think straight."

"What's your plan for Billy?"

"I've scheduled some meetings for today."

Bull takes the paint carriage from Trent and starts back across the fifty, straight and slow, an old man feeling his way with a cane. "Meetings?"

"Yes, Bull. Principal Bradshaw wanted to talk about what happened last night. So I told him to stop by this afternoon. Billy and his mother are coming in after we finish up."

"Billy stomps a mud hole in Austin Murphy on Thursday, then does it again on Friday—on Senior Night—and you schedule some *meetings*?"

"So we can talk about it."

"Don't take Billy for the talking kind."

"What's that supposed to mean?"

"Means don't get in a hurry, Hollywood." Bull produces a buck knife from the back pocket of his jeans, flicks the blade open, and goes to picking his teeth.

"Is that necessary?" says Trent.

"Always thought it a fitting nickname."

"The knife, Bull. Is that even legal to have on school grounds?"

The old man studies the young coach, trying to make sense of him. The locals have had trouble drawing a bead on Trent Powers, too. In Denton, football is as big as it gets: pride and pageantry, parades on homecoming, all the shops closing down on Fridays, even the Walmart. Now the Pirates are in the playoffs for the first time in years. But when Trent Powers rolled into town driving that silver Toyota Prius, football was about the furthest thing from the townsfolk's minds. Ball coaches, at least in Arkansas, drive trucks—preferably Fords.

Bull walks on, painting the field one slow line at a time. Trent stays behind, gripping the ball tight, but Bull knows he's scared. All the years he's spent watching high school boys step onto the gridiron—the old man can smell fear. Bull reeked of it nearly thirty years ago when he had his one shot as head coach of the Pirates. He was younger than

Trent but just as eager. He was in a hurry too, wanting the glory without having paid the price, the pain. And then he pushed those boys too far in the heat of an Arkansas summer.

"You ever think about why we do what we do?" Bull says as he walks.

Trent tosses the ball up. Catches it. "Of course."

"Busted knees, shattered shoulders, not to mention all them shots to the head—that sit right with you?"

"It's part of the game."

"But there's the problem," says Bull. "It's just a game."

Trent stops, staring at the ball in his hands. "Football is a tool, Bull. We should use it to teach our boys how to be better husbands and fathers—better *men.*" He runs his fingers along the ball's white laces. "We should use the game to sharpen them. It's all part of God's plan."

"You're in the Bible Belt now, Hollywood," Bull says, throwing up his free hand but still keeping a steady line. "Everybody's on the same team down here. *God's* team."

"It's one thing to be on the team, and another thing entirely to truly believe," Trent says, still standing with the ball at midfield. "Back when I was a boy—back when I was lost—a coach saved me. And that's exactly what I plan to do for Bill Lowe."

Bull grunts and walks on, already halfway across the field again. He pushes the carriage slower, barely moving at all. Paint hisses from the can. A plume of white rises in the morning sun. Bull hopes Trent is watching, hopes the young coach will at least understand the field before he puts eleven boys on it and sets them in motion.

Bull stops. His chin goes to his shoulder. The field stands half lined and empty behind him.

Before Trent opens the door to his office, he pauses, hand on the knob, and offers up a quick prayer asking for wisdom. Trent prays with his eyes open, just as he'd been taught: *Pray without ceasing*. Memories from California clash with the words in his head, recollections of a meeting that feels eerily similar to the one he's about to have with Denton High's principal. Trent whispers, "Amen," and turns the knob.

As the door opens, a thick waft of Stetson cologne rushes out. Don Bradshaw's just sitting there, wearing Wrangler jeans, Tony Lama boots, and a pearl snap shirt. The top three buttons are undone, exposing a thick patch of curly black hair. He has the same rawhide looks as Bull, but there's something different about Bradshaw, more flare, more style, or maybe it's just his mustache. Jet-black. Like it's been drawn on with a permanent marker.

Jesus hangs from a cross above Trent's head as he positions himself behind his ergonomic metal desk—better suited for a tech company in Silicon Valley—and takes a seat in the oversized leather chair. Trent bought all new furniture over the summer; he couldn't stomach the ratty stuff he'd inherited. The air is thick with cowboy cologne, a leathery floral aroma that burns Trent's nostrils.

Bradshaw gets right to it: "We need to talk."

"What's up?"

"What's *up*?" Bradshaw says, running two fingers down the length of his mustache. "What's *up* is a shit-storm, and you're sitting in the eye of it."

Trent leans back in his chair, shaken by the principal's tone. It reminds him of his father-in-law, Larry Dommers, who also happened to be Trent's former athletic director back in California.

"You don't know the Lowes like I do," Bradshaw says. "They moved in from Eastern Arkansas about ten years ago, a whole horde of them. You ever noticed how Billy kinda talks funny?"

"I've noticed his dialect is different from our other players."

Bradshaw wrinkles his nose. "Yeah, he talks Black, Coach, and it's because all the Lowes come from the Delta side of Arkansas, over close to Memphis. And that's dark, *dark* country."

"Mr. Bradshaw, I don't see what this has to do with anything."

"It's different over there. Don't know how to put it, but I know one thing—you got to know how to handle a Lowe."

"Handle them? Come on. I believe God—"

"Wait till you meet Jesse Lowe," Bradshaw says, popping a can of tobacco, "then tell me what you think about God." The principal licks at the snuff, great heaps of it sticking to his tongue. "Jesse was the first. Came through here about ten years ago and was as good a quarterback as I've ever seen."

Trent sits forward at the mention of a quarterback.

"Jesse's dumb as shit too. I'm talking dumb, dumb, *dumb*. And you know a quarterback got to be kinda smart, right? Not Jesse. He was that damn good. Fast, strong, and could throw a ball a quarter mile."

Bradshaw pauses, working the wad of tobacco around with his tongue.

"Jesse's senior year we're playing Taggard. Only takes Jess three plays to score. Runs the ball twice himself. Then on the third play, he throws a pass. It gets tipped up—and I shit you not—he runs under the thing, catches it, and goes on to score a touchdown. Jesse Lowe threw Jesse Lowe a touchdown pass. I shit you not."

Trent licks his lips. Swallows.

"Taggard scores quick. So we get the ball back, and on the first play we call another run with Jesse. Figure if it ain't broke, don't fix it. But Taggard knew it was coming, so they stuffed him at the line."

Bradshaw picks tobacco from his tongue, eyes scanning the office for a place to spit.

"And?" says Trent.

"Big Jess yanks his helmet off, throws it about ten rows into the visiting stands—the Taggard stands—and storms off the field. Bull goes in to check on him, but Jesse's long gone. Left his mark, though. Coaches' office, locker room, three cars in the parking lot—all beat to hell. Looked like he took a sledgehammer to them. But it weren't no hammer, Coach. No sir."

Trent leans back in his chair, arms crossed, hugging himself. "What was it? What'd he beat the cars with?"

"Used his bare hands, like a goddamn animal. Then, not two days later, Jesse Lowe came right back into this office we're sitting in now, before you went and bought all this fancy furniture." The principal paws at the ergonomic desk. "And asks that coach when he was getting his starting spot back." Bradshaw laughs, tongue out. "You believe that?"

Trent shakes his head.

"Well, it's Gospel. Saw it with my own eyes. But now here's the shit-kicker."

"The shit-kicker?"

"Yeah. That coach—four coaches before you—he *let* Jesse come back. Let him start at quarterback the next week. Didn't even sit him for the first half. Nothing." Bradshaw runs his fingers through his mustache again. "That's the beginning of the end."

"Right," says Trent, waiting for Bradshaw to say more, eyes drifting around the office, landing on a picture hanging by the door. It's a photo of Trent's daughters after one of the few wins back in California. The older one is wearing Trent's hat. The younger chews on his whistle. They are both smiling. Trent doubts if he's seen them both smile at the same time since the family arrived in Arkansas. The memory is broken when Bradshaw huffs, "So what's your plan?"

Trent clears his throat. "I've spoken with Sheriff Timmons. He said the altercation is out of his jurisdiction. I'm going to meet with Billy and his mother later this afternoon."

Bradshaw puckers his lips as if he were finally going to spit, but instead swallows. "If I's you, my plan would be to call Timmons back and have him scare the boy a bit. You got to train boys like Billy, same way you would a dog."

"Stop, just stop," says Trent, waving his hands. "He's a boy, Mr. Bradshaw."

"Eighteen. Checked his records before I came down."

"Eighteen, whatever. Listen, I believe in second chances. I'm here to make a difference in these boys' lives."

Bradshaw rolls the tobacco to the front of his teeth. Trent cringes, offering up his favorite coffee cup, a Father's Day gift from a few years before. The wad makes a wet, sucking sound when it hits the bottom.

"If you don't put a collar on that boy," Bradshaw says, standing and licking his lips, "he'll tear your whole world apart, one piece at a time, just like he done Austin."

"We'll see," says Trent, but it comes out sharper than he intended.

"Damn straight. We'll *see*."

The way Bradshaw's tone shifts reminds Trent how his father-in-law—his old boss—could make him feel like a child just by lowering his voice, the same tone Coach Dommers used right before the Powers family packed up and headed for Arkansas.

Trent stands despite the memory. "Wait. Are you trying to tell me something?"

"Feel like I already said it."

"If this is about Bill—"

"Nothing around here's about Billy Lowe," Bradshaw snarls. "But Mr. Murphy—Austin's daddy—he's a good man. A manager over at Tyson's big chicken plant. Helps out with the school and the boosters. Helps out in a big way."

"Austin will be fine. He just—"

"You and I both know Austin Murphy's soft as shit, but that don't mean he needs to get skull drug by a Lowe boy on the sideline during goddamn Senior Night."

"I told you, I'll get a plan together for Bill."

"You do that, Coach," says Bradshaw. He takes a step toward the door but stops, studying the picture of

Trent's daughters hanging on the wall. "Pretty girls you got there."

The bald spot on the back of Bradshaw's head has thin, sideways hair, slicked down in brittle lines with gel. He gives Trent a moment more to respond then says, "Must be hard on them. Moving to these hills. Like living in a new country."

"We've all made sacrifices," says Trent.

"You ever notice that sign when you drive into town?"

Trent knows the sign but doesn't answer, afraid he's already said too much.

"The GATEWAY TO THE OZARKS sign?" Bradshaw turns, smiling. A brown line of tobacco juice drips down his chin. "Denton's about thirty miles from anything. Folks come up here to get away from the things they don't like. Don't want people bothering them, especially certain kinds of people."

Trent puts a hand to his own chin and rubs it.

"People that talk like Billy," Bradshaw adds.

"But Bill is—"

"There's been some speculation as to his daddy's blood." Bradshaw drags a hairy knuckle across the tobacco stain. "And it don't help matters that one of them Lowe boys got LaCreesha Montgomery pregnant about a year back."

"Come *on*," says Trent. "If I'm not mistaken, Denton has a deputy that's of color."

"Rome?"

Trent shrugs.

"High yella," Bradshaw says. "Deputy Montgomery about as Black as they get around here."

"So you're saying I shouldn't play Bill because you think his father is Black?"

Bradshaw coughs into his fist, shaking his head. "I'm saying there's an order to things in Denton. Hell, even Jesse Lowe didn't curb stomp the son of the school's biggest booster."

Trent studies the principal's forehead; the wrinkles there are almost perfectly straight, like the lines on a field. "Why didn't you tell me all of this before?"

"Seemed like you had everything figured out when you got here," Bradshaw says. "And I'll tell you what else. You need to let boys like Austin Murphy get a chance to score every once in a while. Or things could go from bad to worse."

"Are you threatening me?"

Bradshaw hustles the crotch of his pants, an old football tic. "That little fancy car you drive's hard to swallow, and you're way out of your league with Billy Lowe." He pauses, popping the tobacco can again, adding another pinch. "But it's damn hard to argue with a state championship."

The air conditioner clicks on and cold air fills the room. Trent tries to think of something to say, watching as Bradshaw pockets the can and turns to leave.

"You're not worried?"

Bradshaw stops. "Worried?"

"That stuff you're cramming into your lip, isn't it dangerous?"

Bradshaw digs the can out of his pocket, bringing it up close to his face, reading the label: "Molasses, corn silk, kudzu root, salt, and cayenne pepper." He grins as he tosses the can onto Trent's desk. "No real bite and it tastes like shit, but damn if I ain't three weeks tobacco free."

Trent takes the can, turning it over in his hand. HERBAL SNUFF is written in blocky letters across the front. Bradshaw shuts the door easy on his way out. Trent melts into the oversized leather chair, letting his head fall back. A teary-eyed Jesus stares down at him from the cross.

Thirty minutes later, Trent is still trying to digest Bradshaw's ultimatum as he waits for the Lowes to arrive. There's a piece of white paper on his desk. His new plan. It's written in *Impact* font, complete with a bulleted list and a little space for both Billy and Tina to sign their names. Everything is outlined in black-and-white.

Trent's fingers tremble as he runs them across the paper. His coffee mug, the one with DADDY'S BIGGEST FAN stamped across the front, is empty, scrubbed clean of Bradshaw's herbal snuff stain. Trent sets the paper perfectly in the center of his desk and rummages for a pen. When he looks up, Billy and Tina are standing before him, effigies of themselves: a clown-faced trailer woman wearing too much makeup, and a sullen, angry boy dressed like a rapper in a music video. Billy's little brother claws at his mother's arms, takes one look at Trent, and begins to wail. Billy steps forward, offering his hand. Trent takes it and feels the rough calluses of the boy's palm, the warmth there. The heat.

Trent wants to tell them everything will be fine, wants to ask them to pray, but thinks of his conversations with Bradshaw and Bull. Trent clears his throat before he says, "I have some good news and some bad news."

The smile drains from Billy's face.

3.

"*Some good news and some bad news*"?

Who start a meeting like that? Really, who even say something like that? Keep my mouth shut. Momma bite, though, saying, "Tell us the good news first."

"The good news—" say Coach, but Little Brother still howling.

"Sorry," say Momma.

"It's fine," say Coach, but the way he say it—his face, his mouth—tell me it ain't. Hadn't figured him for a liar until right then. And now I'm worrying, worrying even more when he finally decide to just talk over Little Brother, like he talking over the school bell.

"The good news is Bill will remain on the team."

"What the bad news then?" say Momma, bringing it on faster than she got to.

"The bad news," say Coach and he take hold of the paper on his desk, push it toward us, "is Bill will be suspended for the first half of the playoff game."

I'm still trying to read the top that paper, the little black letters that say BILLY LOWE SUSPENSION PROTOCOL, some shit like that, when he say that line about me being suspended and it all come down fast. Feel so stupid cause I should a worn a cutoff shirt instead of my LeBron jersey.

Shouldn't a combed my hair none. And Momma, God, Momma probably put ten bucks' worth a makeup on. For what? To come hear this shit?

"Billy?" say Momma. "You hear Coach?"

I just keep staring, making my way down each little line on that paper.

"And as for the police," say Coach. "I've spoken with Sheriff Timmons. As long as you complete all of your community service hours, you are good to go."

I look up from the sheet. "Community service?"

"You know, pick up trash, stuff like that, on the weekends."

I hear Momma click her teeth cause she know. She know He the one that pick up trash. He a garbageman, and I'll be goddamned if Coach think he gonna make me one, too.

"That ain't so bad," say Momma.

"Bill?" say Coach.

"Ain't picking up no trash."

Momma start explaining to Coach how I don't like Him, how her boyfriend and me don't get along, but it bullshit. It all bullshit. I make a fist. I stand.

I slap the paper on the desk. Then I start punching it. Hit that paper again and again. Turn it red. Feel like I'm watching it all on camera. Feel like I'll probably be watching it on replay in Principal Bradshaw office on Monday when he telling me why I'm in trouble. But I just keep punching that paper cause I don't know what else to do. Little Brother go quiet. This something he know. This fancy office, that big ass desk, those leather chairs—them things outside Little Brother mind. But me beating that paper to shit? He know that.

Momma scream, "Stop it, Billy! God, stop it!"

My knuckles drip red on the fancy desk. Coach look scared. There power in fear. If He ain't taught me nothing, He taught me that. I can see again. I breathe out, slow, count to ten like them counselors been telling me to since first grade. Then I nod and start for the door. See if Coach gonna call my bluff.

"Wait, wait," say Coach, and I know right then I got him—he want it too bad. Momma know too. Crying like she really mean it now. Crying and bouncing Little Brother. Putting it on thick.

I open the office door. See a picture of Coach weird-ass daughter hanging there. She smiling, almost laughing, like Austin Murphy laugh at Momma on the sideline. I take one step out the door.

"Wait, Bill," say Coach. "I'm sure we can work something out."

"I ain't picking up no trash."

"It the trash that got him so hot," say Momma. "Travis, my boyfriend, Billy just cain't stand Travis."

Coach stand now too, and Momma stop talking. "This boyfriend," say Coach, "he sounds like a source of pain."

"Naw," I say. "He ain't nothing."

"Has he ever," Coach pause, looking from Momma to Little Brother then back to me, "caused you any harm?"

Just stand there, don't say nothing, knowing damn well Coach saw that burn on my neck. "He ain't hit me, if that what you asking."

Coach got a look in his eyes, something I ain't never seen from him. "Are you sure, Bill?"

"He ain't hit me."

Momma still crying, but it different now. It real. There a little gash right below her left cheek that say everything she ain't never gonna say to Coach.

"Okay," he say, his voice low. "Let me get my pen."

The first pen he grab is red. He go to write on that sheet of paper, go to scratch out "community service," and it don't make no mark. I done made my mark on that paper, got my red all over it.

He find another pen, a black one. He draw a line through "community service." He push the paper to me. "How's that?"

I look down the list. He probably think I cain't read. So I prove it. "'Read apology to team'?"

Coach take the paper from me and look at it hard.

"You'll need to write an apology and read it to the team. Let them know you're sorry for what you did to Austin."

I swallow. Momma done crying now. I hear her sniffle like she about to start up again. I cut her off. "What if I ain't sorry?"

"*Billy*," say Momma.

Coach lean back in his fancy chair.

"Is that how you really feel, Bill? Have you prayed about it?"

"Nah," I say, knowing God don't wanna hear none a my shit. He got bigger things to worry about than Billy Lowe. "I ain't prayed about it."

"Would you?" say Coach, holding that paper tight. "Would you at least pray about it?"

Momma ain't crying no more but I know she could start up any second.

"I guess."

Coach smile like I ain't never seen a man smile before. Smile bigger than when we won all them games before Lutherville. But what he smiling for now ain't real. Ain't got nothing against Austin, not really. But if he laugh at me again, I kill him. Know that much. It ain't Austin I's mad at. Just mad. You supposed to be sorry for being mad? God forgive something like that?

"Okay," say Coach, still grinning as he slide the paper over to me. Don't look much like a paper no more. He pass me the black pen. Momma kinda smiling now too. I sign it: *Billy Lowe #35.*

Momma driving His shitty little Nissan Sentra. Empty bottles so thick in the floorboard cain't help but step on them, getting my Jordans all nasty. I already told Momma not to say nothing: don't say nothing about Coach, about the suspension, none of it. Told her just to keep it between us.

"Alright, baby."

She put the car in park and cut the lights. The trailer go dark, looking tiny and rusted like His shit car. There one blue light glowing through a window. I know He in there. Can almost smell him. Drunk already, watching TV, and still pissed cause I didn't play on Senior Night.

"He just mad cause it mean so much to him," Momma say.

"To *Him*?"

"He care, Billy, more than you know."

"He don't care about nothing."

"You ever see him up in them stands? Always got his little headphones on, listening to that radio, wanting to hear what them men say about you."

"Don't mean nothing."

"He just wanted to walk out on that field, hear the announcer call all our names, like a—"

"—family?" I say. "Shit. He weren't gonna walk with me anyway."

"Just trying to tell you how he think."

"I know how He think."

"I won't say nothing," say Momma.

"Promise?"

"I'd jump the moon for you, baby. Ain't you learned that?"

"Yeah, Momma. I know."

Momma the first one through the door. Trailer small, one bathroom, two bedrooms, and this big room with the kitchen and the TV and the sofa. Momma eyes go wide like she happy to see Him, but she ain't. I know it fake. He got a job at Denton Waste Management, tossing trash cans all day. Momma like the money cause she ain't got no job, just kids, and she only get paid so much for her boys.

"Hey, baby."

He don't say nothing, just sitting there, Waste Management work shirt unbuttoned, one hand down His pants, the other balancing a bottle of NyQuil on His gut. Got those stupid headphones on too. Don't nobody wear headphones like that no more.

"Travis?" say Momma. "You hear me?"

"Yup."

"You ain't gonna say hello?"

"Nope."

Momma huff and set Little Brother on the floor. "Well, I's gonna fix something to eat."

"Saturday night," He say and raise up His little radio. "Talking Pirate ball on the local channel. I ain't hungry."

"These boys hungry."

"Let Billy fix supper. He gone be a bitch, let him do bitch work."

"*Travis.*"

Feel it now, this what I been waiting for. He been waiting for it too, probably sitting there, getting good and drunk, listening to them men talk about how Billy Lowe the reason the Pirates lost, working up the balls to come at me. I take one step toward Him, one step that way, but Momma feel it. She heading toward the sofa now, and I can tell by the way she moving, the way she plop down in His lap, she trying to save me the only way she know how.

Little Brother just sitting there, staring off into nothing. This the worst part, maybe worse than the cigarette, or even the dog pen. The way they just woller like that on the sofa. Don't even care they kids around.

"So you gonna try and fuck for Billy now?" He say.

Momma put a finger over His lips and giggle. Momma used to be pretty. I seen the pictures, but them pictures ain't been through what she been through. Momma dark hair shine wet in the blue glow of the TV. He keep pulling at her shirt.

"Come on, Travis," she say. "Let's gone back to the bed."

He don't say nothing, just grunt and keep tugging at her. He wanna do it right there. Want me to see what He gonna do to my momma. Gonna have to hear it—ain't no way not to hear it, or feel the trailer shaking—but I ain't got to see it.

I pick Little Brother up. We walking back to our room when all the grunting and slurping stop and He say, "The hell?"

My feet go cold.

"*Billy Lowe Suspension Protocol?*" He say. "Coach sitting you for the first playoff game too?"

I ain't got to turn to know what He got in His hand. Guess it fell out Momma pocket. There won't be no stopping Him now, no stopping what's coming. I set Little Brother on the floor, look up at Him waving that little white paper in His hand, pointing at it. His yellow underwear sticking straight out from Momma, and I know, right then, this what I been waiting for my whole life.

4.

Trent pushes the pedal on his Prius all the way down. The engine doesn't roar, but instead purrs electric, like a golf cart. The car zips down Main Street, over the Arkansas River, cutting its way through downtown and past Denton's lone McDonald's. Trucks line the parking lot. Trent knows they're in there—old men wearing camouflage and fluorescent orange, talking about deer hunting, liberals, and football. Trent knows too, if they saw him they'd say something about the Prius. His little car was all anyone could talk about when he'd first arrived.

"What you driving, Coach?"

"A Prius. Gets fifty miles to the gallon."

"That right?"

"Yes."

"Alright then, *Coach*."

A month ago, Trent added a Pirate helmet decal to the back window, a gnarly flag with a skull and crossbones. It had helped, but not enough. As the Prius purrs into the driveway, a FOR SALE sign hangs next to the pirate flag decal on the car's window. The engine clicks off, and Trent hustles out.

Their house sits at the end of a cul-de-sac, fiery-leafed maples with shadowy trunks lining the expanse. Not another house around for miles. Inside, there are more square feet than Trent and Marley could've ever afforded in California, but the living room is almost empty. Unpacked boxes stacked high in the halls. Spaces on the walls where there should be faces, family portraits, close-ups of the girls doing everyday things. A leather sofa and a threadbare recliner are the only pieces of furniture in the room. On a table in the corner sits an oversized flat-screen television, cords dangling out from behind it like the gloomy maple limbs casting shadows in the front yard.

In the kitchen, Trent's wife, Marley, stands with her back to him, waiting for the microwave to ding. She's wearing the same ratty sweatpants and the shabby Valley T-shirt she wears almost every day, but sporting them well, sharp curves at her hips and thighs. After they arrived in Arkansas, Trent couldn't get Marley to leave the house. She said she didn't want the players' parents—especially the boys' mothers—getting the wrong idea. Marley was not here to be anyone's friend; she was here to win ball games. Victories required time and effort, warm meals, dishes, laundry. She even watched scout film on all the opposing teams. On Friday nights, Marley sits down on the field, behind the south end zone, away from the gossip and the whispers of all those Booster Club parents, alone except for their youngest daughter Ava, crawling around beneath her feet.

"*Shhhhh*," says Marley, turning, finger to her lips. "If you wake her up, Trent, I swear to God."

"Ava's napping. Got it," he says, nodding. "Lorna home?"

"Play practice."

"Right."

"And she got the lead," says Marley, eyes rolling. "Of course, she got the lead."

In a way, Lorna was the start of everything: Marley pregnant at eighteen, the couple rushing to the courthouse to elope, the long nights and the crying baby. Then Trent went to work. He was a father; he had to provide. So he volunteer-coached until he graduated college, then got a job with a small high school, and then another, and another. Four jobs before he was the head football coach of the Fernando Valley Jaguars, his alma mater. It was a fast climb, and it helped that Marley's father, Larry Dommers, was the Jaguars' athletic director. It helped a lot.

But then the Jaguars started to lose and just kept losing.

Coach Dommers let the grim carnival ride spiral on for three full seasons, and after the plug was finally pulled in the Valley, Trent was left with a dismal 3-27 overall record, a death sentence in the world of coaching. There was no school in California that would hire him, so they left. And now there is only Arkansas and Billy Lowe, Lorna miscast in the halls of Denton High: amber hair, hazel eyes, skin still warm and tan like the Gold Coast sun, the same shade as her mother's.

Trent plops down at the kitchen table.

"Eat," says Marley, opening the microwave door before it dings, pushing the hot plate toward her husband.

"God, babe, I can't quit thinking about—"

"Eat," she says again. "You have to be strong."

Trent takes the sandwich in both hands, closes his eyes, and says a silent prayer of thanksgiving. When he opens his eyes he says, "I've never seen a boy act so—"

"It was ugly," says Marley. "There's no disputing that."

"But deep down, I think he's a good kid."

"You had your meeting today, right?"

Trent sticks the warm sandwich in his mouth.

"Did you call Dad?"

Trent chews.

"We're in the playoffs now, Trent. You should call him."

Trent mumbles around the food in his mouth.

"And these people," says Marley. "They'll worship you if you bring them a state title."

Trent takes another bite.

"We gave up everything for this. And I can stomach the stinking chicken houses and chatting up rednecks at the Kum & Go—but not for much longer. You have to hold up your end of the deal."

Trent's mouth opens like he's about to speak, but then baby Ava screams, her cries erupting from the monitor on the kitchen counter. Marley turns to the sound. Trent stares into his sandwich.

"If we win," Marley says, reaching across her husband and silencing the monitor, "then we can get the hell out of here."

When Lorna comes home Trent is in the shower, letting the water wash him clean. He takes his showers cold, the knob turned all the way toward blue. It's a form of meditation, a practice he learned during his childhood, bouncing from foster home to foster home, temporary dwellings where the warm water ran out quick.

Trent's hair is still wet when he enters the living room. A football game glows across the massive television, the players nearly life-sized on the screen. Lorna sits cross-legged on the floor, nose buried in a collection of Shakespeare's sonnets. Baby Ava bounces on her mother's leg, all giggles and gurgles. Trent holds tight to the iPad in his hand and reaches for his youngest daughter. Marley's eyes never leave the game. The announcers' voices echo across the almost-empty room, discussing the running back situation at the University of Southern California.

"Hey, Lo," says Trent. "How was play practice?"

Lorna looks up from her book. "Nothing fancy like back home, but it's fun. Did the team practice today?"

"Saturday. It's our day off. We'll get back to work tom—"

"Shhhh," Marley hisses, jabbing her finger at the television. "I want to hear this."

Lorna marks her spot in the book. "Could we please—just, like, once—watch something besides football? I'm sick of it."

"Sick of *football*?"

Trent can still taste the microwaved sandwich from earlier, his mushy excuse for not telling Marley about Bradshaw and Billy. Marley is just like her father—just like his old boss—she never forgets.

"Are you sick of eating?" says Marley.

Lorna rolls her eyes.

"Football puts food on our table."

"I'm not hungry."

"Not yet."

Marley turns to Trent. He reaches around Ava and taps the iPad's screen. Game film of the Harrison Goblins, their playoff opponent, begins to play. Trent brings the device in close. Baby Ava's eyes light up in the glow.

"*Not yet*," Lorna says, shaking her head as she opens the book again.

"Coaching is all about choices," says Marley. "Doing what's best for your family—what's best for the team. Isn't that right, Trent?"

Trent stiffens. "It's about building up young men."

"It's about hard decisions like the one this USC coach had to make." Marley leans in closer to the screen. "Do you think he made the right call?"

Trent lays the iPad down, pulling Ava into his chest. "I didn't even hear what they were saying. What's the story?"

"Just listen."

One of the announcers—the one with the blue suit, red tie, and more makeup than Tina Lowe had worn earlier that day—is defending USC's star player.

"What'd he do?" says Trent.

"Had a scuffle with a girl at a bar," says Marley, nodding. "They say they have video evidence, but they haven't shown it."

"No way." Lorna slaps the book closed. "And he's still getting to play?"

The conversation with Principal Bradshaw pulses on repeat through Trent's brain. He feels both Marley's and Lorna's eyes on him now. He nuzzles baby Ava's hair.

"*Dad*," says Lorna, standing and moving directly in front of him. "You wouldn't play him. Would you?"

Trent is thankful for the school play. Thankful Lorna got the lead and didn't see the violence that had transpired on Pirate Field the night before.

"Listen, Lo—" says Trent, but then the television screen flashes. The beastly running back slices through the defensive front, plows over a defender, and trots into the end zone. The crowd—over fifty thousand people crammed into the Los Angeles Memorial Coliseum, cheering, clapping, stomping, their faces covered with red and gold paint—rumble beneath Trent's words. "You let me worry about boys like that."

Marley nods. "It's your father's job."

"How could I forget," says Lorna, yanking Ava from Trent's arms, "about your *job*." And then she's gone, feet pounding as she climbs the stairs to her room, Ava giggling with every step.

The video on Trent's iPad plays on repeat. Marley turns the volume up on the television. The announcers marvel over the touchdown run.

Trent falls asleep with the iPad in his lap and the television still broadcasting USC's victory over Washington State. When he comes creeping into their bedroom, Marley is already in bed. Trent knows she's naked beneath the covers; she always sleeps in the nude. She was a basketball player in high school, a bruiser, but to look at the shapes rising up from the sheets, you'd think she was all finesse, a point guard or shooting forward—something smooth.

Trent says, "Hey, babe."

Marley closes her eyes and pulls the covers up to her chin. Her lips barely move when she replies, "You still haven't told me about your meetings today."

"They were"—Trent pulls his sweatpants down and steps out of them—"fine."

"Don't even *think* about getting in this bed. Not until you talk to me."

Trent slides his legs back into his pants. "You don't have to act like this, Mar. I'll tell you about the meetings."

Marley doesn't move, doesn't blink, staring directly into the ceiling fan. The fan is on. Trent cannot remember a November this hot, not even in Southern California.

"I suspended Bill for the first half of the Harrison game."

In one quick roll, Marley is out of the bed, standing before him. "You're kidding. You *have* to be kidding."

"It's only the first half," says Trent, trying not to look at anything but her eyes. Marley's body still tugs at him the way it did when they were in high school. "It was the right thing to do."

"You didn't call Daddy?"

"No."

"Well, I did, and he said—"

Trent raises his hand and Marley stops talking. He's almost surprised. "I am not your father," he whispers. "I'm your—"

"I know what you are," she snaps and folds her arms tight across her chest, pushing her breasts up and out, like maybe she knows the power she still holds over him. "You're the reason we're in *Arkansas*."

Trent shakes his head. Had it always been this way? He and Marley had been together so long it was hard to remember. Trent was fifteen when Larry Dommers adopted him, baptized him, and brought him into his home. Coach Dommers gave Trent everything: a Bible, the starting quarterback spot for the Valley Jaguars, and his daughter's hand in marriage.

"I see a lot of myself in Bill," says Trent.

Marley unfolds her arms, placing both hands on her hips.

"The foster homes, Mar, all that."

"This is different."

"I went through six foster homes in five years."

"I know," says Marley, softening, just a little. "I know it was tough."

"We fought, like big foster family fistfights. Look, look here."

Trent bends down, pulls his hair back, and shows his wife what he's shown her a thousand times—a small scar on his forehead.

"That was from a fist," he says. "Have you ever been punched in the face?"

"No, Trent. I've never been punched in the face."

"But I bet Bill has. I'm sure of it."

"What on earth does that have to do with football?"

"I can use the game to teach him lessons." Trent takes the pillow from his side of the bed, bringing it into his chest. "You know, about life. Just like your dad did for me."

"This is your job we're talking about," says Marley, hands falling by her side, exposing the whole of her body, everything out in the open now. "Our *life*. I'm sure Billy has it tough, but have you thought, for just one second, about us?"

"We're fine," Trent says and tosses the pillow back on the bed.

"You're not home every day. You don't see the girls like I do. Ava was walking when we left California. Do you remember that?"

"The doctor said it's all the ear infections, throwing off her balance."

"Stress, anxiety, babies can sense that sort of stuff. This place isn't good for us." Marley squeezes her eyes shut. "It's backward and sad. Everybody is fat. They all want to talk to us, about nothing, talk and talk and—"

"It's called Southern hospitality, Mar."

"It's fucking *Deliverance*, and that principal looks just like Burt Reynolds," she says, standing there, waving her arms as if she were fully dressed.

"*Marley*."

"Save your sermon for the boys, Trent."

"You know I don't like it when you talk like that."

"You know what I don't like?" Marley snaps. "Living in this shithole town. And the only way we're getting out of here is if you win enough games to make everyone forget the fact that Daddy had to fire you."

Trent breathes in deep through his nostrils and swallows Marley's rage. The cold showers, the breathing exercises, all of these small practices help him weather her storms. He knows his wife is a believer, but her faith is sharper than his. Jagged. Old Testament versus New. Marley's anger is righteous, like Jesus in the temple courts. Of course, she has every reason in the world to be upset with him. She's a thousand miles from home because her husband has failed, repeatedly, and she doesn't even know the worst part yet—Bradshaw's ultimatum.

A shabby Fernando Valley conference championship shirt hangs loose from Trent's shoulders, something he'd earned as a player, not as a coach. He remembers Billy's nasty scene on the sideline, puts both hands on his head, and tries to push it away. The boys were wild in California, sure, but nothing like this one. Billy is like a violent car wreck. A semitruck and a red convertible. Something strong mashed with something beautiful. He's the only reason they've made it this far. Without him, the Pirates don't stand a chance.

Trent reaches out, taking Marley by the waist. She doesn't resist, letting him pull her in close. "What should I do, Coach?" says Trent, the corners of his mouth turning up in a grin.

"You should go." Marley doesn't smile. Doesn't blink. "And don't come back until you've done something about Billy Lowe."

Trent lets go of his wife and looks up, searching for a response, watching as the ceiling fan spins round and round, thinking at some point, somewhere a long time from now, that fan will give out, just up and stop.

And then he thinks, Marley's right: Bradshaw does look like Burt Reynolds.

5.

After it was over, I took His best bottle of whiskey and left. Got all the way down to the river, thought about going over to my brother Jesse trailer, telling him how I whooped His ass, but I didn't. Just sat by the bank and watched the water. Hard to drink after you see what the drink take from everybody, but I did.

Drank the bottle dry.

Some logs still smoldering in a fire pit. Bud Light cans and cigarette butts everywhere. Just been trying to catch my breath, figure out what I'm supposed to do next. What you do after something like that? After He got up from the sofa and started coming at me with His pecker still hard, Momma jumping up, taking Little Brother, saying, "Travis, don't."

"First playoff game too?" He said, holding up that little bullshit paper.

"Yeah," I said. "The fuck you gone do about it?"

He nodded, coming at me slow, almost grinning. "About to show you what the fuck I'm gonna do about it, Billy."

"Stop, goddammit," shouted Momma. "Y'all *stop*." But she knew what was coming. She been knowing for some time.

"Get on out here, Tina," He said, not taking His eyes off me. "I'm about to teach your boy a lesson."

I watched her go, watched her slide her feet in her house shoes and run out the little screen door. Everything you need to know about Momma in them slippers. Don't even take the time to pull the backs up, just walk them down flat.

His little shitty Sentra revved up outside, Momma gassing it. And then she's gone. And that's good. She didn't need to see what I's gonna do to Him.

We stood there a while, just staring at each other. He used to play basketball, but He soft now. Probably soft back then. I thought about just going back in my room, locking the door, and waiting for tomorrow. Tired of fighting. Knuckles already scabbed over. But He was drunk, and even NyQuil make a man brave if he drink enough of it.

"Me and my daddy used to tussle," He said and looked past me, kinda smiling. "Yeah, we used to get after it. Taught me a thing or two."

"Could a fooled me."

"Didn't get to walk with my daddy on Senior Night, neither," He said. "Way it was for basketball, you had to be one of the starting five to get your name called out."

"Sound to me like you weren't nothing in high school."

"Naw, I weren't, but I'm all you got now." He looked at the bottle in His hand, but the bottle empty. "And I tell you another thing, you gone start calling me by my name."

I bit my cheek and felt it coming back.

"You hear me?"

"I hear you."

"Say my name then, boy. Maybe that'll keep you from this ass whooping you about to get."

"You ain't got no name when it come to me."

He took a step back, almost smiling. "I's hoping you'd say that."

Something about Him wanting to fight so bad made me turn away. Don't never wanna give Him what He want. I's almost back to my room when I heard Him flick his lighter.

Whole body go tight at the smell, feeling that burn all over again. I turn quick. He ain't even looking, just standing there smoking a cigarette like He was the other night when He stuck me. I's sitting on the ground against the sofa, holding Little Brother, watching *Wheel of Fortune,* and then He stuck that red tip in my neck, like it was some kind a joke. I just squeezed Little Brother tight. Just took it. Been taking His shit for years. Back when I's a kid and He's still bigger than me—I *had* to take it. Didn't have no choice. Don't know if that's what I's thinking when He stuck me, but I knew I couldn't let Him see me hurt. Little Brother started screaming, loud and crazy, like he could feel the fire in my blood. Then Little Brother got the pen. Too much crying. Too loud. Should a whooped His ass right then, but I went to practice instead, and there weren't no way that sophomore linebacker could a known what he had coming.

I blinked and saw Him still standing there, moving His mouth.

"You hear me, boy?"

I heard Him. He just asking for it now.

"Don't say it again."

"Say whatever the hell I want. Shit, I been living here going on five years."

"Don't say it again."

But then He did.

"Best get used to saying my name, Billy." His words hissing out evil and slow around that cigarette. "Cause your daddy ain't never coming back."

He didn't say nothing else. Didn't get the chance. Felt my knuckles crack open as they hit right above His left eye. He so drunk, so soft, went down easy. Knocked His bitch ass out with one punch. Just stood there over Him, watching that big belly go up and down.

"You ain't got no name. You hear me?"

He started pawing at His face, squirming. Looked real weird the way He was twisting around on that floor.

"You hear me?"

Don't know why I did it, but I took a bottle of His good whiskey from the cabinet, some Early Times. Reached over Him, took Coach little bullshit paper and started ripping it up. Then I took a big long swig, letting Him know who the man of the house was now.

He said something, but I barely heard Him. Just shook my head and said, "Ain't nobody gonna help you now. You wanna go to the hospital, you best start walking."

Crawling.

That's what He's doing when I left the trailer, crawling right behind me, reaching up, saying my name. Didn't look at Him though. Didn't look back till I heard the screen door slap shut, heard Him fall. His fat ass rolling down the steps, almost pulling the door off the hinges. He was down on all fours, shaking His head, when I started running.

Ran all the way to the river. Thought about wading out in the current, letting it wash me clean, but instead I kept drinking. The bottle just about full when I got to the water. It almost empty now.

Fell asleep and woke up whiskey drunk. Watched the sun come up over the river through crusty eyes and decided it was time to go home. He'd be awake now, Momma in the kitchen frying up some eggs, and maybe He'd a learned His goddamn lesson. Maybe things would get better.

I toss the bottle in the river and watch it float over the dam. Don't make a sound. Walk the whole way home. Ain't much a walk. Denton small and smell like chicken shit. Chicken houses everywhere. Even got them in town now. And Mexicans. Damn. The Mexicans taking over.

When I get up to the trailer, His Sentra ain't in the driveway. Tire tracks deep in the dirt. Look like He peeled out, probably embarrassed cause I whooped His ass. Stand there on the porch and don't hear nobody inside. Don't hear nothing. It the quietest I ever heard the trailer and for some reason, that scare me. When you raised in Shady Grove Trailer Park, it the quiet that scare you.

The only light in the kitchen coming from the stove's overhead dome light, glowing orange like Halloween. I take a step inside. Don't see nothing at first. Damn sure don't hear nothing.

"Hey?"

Nothing.

"*Momma?*"

The window unit kick on and I just about shit my pants. "Come on, Billy," I say to the dark. Still woozy from all that whiskey. And that orange light, God, I can barely see.

Like a dream, like walking through a fun house, a room full a mirrors and clowns.

Thinking about how much I hate clowns when I step on Him.

Feel like a trash bag filled with wet grass, stink like one too. My left toe jab right in His ribs and He don't move, don't grunt, nothing. He out in the middle of the kitchen, lying over on His side, like He'd crawled back up them steps and just rolled over.

I think about leaving right then. Just getting my shit and going out the door. But I don't. Cain't. It the fact that He so damn quiet. I bend down. He really stinking now: smell like stale cigarettes and NyQuil. So much He couldn't piss it out, had to sweat it out. And ass. He smell like ass. I try not to think about His stank-ass wollering around with Momma. The orange light cover every pimple on His face, every mole, every hair. The glow make none of it seem real.

"Wake up," I say and shake Him.

He don't move.

"Wake the fuck up. Where's Momma?"

Nothing.

It's when I shake Him again, shake Him good and hard, that I see He lying in a pool of something. So dark in here, I cain't see nothing but this big wet circle all around Him, like He pissed hisself. Smell worse than normal. There some different stuff up around His shoulders. Gooey stuff. Thick like syrup. I lean in closer, and that when I see it. His head lying flat on the kitchen floor, got this gash just above His left eye, deep and red, so red it look kinda purple.

Ain't no way I did this. I hit Him once. Was He bleeding when you left? Don't be stupid, Billy. He's still breathing when you left, still talking, still moving. Asking you for—

Help.

The glow, it on me now, all around me like the syrup on the floor. Feel like it pulling me down to Him. Don't feel real.

I try to stand, but cain't. I shake Him again. He don't move. Don't grunt. Nothing. The syrup on the floor got me stuck. But I'm Billy Lowe. I'm strong and can run the hell out a football. That's what it feel like. Feel like I'm running through that little crease, that alley—*Blood* Alley—as I pull away from the mess a Him on the floor.

I'm running again, acid burning in my lungs, my legs, as I tear down the road and away from the trailer. Not even thinking about where I'm going. But there only one place for Billy Lowe on a Sunday afternoon in the fall. My feet, they feel it, too. They carry me. And before I can make sense of His busted head and that orange glow, the clowns and the syrup—I hear a whistle, and I stop running.

6.

Early Sunday morning Marley hears a noise: the spigot just outside the master bedroom window, turning. That awful sound before the water begins to flow. She rolls out of bed, bare feet slapping against the hardwood floors. A Sunday sort of silence hangs thick through the house. Marley's at the window now. What she sees in the driveway does not make sense, a green garden hose snaking its way into a five-gallon bucket. The bucket is overflowing. Trent bows before it, down on his hands and knees.

Why is her husband washing the Prius at this early hour? Marley tries to remember the night before. Had Trent come back? Had she felt his heat, under the covers, in the bed beside her? The air is warm and sticky but the floor is cool. Marley's toes curl as she turns from the window and wraps both arms around her chest. The baby monitor relays a gray-scale image of Ava, asleep, with her mouth open. Marley picks up the monitor on her way out the door.

The garage opens, the Prius revealed from the tires up. Dust covers the grille. Mud streaks out behind a yellow sponge as Trent drags it across the hood then dips it in the water again.

Marley says the first thing that comes to her mind:

"It's five thirty in the morning, Trent. What are you doing?"

"I went there," he says, elbow deep in the five-gallon bucket.

"Where? Wait. Why is the car so dirty?"

Trent stands and continues scrubbing, working hard to get the dark, swirling stains off the driver's side headlight. He stops and drops the sponge in the bucket, turning to his wife.

"I went to Bill's trailer. They live down a dirt road." Trent squats and puts both hands on the bucket, one on each side. "When I got there, they were already arguing."

The baby monitor in Marley's hands cuts out then comes back on. She looks at it. Ava rolls over but doesn't wake.

"Tina's boyfriend, Travis," Trent says, "he was upset about Bill being suspended for the playoff game."

Marley almost asks her husband why he'd gone to their trailer, but she knows the answer. He went because she told him to. It was as simple as that. Marley squeezes the baby monitor and the plastic creaks between her fingers.

"I was just sitting in the Prius, pretty far out, but I could see straight through the window." Trent's voice is soft, barely louder than the water bubbling out of the bucket now, splashing in pools on the concrete. "Right when they really started screaming, Tina ran out, got in the car, and drove away. Can you believe that? She left him."

Marley can believe it.

"She left Bill in there with the man who has hurt him the most."

"Did she see you?" Marley says. "Did anyone else see your car out there?"

"I-I don't think so," Trent says, staring through his wife like he's at the trailer again, watching the scene play out. "It doesn't matter."

"Tell me exactly what happened," Marley says, "and I'll tell you if it matters."

Trent blinks and turns away from his wife, eyeing the bucket. The world outside is gone. There is only the water. It reminds Trent of his baptism. He can still feel Marley's father's hands on his sixteen-year-old chest, the back of his neck, pushing him down and holding him under. When Trent had emerged from the salty San Pablo Bay, the world was cast anew: the foster homes, the fights, even the memories of his negligent parents—gone. With Jesus by his side, Trent was no longer alone. He'd tried telling Marley all of that before, tried getting her to see the world through the eyes of his Savior, but she was blinded by a life of luxury. Marley hadn't survived what he'd been through. She didn't know true pain.

Trent stares into the bottom of the bucket. The water is soapy instead of salty, but Trent can see it all again: the way the man fell, the way Billy ran, the blood. The water burns crimson as he turns to face his wife.

"Bill hit him," Trent says, still kneeling before the water. "I think he-he—"

Marley says, "*No*," sharp enough to cut Trent off.

"The way he fell," Trent continues, trying to say what he has to say, trying to make sense of the pictures in his head. "I mean, the way *Travis* fell. I knew it. Bill knew it too. That's why he ran. That's why I—"

"You?" Marley says, and Trent turns, eyeing the puddle of water as it expands across the concrete, almost to Marley's toes now. "What did you do, Trent?"

"I-I—"

Marley steps back. The water runs off the driveway and heads into the grass.

"I didn't do anything."

"You just drove away?" Marley says. "And where did Billy go?"

The yellow sponge floats across the top of the bucket. Trent focuses on the holes dotting the surface, porous and dark, like the acne-scarred cheeks of Travis Rodney. The man goes down again and Billy runs. Trent watches the scene on repeat, not letting his mind go any farther than the fall. He feels Marley, squatting beside him now, reaching her hand into the bucket for the sponge.

"I should call the police," Trent says.

"Call the police?" Marley squeezes the sponge with both hands. The water splashes the tops of her bare feet. "I want you to consider something for me. Okay?" She waits a beat, stands, and continues. "Travis Rodney is a bad man, Trent. Think of all the pain he's caused Billy."

Trent remembers the burn on Billy's neck, the small red dot that led to the fire they're up against now.

"It's the same pain you endured as a child," Marley says, twisting the sponge tighter and tighter. "Maybe Billy had had enough. Maybe—" Marley pauses and lets the sponge uncoil. "Maybe Billy decided to do something about it."

Trent's mouth barely moves as he whispers, "What are you saying?"

Marley does this weird thing Trent remembers her father

doing, like she's looking at his forehead instead of his eyes. Her voice flat, emotionless. "We should help Billy. That's what I'm saying."

"*Help* him?" Trent says. "I know what Bill did. I mean, God. I saw him do it."

"You saw Billy hit him. One punch. And now you think this man is," she pauses, whispering the next word, "*dead?*"

Trent watches Travis go down a final time, watches Billy run, but the memory stops there.

"No way," Marley says. "The guy might be unconscious, probably hungover with a nasty headache, but he's not dead." She takes a breath, watching Trent, waiting. "Right? Doesn't that sound right?"

"I know what I saw, Mar. It didn't—"

"Look at me."

Trent stares at his wife, straight on, the way he used to look at her back before the girls came along, before football. Marley's eyes are this wild shade of amber, two glowing hot coals.

"A few days from now," she says, "when some redneck asks you, 'You hear about Travis Rodney?' You have to be able to look him in the eyes and say, 'Oh my God. Really? I had no idea.'" Marley nods a few times to herself. "And it should be easy, because it's the truth. You don't know what happened. You just saw him fall. Am I right?"

Trent peers into his wife's smoldering eyes.

"That's it," Marley says, dipping the sponge in the bucket again. "That's all there is to it. Now go inside and take a nice warm shower. Not a cold one. I'll get some breakfast going and make sure the girls are up and around."

"For what?"

"Church starts in a few hours," Marley says, and there's a tone to her voice that Trent can't quite place. "You need to stick to your routine: church on Sunday and then practice in the afternoon. Regardless of what has happened—or what hasn't happened—your team is still playing in its first playoff game this Friday. The boys need you, Trent. I need you." Marley slaps the sponge onto the driver's side headlight, washing away the mud. "We could all use a win."

The Powers family is a portrait of innocence in their Sunday best. Marley made sure of it, telling Lorna to get the hell out of that flowery dress that was too long anyway, and put on a bra. Baby Ava hates bows like her mother hates losing, but she is wearing a gray and black one—Pirate colors—sitting nice and quiet in the front row of the East Mount Zion Baptist Church.

The preacher's voice drones on, but Marley isn't listening. Instead, her eyes are on Trent, trying to forget what he'd told her only a few hours before.

Ava squirms and Marley pinches her thigh. Just hard enough to let her daughter know she's serious. Marley has never been one of those mothers—the kind who takes her child out of church if the kid gets upset; the kind of mother who lets her child control her life. No. Marley has too much of her father in her for that.

Ava paws at her mother's hair, giggling. Marley squeezes the soft spot on the toddler's inner thigh again, harder this time. Ava's body goes tight, but she stops. Marley thinks about control, remembering how Ava was her final chance to regain any semblance of it when Trent started losing at Fernando Valley.

The pew creaks as Trent adjusts his weight. Bits of the preacher's sermon disrupt Marley's memories, words like "sin" and "repent" and "salvation."

Ava was as simple as not taking the pill. It worked the same way the first time, except with Lorna, Marley had just turned eighteen, almost a college girl, the world budding and green out ahead of her, until she got pregnant. At that age, Marley hadn't even considered taking the pill. It seemed so strange now, but deep down she knew the reason—her father.

Larry Dommers had a voice like this preacher and a way about him that Marley feared. He'd become infatuated with Trent in high school, and that confused Marley. When the young boy with the dark hair and the long fingers moved out of his foster home and into their basement, the only things Marley liked about him were his hands. Trent had strong hands with veins like rivers on a map. After a while, her father's interest became obvious, devoting more and more time to this young man who could throw a tight spiral, and, well, Marley decided she'd show the boy some interest, too.

It was late November, right around the last game of the Jaguars' season, when Marley snuck into the basement and found the star quarterback asleep in the dark. Nine months later, just after Marley arrived on campus, two new lives began.

Lorna's and Trent's.

Marley stuck on the sideline, watching as Trent worked his way up through the ranks until finally her father had given him the last thing he had left to give, his title as head coach of the Fernando Valley Jaguars. When the losing started, Marley felt her control slipping through Trent's capable but somehow shaky fingers. So Marley stopped taking the pill.

The preacher is sweating as he asks the congregation to bow their heads and close their eyes. Ava rests her cheek on her mother's shoulder. Marley rubs her baby's back, thinking this situation they're up against now, what Trent says he saw happen with Billy, it's no different than motherhood. It's all about sacrifice. It's about doing what is best for your family. If the Powers family ever wants out of Arkansas, the Pirates have to win, and the only way they're going to do that is with Billy Lowe.

Marley watches her husband, head bowed, eyes closed. Small flickers of his lashes pulse like a dreaming dog's leg. The preacher says, "Amen," and still, Trent's eyes remain closed.

The boys enter the locker room with long faces that remind Trent of the congregation at East Mount Zion Baptist Church. The townsfolk were restless after the Lutherville loss. The power of football is strong in Arkansas, strong in the South, like religion, a distraction from the trailers and the pain of everyday life. The chapel was a far cry from the megachurches in California: the smoke machines, the laser lights and electric guitars. But still, they sang hymns and sat in wooden pews and Trent felt the peace of the Lord wash over him.

In the locker room, chinstraps pop like Black Cats on the Fourth of July, the boys getting ready for Sunday's practice. Trent is proud of their attendance. It had been tough convincing them to practice on the Sabbath when he'd first arrived, but now, eleven weeks into the season, the locker room is packed full. Trent can't help but wonder how many of their parents have talked with Principal Bradshaw. If that is the sort of conversations these boys endure around the dinner table, after their fathers have had one too many beers and their hearts get heavy, mouths loose.

Trent blows his whistle. The boys look up, expecting the game report, a pep talk. Trent eyes the single empty locker. Number thirty-five. He turns away then looks back again, but still, the locker is empty.

"Alright, guys," says Trent. "Listen up."

The boys go quiet.

"The point of this meeting isn't about the loss, or even to discuss the playoff game. The point of this meeting is *us*."

Trent glances at Bull. The man is a statue. He doesn't move, doesn't blink, just stares at Trent, a blank gaze like an empty locker on a Sunday afternoon.

"Are we *okay*?" asks Trent. "Are we *good*? These are questions we must constantly ask ourselves. We must be honest. It's the only way we'll make it to the championship game."

A senior offensive lineman, Jarred Trotter, is sitting by his locker wearing only his tight, white football pants. His legs sprout black hair. His gut hangs loose as he fingers his belly button. He's the sort of player high school football teams are built upon: true believers who will fill the stands long after their time on the field is through. The boy raises his hand.

"Hey, Coach?" says Jarred, turning to the rest of the team. "Everything looks good to me."

A few of the younger boys giggle.

"Right," says Trent over the snickers. "I think everyone knows what I'm talking about. We had a difficult situation on Friday and—"

"We know what you're talking about," snorts Jarred. "We know, but don't nobody care. How's that for honesty?"

Trent reaches for the whistle around his neck. "That's good, Jarred, honesty is good, but we're a family. We take care of each other."

"Naw, Coach. *We're* a family. Billy Lowe's a piece of shit—always has been, always will be—and we're sick of it."

The boys mumble in agreement.

Trent brings the whistle to his mouth and blows. "Watch your language, Jarred. That's enough."

Jarred stands despite the cry of the whistle. "I'm speaking as a senior member of this team, and what I'm saying is—we're done with Billy Lowe."

Trent looks over Jarred's shoulder to the rest of the team, scanning their faces, trying to decide the best way to reach them. "You don't understand this situation at all. Bill is going to issue an apology to the team. He's on a path to recovery—"

"You think I go home to hugs and kisses?" says Jarred. "Think my daddy ain't crazy? My parents got divorced two years ago. That shit's hard."

"It's different for Bill. His situation is—"

"Life's tough," Jarred barks, "that's why we got these hard-ass helmets."

"*Language*. I'm not going to tell you again." Trent's mind drifts back to his conversation with Principal Bradshaw, back to the trailer from the night before.

"Sorry, Coach," says Jarred and pauses, like maybe he's just going to sit back down and let that be the end of it, but he doesn't. "Want me to write you a fucking apology?"

The locker room goes silent. Trent's mouth is dry. He tries to swallow, tries to speak. His cheeks puff as he struggles to blow the whistle again, but it doesn't make a sound.

Bull's words thunder across the room: "Jarred Trotter, four-hundred-yard keg lunges, *pronto*."

"Yes," says Trent, his voice coming back to him now, watching as Jarred grabs his helmet, his pads, and sulks out of the locker room. "And watch your language."

When Trent walks onto the practice field, the afternoon sun blinds him. Billy is in the darkness, running away from the trailer with blood on his hands. Bull's whistle blows hard and sharp, ringing out like an alarm, and then Billy is gone. It's just practice, football practice. Trent tries to recall the peace of Sunday morning, humming the tune of a hymn he knows by heart.

Bull has Jarred over near the sideline. Again and again, the boy drops to a knee with an empty keg held high above his head. *Four hundred yards:* that's the rule. Any infraction the coaches deem worthy earn the boys four fields' worth of keg lunges. Jarred moves slow, one yard at a time, shaking his head and cussing with every step.

The rest of the team has already begun their warm-up: high knees, skips, and sprints. The linemen are having a tougher go of it. Trent trots across the field toward Bull and Jarred.

"Still got about two hundred yards left," says Bull, not missing a beat with his whistle. Already the volume of it is giving Trent a headache.

"I got it," says Trent.

Bull grunts then takes off across the field. Trent watches the old man jog toward the rest of the boys, chin up, chest out, skinny legs making choppy strides.

"You gonna blow that whistle or what?"

Trent looks from Bull to Jarred. "Yes, I'm going to blow this whistle."

"My senior year and we get a Cali-boy for a coach."

"What'd you say?"

"Nothing."

"I heard you."

"Didn't say nothing."

"*Anything*," says Trent. "The correct way to say it is, 'I didn't say *anything*.'"

"Holy shit," says Jarred and drops the keg.

It hits the grass, the hollow gong reverberating through Trent's gut, taking him back, all the way back to the last foster home, the worst. A bell controlled everything they did in that house. When it was time to eat, the "Mom" rang a bell. Time to wake up, time to go to the bathroom, time to watch TV—the bell marked every minute of their lives.

"Pick it up."

Down on one knee, Jarred shakes his head, glaring up at Trent. "Nah, Coach. I'll pass."

"Pick it up."

Jarred smiles as he unbuckles his helmet. The first thing Trent notices is Jarred's hair. It's blond and thick, like he washes it twice a day, a stark contrast to Billy's greasy black mane. Trent's hair didn't look like that, not when he was in the foster homes.

"Pick up your helmet."

"What you gonna do if I don't?"

Trent remembers the bell at the foster home chiming, signaling it was TV time. He just wanted to watch one football game on a Sunday afternoon—he was even wearing his Dan Fouts jersey—but that big boy, a boy the size of Jarred, kept changing the channel and standing in front of the television, bouncing a football off Trent's head.

Trent bends down and picks up Jarred's helmet. It feels solid in his hands, heavy. Jarred stands, muttering something under his breath. Then he starts to laugh, just like the bully had done until Trent couldn't take it anymore. When the "Mom" finally came rushing into the living room, the bully was unconscious.

Jarred's mouth is moving now, but Trent doesn't hear him, lost in the depths of a dark hole he thought he'd left behind.

"What?" says Trent. "What did you just say?"

"*Billy*," Jarred says and points. "He's coming down the road."

7.

I quit running when Coach holler for me. Something about the helmet, or maybe it the way Coach hollering, remind me why I'm running in the first place.

"Bill!"

I don't say nothing, just sit down, right there in the road.

"My God. Are you alright?"

"Yeah."

"You look—*bad*," say Coach.

Then he don't say nothing else. Just stand there holding that helmet. Even look down at it like he don't know why he holding it, like it got ahold of him.

"What about you?" I say.

"What about me?" say Coach.

"You alright?"

Coach shake his head and drop the helmet. It roll on the blacktop, turn, and sit straight up like it watching us.

"I'm fine," he say, looking back over his shoulder to the field. "Come on."

Coach start blowing his whistle, blowing it right there in the street like he gonna stop traffic. But it ain't traffic he worried about. It practice. Bull out there running defense with the team. When Coach start blowing his whistle, they all stop. They looking at me now. I feel they eyes and know what they thinking. Thinking, *Here come fucking Billy.*

Coach got me under the arm like I'm some little kid. He pulling me out to the field. I got Momma shirt on, BUD LIGHT across the front. Embarrassing. And Coach still blowing that damn whistle, hollering for the team. Bull ain't even looked up from his drill, but the boys did. They see me now. I think about running, but I ain't that fast.

"Bill has something he'd like to tell you all," say Coach and the way he say that last part make me cringe. "Go on. It's alright."

The words in my head all ripped and torn like that little paper Coach made me sign. I know this the only way I'm gonna make it right, but I cain't see the words. All I see's the glow. His busted head lying in syrup.

"It's fine," say Coach again. "You can do it."

They all staring at me now. Even Bull staring, probably thinking I wore Momma's Bud Light shirt to practice on purpose. But it ain't like that, Bull. For the first time I think about Momma. Think she probably the one that busted His head. Came home, saw Him down, and did what she always wanted to do. Don't blame her. Not one bit. Little Brother probably saw the whole thing.

"Bill," say Coach. "*Please.*"

His voice sound like a kid voice. Sound scared. Then big Jarred come walking up, got a shit-eating grin on his face, already nudging somebody, pointing. But he ain't pointing at me. He pointing at Coach, laughing. Jarred ain't got his helmet on neither. And Bull see him and don't say nothing. Every Pirate know when you step on this field, that helmet stay on. But Jarred helmet off and Bull ain't saying nothing.

I look at Coach. He looking at Jarred, looking at him like he scared. Almost feel sorry for Coach. Almost.

"I guess," I say and take a deep breath, "I shouldn't a done Austin like that."

And there ain't no paper, there ain't no fancy words, there's just that. Austin Murphy don't even look up, probably scared too. I hear Jarred laugh from the back, but he ain't laughing at me. He laughing cause Coach clapping now, clapping and reaching out like he wanna put his arm over my shoulder. I turn away. If the guys see me hugging Coach, that'd be the end of it. Coach stop and look down. I follow his eyes. There's red on my Jordans. Got red all over them. It ain't syrup, though. I see that now. Coach do too, but he turn away, like all that blood don't scare him one bit.

8.

The dead man's Nissan Sentra sits outside a trailer down near the Arkansas River. The trailer belongs to Jesse Lowe, oldest of the Lowe boys, and resembles a cheap beer can, its contents bitter and volatile. Tina Lowe is asleep inside the car. She let baby Stephen stay in the trailer. She even covered him with bath towels after he fell asleep on Jesse's sofa.

Tina's eyes open, small slits like crescent moons. She stretches, then walks up to her son's trailer, opening the door without knocking. Over the last few years, she'd grown accustomed to Travis's scent, but her oldest son's stink is different: musty like a scab, a stench that draws you in. The odor is so strong she holds her breath as she walks to the sofa where Stephen sleeps. When she gets to him she exhales in a long steady stream and breathes in Jesse's world. Something rises in the back of her throat. She holds it down.

She'd not wanted to stay at Jesse's, but there was nowhere else to go. All she had left was Jesse and Billy. The first and the last in the line of Bill Lowe, the man who started it all, a man she still sees in the eyes of her sons.

Stephen wakes slowly. He's almost two, and has a

different look than her other boys. Softer maybe. Less dangerous.

"Morning, baby."

"Shit, don't remember you talking to me like that."

Jesse appears behind his mother, shirtless and bulging, scratching at his chest with a hairy pinky.

"You don't remember nothing, Jesse. Done drank your brains away."

"Never had none to begin with."

"Yeah, hon, you did, before you took all them hits in football."

Jesse's laugh sounds like his father's. "I's the one doing the damage."

"You doing the damage now. All that drinking."

"Maybe you right. Cain't even remember most them games."

"I can."

"You gone cook some breakfast?" says Jesse.

"This your place, ain't it?"

"When Creesha get up we just go on down to McDonald's. Ain't nobody cooking around here."

"I'll cook for you, Jesse. But I got to feed Stephen first."

"That boy still on the titty?"

Tina already had her shirt halfway up, revealing a soft white fold of skin, but she stops, pulling the shirt back down. "Don't call it that."

"Titty?"

"Yeah, don't do that to me."

"What you want me to call it?"

Tina brings Stephen to her breast. He's big enough to just stand between her legs and drink.

"I don't know, but it don't got to be ugly. You's just like this right here till you were three year old. Billy stayed on till he's almost five."

"Sound like Billy. Always the baby, till this little shit come along."

"Jesse, I swear."

"You really let us hang on that long?"

"Don't bother me none. Hell, it's free."

Jesse is laughing when Creesha enters the room, holding tight to her baby girl, Neesy. Neesy looks like a Lowe through and through, except she has Creesha's coarse hair, wiry at the temples, and skin the color of dried red dirt. But there is no denying those ears. Biggest thing on her. Lowe ears.

"What's so damn funny?" says Creesha.

"Momma spoiling Travis's boy over there. Shit, soft as Travis is, bet that baby gone break Billy's titty-sucking record."

"Dammit, Jesse."

"Sorry, Momma," says Jesse. "You still gone cook me some breakfast?"

"Yeah," says Tina, plucking her nipple from Stephen's mouth, tucking her breast away and standing. "But then I need to get back to Shady Grove. Clean up whatever mess Travis and Billy done left me."

"Thought you went over there already?" Jesse says.

Tina's back goes tight.

"Yeah, Tina. You left out here about as soon as you got that baby down last night," says Creesha, scrunching up her brow. "You probably don't remember. You was high as a kite."

"Naw."

"Yeah, Momma. You tore outta here, said you had to go check on Billy."

"Went to McDonald's. Got to feed myself sometime too."

"That ain't what you said last night," says Creesha.

"Y'all should know better than to trust me when I been smoking. Them Mexicans lace that dope these days, make me half crazy, but damn if it don't help me sleep."

Creesha's gaze moves from Tina to Jesse. "You supposed to be smoking that shit while you still breast-feeding?"

Tina looks at Creesha and forces a smile. Baby Neesy squirms in the girl's arms. She's probably hungry. Tina doesn't know if that baby is Jesse's or Billy's—or somebody else's entirely—but she knows it's hungry.

"Smoking don't hurt no baby, Cree. It's natural."

"You brought him to our *house*?"

Marley stands beside the running water in the sink, but she doesn't wash a dish, doesn't fill a glass. The water is simply a sound to hide their voices. They've already talked all around it, been in the kitchen for nearly an hour. Trent leans back, looking past the swinging doors and into the living room: Billy sits in the recliner, Lorna and Ava on the couch.

"This morning," Trent says, "all that stuff you said. How we should *help* Bill."

"This," says Marley, pushing the faucet's handle, steam rising in the sink, "is different."

"It's just like what your family did for me."

"No, Trent, this is different. *Way* different. What you said you saw—"

"I'm literally doing exactly what you told me to do."

"How do you not remember," Marley says and turns to him, perspiration dotting her upper lip, "what happened with us?"

Trent remembers, of course he remembers. Lorna is exactly half the age of Marley now. That fact alone makes it hard to forget the final year they spent together in the Dommers' house.

"Do you want Lorna to make the same mistake I did?"

"*Mistake?*" says Trent.

"You know what I mean."

Billy's knuckles looked like they'd been sandblasted. And his eyes, God, his eyes were black and deep. Trent saw fear in Billy's eyes and remembered what real fear felt like.

"I just thought maybe this would work," says Trent.

"Maybe," says Marley, fanning her neck. "Or *maybe* he'll sneak into Lorna's room when we're asleep and—" She stops. Exhales. "Did you even think of that?"

Everything is hot now. The kitchen like a sauna, air so thick Trent feels the weight of it in his lungs. "It was right after practice. Bill had just apologized to the team and was standing there in the parking lot. He looked pitiful, babe, pitiful. So I asked him."

"To come to our house?"

"Yeah. If he wanted to stay with us."

"*Stay* with us? God. How long do you plan on him staying with us?"

"Maybe just for the playoffs?"

"That could be two more weeks."

"I know, but think of the good that could come from it."

Marley rolls her eyes. "We would be able to keep an eye on him, make sure he's out on that field," she says. "But I don't know. You need to call Dad."

"No," says Trent, a sharp edge to his voice.

"What has gotten into you?"

"This is what's best for Bill." Trent pauses, sure of himself now. "What's best for us."

Marley wipes a bead of sweat from her brow. "And you're sure he didn't see you out there, at that trailer?"

"*Mar,*" says Trent, standing, stepping toward her. "He didn't see me, okay?"

Marley's hand goes to a 1990 state championship ring dangling from a chain around her neck, years before Trent's reign as the Jaguars' quarterback. She'd been a "water girl," always on that sideline, always close to her daddy.

Trent reaches for his wife's shoulders. "What you said this morning, about Travis being a bad man, about us protecting Bill—I prayed about it." Trent takes the ring from his wife's fingers and lets it fall to her neck. "It makes sense. It's the right thing to do. So for once in your life, I'm begging you, please, just trust me."

Marley's eyes move to the refrigerator, Lorna's junior year report card, Ava's handprints in pink. She pulls away. "Billy has to play, Trent. That's all that matters. So, yes, he can stay here. That way we can keep a close eye on him, but you better make sure he's out on that field come Friday."

Trent feels the heat rising in the sink. He moves that direction, planning to shut it off, or at least turn it cool, the kids can't hear them anyway, but instead peeks back around the swinging doors. What he sees sets his blood to boil: Lorna and Ava remain on the couch, but the recliner is empty.

The swinging doors slam into the kitchen walls. Trent's hands gnarl like paws at his waist. He scans the room, head twitching from side to side, searching for something—for someone—that is not there.

"Where is he?" snaps Marley from behind, at the doors now.

"I-I don't know."

"Jesus," says Lorna. "He went to the bathroom."

Trent bends at the waist, hands on his knees. "Thank God, I thought he was—"

"Thought I's what?" says Billy, stepping out from the bathroom. Voices on the television laugh as he stands before the speechless family. Trent watches the boy and for the first time reconsiders bringing him home. There is a moment, when the screen blinks to commercial, where everything in the house is silent, everything except the sound of the rushing hot water, steaming in the kitchen.

9.

Don't ask people for nothing. Never have, never will. Didn't ask Coach to bring me here neither. I's just standing in the parking lot after practice. Didn't wanna go home. Ain't never going home again. So I's just standing there, pissed, when Coach pull up in his little car and say, "Hey, Bill?"

Feel like maybe, if he'd a just called me Billy, I might have said no—saved him the trouble. But he didn't, so I didn't. And now here I am in a leather recliner with Coach weird-ass daughter on the sofa, that little baby girl sitting right next to her.

Denton a small school, only about a month left before Christmas break, but I ain't never talked to this girl. Every time I look at her I think about what everybody say. How she talk funny, like she speaking a different language. She keep looking at me, cutting her eyes like she gonna try something. But she ain't. Girl like her far, far from Billy Lowe.

Coach and his wife in the kitchen, arguing. They got the water on like we cain't hear them, but we can. Parents so dumb. Don't matter if they rich, they still dumb.

I hear a click and turn my head in time to see Coach daughter try and hide her phone. I know she just took a picture of me. She lost in the thing now, fingers tapping on the screen. Bet she already posting it somewhere. Saying something bad about Billy Lowe. *Got this skank boy in my house*. Something like that.

Feel it rise up in me like the heat from the kitchen. Why Coach keep it so damn hot in here? It a thick, wet kind a heat. I want to take the phone from her, throw it through the window. I watch her tapping away on the screen and I know if I sit here any longer, I'll do it.

I stand.

The news playing on the TV. Ain't never watched the news in my life. She stop tapping the phone. She look at me.

"What are you doing?" she say.

I keep standing, my eyes stuck on the TV. A good-looking woman on there talking about rape and murder. Only rich people watch the news. Got to keep tabs on people like me, but they don't know. Coach daughter, she don't know neither. Whatever she got on that phone don't tell her nothing about Billy Lowe.

"Did you hear me?" she say. "I asked what you were doing."

Sound like a damn teacher, the way she talking. I turn to her. She looking at me now, but then look back to her phone quick. She look like a teacher too, one of them lazy teachers always trying to look like the kids. Wearing some kinda wrap on her head, and a dress, a full-length hippie dress. Who she think she is? Where she think she is? This ain't California.

"I hear you," I say.

"That's no way to respond to friendly conversation."

"That what this is?"

"I don't see why not."

She look different. That's the only way I know how to put it. Don't look nothing like the woman on TV, or the cheerleaders at school. My old girl, Creesha, she used to wear so much makeup couldn't tell it was her when she took it off. Made her face almost white, cheeks pink. Coach daughter don't got no makeup on, don't even look like she wearing a bra under that hippie dress. And her eyes huge, biggest things on her face. She ain't cute, though. That ain't the word for what she is.

"Come here," she say, and pat the sofa like she calling some dog. Her baby sister sitting on the other side of her start to laugh and reach for Coach daughter's hands. I try to remember Little Brother laughing, but I cain't.

"Nah," I say. "Good where I'm at."

"Standing in the middle of the living room? That is no place for socializing."

I ain't got a clue what she just said.

"For talking," she say. "You know, friendly conversation."

"Told you, I ain't trying to have no—" but before I can get it out, she lean over from the sofa and grab hold of my wrist. Her hand cool, smooth, like limestone. Like the walls in Eden Falls Cave, that crack in Linker Mountain where Creesha was always wanting to go and make out, like we cain't do that in the trailer, or at the river, anywhere other than Eden Falls. That cave scare the shit out of me. So damn dark you cain't see nothing. Just got to feel your way along the walls all slick and cool, almost cold, like Lorna fingers on my wrist, pulling me to that spot on the couch.

"See," she say, smiling. "Was that so bad?"

When she smile her teeth like her eyes, big and white. Whitest teeth I ever seen. Straight and square, just like I'm guessing Coach wanted them to be.

"Still with the silent treatment, huh?"

I don't even realize she still got ahold of my wrist until she jerk her hand away. Jerk it like she touched a hot skillet, a burner on the stove. She rubbing her hand now like it really burnt. Cain't imagine what she felt from me. Whatever it was, it weren't something she could hold on to long.

"Sorry," I say.

"It speaks?"

I push up from the sofa. She making fun of me? Who the hell she think she is? She take hold of my wrist again, and this time it ain't so much the cool I feel, this time it burn, almost electric, like a fence wire, and it enough to stop me from standing.

"I want to show you something," she say and take the phone from her lap.

"Nah," I say, but she already got the thing out, already showing me. I was right, she took a picture of me, but it weren't like what I thought. It a good picture. She done some weird stuff to it, but I look tough, mean. Look like I think I look. Just sitting there, kinda hunched forward, kinda pissed off. She changed the colors, whatever the hell it is girls do to pictures. And then, in a red that make me think of Him and syrup, she wrote something just above my head.

"Are you familiar with Theogenes?"

I feel like maybe she videoing this whole thing, gonna try and make me look stupid then show all the kids at school. I don't say nothing.

"You remind me of him."

"Who?"

"*Theogenes*—he was a beast."

I fold my arms tight across my chest, stare at the good-looking woman on TV. Bet she don't know who Theo-genes is.

"It's a compliment, man. Don't be so sensitive."

Sensitive? I try and stand, but she hold me down again. My older brother Jesse always say, "Let them bitches think you don't want none, then they'll come crawling for it." That worked with girls like Creesha.

"Theogenes was an ancient Greek pugilist—a boxer—and he was the best."

"What that got to do with me?"

"Back then boxing was different," she say. "They'd strap guys to these gigantic stones. Place them only an arm's reach away from each other, and then tell them to go at it. One man would beat the other to death, and that was that."

"So?"

"*So?*" she say and smile. "That's sport, right? Like, that's football. I don't agree with it, but Theogenes was strapped to the stone fourteen hundred times, and fourteen hundred times he emerged the victor. That's badass."

Did she just say *badass*? She did. And now she looking at me, got ahold of my wrist again, and she ain't jerked away. Creesha used to jerk away, always teasing until I couldn't take it no more. That's how babies happen. Get a man so worked up he cain't think. But this girl, she ain't teasing, she squeezing me like she feel the burn, like she want the burn, like she tough. Everything inside me start to churn in a way that feel like fire, but it ain't—this something different.

"My name is Lorna."

"I know, you Coach daughter."

"My *name*," she say again and kinda lean into me, "is Lorna."

I don't do nothing, cain't, just sit and watch her coming for me. But before she get there her little sister start howling, like she feel the fire too. She start howling and Coach daughter—*Lorna*—she turn to that baby, and I'm gone.

In the bathroom I run water across my face. It ain't cold. Lukewarm at best. Still, I splash the water on my cheeks and look in the mirror. Forgot I got Momma's Bud Light shirt on. Stupid. In there with Coach daughter wearing a ratty beer shirt. Stupid.

I put a towel on my face. In the darkness, He's there. But He ain't got the busted head yet. He talking some shit, talking about me not playing ball no more. Momma crying.

Above the towel rack there a picture of Coach family from back in California. Only picture in the bathroom. His wife got them big eyes like Lorna. Even the little one got them eyes. Coach look like a man should look standing there with all his women. I try to imagine how Billy Lowe'd look like in a picture like that, but all I see is Creesha and baby Neesy, and they ain't with me. They out in the trailer with Jesse.

When I open the bathroom door everybody in the TV room now. Coach standing there in a hit position, crouched down like he ready to fight. His pretty wife look pissed or scared, cain't tell the difference, and that baby still crying.

"He's in the bathroom," say Lorna.

I watch Coach breathe in deep and stand, like maybe he thought I's in the garage beating his car with a bat, or in the room where he sleep looking through the drawers for money. He say, "Thank God, I thought he was—"

"Thought I's *what*?" I say and walk back to the chair.

"Bill . . ." say Coach, mouth turning funny.

"Thought I's what?"

They all staring at me but Lorna. All them eyes, staring at me like I crazy. And that little baby girl still crying. But she ain't got nothing to cry about. I cain't breathe. My fists clench. I want the rock. I want the straps. I want another man across from me.

I look to Lorna.

She looking at me now too, but it different. Like her cool hand on my wrist. She shaking her head, those big eyes speaking to me from across the room. Her look so steady, so calm. She take the fire out of me just like that. I look away to that crying baby girl on the sofa and I see why she crying. There a bottle about two foot out her reach. She hungry. But don't nobody see why baby girl crying cause they all looking at me.

I go to her.

"Now, Bill," say Coach.

The wife tense up as I walk past her. Coach grunt too, like he ready for it, but ain't nothing coming for you, Coach, not today. Lorna smiling already cause she see.

I pick the bottle up, slide it into baby girl mouth like I done Little Brother a thousand times, and finally, she stop crying.

10.

The tiny Sentra is packed full. Tina and Creesha ride in the back, holding the babies while Jesse drives. Denton flies past in shades of crumbling rust and gray. Another Dollar General went up a couple months ago. Its new yellow sign shines in stark contrast to the decay.

The car turns into Shady Grove. Rows of trailers run as far as the eye can see. Tina's trailer is in the back. There's a fence that puts an end to the park and marks the beginning of a chicken farm. Six chicken houses sit less than a hundred yards away, roasting in the heat, their sharp stench all but unnoticeable to the inhabitants of Shady Grove.

Jesse puts the car in park and wraps an arm around the passenger seat, turning back to his mother. "Want me to go in with you?"

"I got it, Jesse."

"You sure?"

"Shit, you heard her," says Creesha. "Besides, me and Neesy hungry. Tina didn't cook nothing like she said."

Jesse huffs and jerks back to the steering wheel. The car shakes as he turns.

"Thanks, Jesse," says Tina, and then she's up and out of the backseat, walking toward her trailer.

Stephen is asleep in her arms when she gets to the

screen door. Tina notices it's broken. She wonders, for a moment, who has broken the door. It could be any of them. She remembers the night, how Travis had gotten so upset over that silly piece of paper, like their life wasn't already filled with enough pain. And then she left. Stayed gone. Surely she'd remember if she'd come back to this place, no matter how much she'd smoked. She'd smoked a lot, trying to forget, trying to sleep. But there's something about that screen door, something about how it's broken—just barely hanging on—that makes her question everything.

She looks back over her shoulder to Jesse and Creesha and the Sentra. Creesha's letting Jesse have it, head on a swivel, side to side, probably telling him to get going, they got things to do. Jesse cracks open a beer, chugs it down, and Tina is thankful. When he starts with whiskey this early in the morning, nothing good follows.

"*Jesse?*" she whispers toward the car, trying not to wake Stephen.

He cracks the window, sticks his mouth to it. "Yeah?"

"Y'all wait on me, alright?"

"Wait on *you*?" snaps Creesha.

"We waiting, Momma," Jesse says. "Go on in, make sure everything alright."

"Thanks, baby."

The screen door whines as Tina pulls it back. The trailer envelops her, thick and steamy, cutting through the stink of the chicken houses. The pitiful door slaps shut, a tired sound, like it's just waiting to fall.

At first the trailer is so dark Tina can't see anything. Slowly the dome light from the kitchen casts its orange glow across the cramped room and Tina makes out a shape lying on the floor.

It's not the first time she's found Travis like this, not the first time he's passed out, but there's something hanging in the air, a smell that makes her heart flutter, makes the baby in her arms feel heavy and warm.

"Travis?"

She steps to him on tiptoes, creeping. He's on his side, the light from the kitchen washing over more of his body the closer she gets. After three steps, she sees that this time is different from all the others.

"*Mercy.*"

Tina whispers the word like a prayer, and then she sees it. The cast-iron skillet she's used for years to scramble the boys' eggs, fry their bacon, just about the only love she'd been able to give her boys was fried up in that pan. It's been cast aside, thrown back under the kitchen table, but it's there.

Something catches and breaks through the haze of the night. Had she been here? Had she really come back to this place like Jesse said? Were her fingerprints on that skillet? No. It was impossible. She went to McDonald's. She walked through the drive-thru, ordered a Big Mac and fries. But then she remembers driving Travis's Sentra and can make no sense of walking to McDonald's.

There's a sound in the trailer now. Tina almost doesn't recognize it, distant, far off, like the tornado siren on Wednesdays at noon. Tina blinks and realizes Stephen is crying, wailing, and staring right at the mass of death on her kitchen floor.

She's frozen, listening to the cries of her son, letting them wash over her and take her back to the sleepless nights, so many sleepless nights with mouths to feed.

Tina places her hand over her youngest son's eyes and walks out of the trailer.

The sun is bright, blinding. Tina is thinking of Billy, only Billy. She squints, fearing Jesse and Creesha have left already. But then the car comes into focus, and still Tina thinks of Billy.

"Everything alright, Momma?"

She pauses, turning back as the screen door snaps shut. She can still see the gash above Travis's eye, the skillet slicked with blood.

"Yeah, Jesse, everything fine."

"Alright, then. Cree say we got to go."

Tina nods, hand over her eyes, shielding the sun, watching as they leave. The car is turning off the dirt onto the gravel when she calls for them. "*Wait.*" The Sentra jerks, slowly reversing until Jesse is only a few feet away from her, his arm dangling out the window, too close to the trailer and what lies inside.

"You holler, Momma?"

Tina wedges her body between Jesse's eyes and the door, doing her best to block his view. "Can y'all keep Stephen for a while?"

"*What?*" Creesha flails in the backseat. "Nah, hell nah. We got our hands full with Neesy."

"You sure you alright, Momma?"

"Just need to get some stuff done around the house. It's a mess."

"Like we ain't got shit to do?"

"Shut the fuck up, Cree," barks Jesse.

Tina is thankful for a moment, but then she remembers it is still early, barely noon, and she has never seen a man change so much after beer number twenty.

"We can take him, Momma," says Jesse. "Ain't no skin off my back."

"Appreciate it," she says, opening the car door, placing her baby boy in the seat next to Creesha. The girl doesn't even look at him, doesn't even turn her head, or buckle him in, or hold him. The car drives away.

The porch creaks under Tina's weight. The screen door slaps shut. She steps over the body on the kitchen floor as if it weren't there, pulls out a chair from under the table and sits down.

"Travis?"

Silence.

"What am I going to do with you?"

11.

Coach driving fast, tearing down the road to the field house like something got him stirred up. But shit, it almost been a whole damn week, and I been good.

Ain't been easy, either. The Powers some weird-ass people. Got three trash cans: one for paper and plastic and Coke cans, another for baby diapers. I don't even know what the third one for. Still cain't put my finger on Coach wife, though. She got a mean streak in her remind me of Bull. Lorna alright. Kinda weird. Kinda cool. They let me sleep on the couch. Coach look embarrassed when he ask me if that okay. Didn't tell him nothing about how me and Little Brother share a room. How Momma used to keep all these stray cats and dogs in our trailer. Don't matter we got rid a the last dog about two years ago—right around the time Little Brother come along—the whole place still smell like the pound. That sofa cool with me. Don't really sleep much, just watch TV. Sometimes, late at night, I can hear Coach whispering to his pretty wife. Ain't nothing like what I used to hear in the trailer, but them whispers don't sound that happy either. Started to worry they whispering about me. Then Mrs. Powers bought me some clothes. Lorna made a funny face when she saw me in that black polo shirt, them new jeans. Weren't sure how to take it, so

I didn't say nothing. Been fighting hard not to show them I'm scared. Five days and I only asked to call Momma a few times. Don't got no cell phone. Had to ask Coach to use his. Ain't really worried about Momma. She take care of herself. Little Brother the one got me worried.

"You hear from Momma?"

"I've tried, Bill. She doesn't answer."

"Probably ran out a minutes."

I look over at Coach and see he smiling. Got his window rolled down, hand waving through the air, letting it catch and dance.

"Bill?" say Coach, still grinning. "We need to talk."

My heart drop. Maybe I read him all wrong, maybe he just nervous cause he got to talk to me. But I been good, real good. Ain't even said nothing about being suspended, or the trailer. Ain't nobody said nothing about the trailer. Should a kept my mouth shut about Momma. Stupid. Billy Lowe you can be so damn stupid.

"Yeah?"

"Manners, Bill."

Kinda piss me off, the way he always wanting me to talk like we in the army or something. "Yes *sir*?"

"You and I are similar," he say, and I breathe a little because he ain't got nothing to tell me, nothing bad anyway.

"When I was young, younger than you, I went through six foster homes in five years."

Feel like he lying. Ain't no way Coach soft ass was in no foster home. No way. He must see it on my face, cause he leaning across the console now, pointing to his forehead.

"You see that scar, the one above my left eye?"

I see it. Don't look like much to me, but it there.

"I hit a boy at my last foster home, a big boy, and he hit me back. That's where that scar came from."

I nod, but that ain't nothing.

Coach laugh. "Over something so silly."

I can feel him waiting for me to ask about it, and now I don't want to. I don't care what Coach say, he ain't like me.

"*Football*, of all things, it was over football—a Chargers game."

I hate the Chargers, probably the softest-looking team in the league. That baby blue and yellow, that little stupid lightning bolt. *Soft*.

"Yeah, San Diego, they were my favorite team," say Coach. "And I really wanted to watch the game, and this big boy, this bully, he just wouldn't let me watch it."

I nod, but don't wanna hear it. This some playground bullshit, some kid story.

"So I hit him."

Coach shift the car into park cause we at the field house now. I check the clock. A little past eight. The other boys in there about to start workouts with Bull, but Coach just sitting here with me.

"And I kept hitting him. I can still remember it. He hit me back. Got me good. So I grabbed a lamp and I hit him with it too. I wanted to kill him, Bill. And if they hadn't pulled me off, I would have. Not a doubt in my mind, I would've killed that boy, and I wouldn't be here with you right now."

He ain't looking at me, just staring straight through the windshield like he watching it all over again. And we just sitting there, and there's power in just sitting cause I know

Coach need to be in there with the rest the team but he out here with me, telling me this story, and now I'm thinking maybe it ain't a kid story. Maybe this something real.

"And then a coach took me in," say Coach, still looking straight ahead. "A man by the name of Larry Dommers. I lived with his family until I graduated high school, played quarterback for him, too. Then I married Marley, went to college, and worked my butt off so I could provide for my family." He pause and turn to me. "And Bill, I would have never done any of that without Coach Dommers telling me the secret."

I can hear Bull blowing his whistle now. The weights already banging around in there. Coach turn the car off. I feel them weights, heavy, like my heart thudding in my chest. My heart beating like that cause I wanna know the secret. I want what Coach talking about. He looking at me now. I cain't help it, I turn to him. Something rise up from my gut to my throat.

"Do you want to know the secret?"

I nod, just barely.

And then Coach say, "*Jesus.*"

Kinda hoped it was bigger than Jesus.

"Do you have a personal relationship with Jesus Christ?"

Jesus like LeBron, or one them big-time movie stars, like The Rock. Them people on another planet. How I supposed to have a personal relationship with The Rock—with *Jesus*?

"I-I don't think so."

"That's what I thought."

"What I got to do to get it?"

"First you must confess your sins."

There's something about the way Coach looking at me now. Like this mean too much to him. Like he want me to say it too bad.

"We could talk about it, Bill. You and me. Your sins, your confession. I could walk you through the steps."

"You want me to do it right now?"

Coach laugh, but it sound fake too, like he just buying time. "You can," he say, "but you have to really think about your sins. You have to truly confess. That's the only way it works."

"What'll happen after that?"

"Your whole life will start to get better. Trust me, I know. That's exactly what happened to me."

Ain't no way it work like that. If it was that easy then why ain't Momma confess to Jesus a long time ago? Get us up and out Shady Grove before He showed up? We went to church one Easter back when I's little. Nothing but old people sleeping and a man up front hollering.

"Do you want to confess to me?"

"Like tell you all the bad stuff I ever done?"

"Not all of it, just the big stuff."

"And then things'll get better? Just like that? Sound too good to be true."

"It is," he say. "It's Jesus's gift to you. That's why He died on the cross. He made that sacrifice so you could be forgiven."

I shake my head.

"With Jesus you could go to college, you could be a coach, a lawyer, a doctor—you could be whatever you wanted to be."

I turn from him because it all too much. And it ain't true. It a nice thing to say—it is—but it ain't true. Ain't a single Lowe ever finished high school, sure ain't been to college. Ain't no way.

"Look at me, Bill."

Them weights clanking in my head, my heart.

"I think you're good enough to earn a football scholarship. That could be your ticket. They'll help you with the work and make sure you make it to class. It'd be your way out, but you can't do it alone."

Ain't never thought about it like that. Don't nobody get scholarships from Denton. Too small. We only got one McDonald's. But it kinda make sense—more sense than Jesus. I know football, and ain't nobody ever been any better at running a football than Billy Lowe. Nobody.

"Nah."

"Yes, Bill. You're good enough, and I have a few connections that might help, but you're going to have to work hard and pray harder. You'll have to sacrifice great things, just like Jesus."

"I'll work for it."

"And?"

"I don't know about confessing to Jesus and all that, Coach. Some the stuff I done, you probably wouldn't wanna hear it."

Coach nod, eyes tight but happy. "When you're ready to talk, you know where to find me."

He open the car door quick after that line, like he trying to make a point. And then he disappear in the field house, already blowing his whistle when I step out the car. I walk in and sit down under a bar. All the boys looking at me.

Don't even change out my new clothes. The bar feel good and heavy. I start lifting it, pushing that weight cause it mean something now, and praying. Whispering in my head, *Jesus? Jesus? Jesus?* But Coach blowing his whistle so loud I cain't hear nothing. Just feel that weight on my chest, my heart.

12.

Trent is in his office when the phone rings.

He smiles before he answers it, smiles because he feels good, as good as he's felt since the night at the trailer. The conversation with Billy earlier that morning was a turning point. And then the workout, it was different, a good kind of different. They had perfect attendance for the first time all season. Jarred Trotter even worked hard, showing no lingering ill will from the keg lunges. And Billy—Billy worked harder than Trent had ever seen a high school boy work. Trent had never been prouder of a player, but beneath it all, there was something tugging at Trent.

The phone continues to ring.

Trent knew the type of boys that received scholarships: giants and freaks—a combination of size and speed that people paid money to see. Billy was five foot ten, two hundred pounds: a good size for high school football. He was fast, but not *that* fast. He was tough—there was no doubting his toughness—but tough doesn't earn a college scholarship. It didn't help matters Billy was white and under six feet tall. Trent knew college coaches saw things in black-and-white, inches and pounds. There was the other thing, too. The truth Trent wouldn't let himself think but was there, lingering behind every word he'd said to Billy about Jesus.

How much did the boy really remember from Saturday night? Had he noticed the gray car parked just beyond the trailer? Over the last five days, Trent had been unable to get a read on Billy. All the Sunday-morning questions had gone unanswered and now it was Friday. Game day. A confession would be good—for Billy *and* Trent.

On the fourth ring, Trent takes the phone from the receiver and puts it to his ear.

"Pirate Field House," says Trent, surprised by the voice on the other end but still able to keep his tone steady. "Hello, Sheriff. Yes, I have a minute."

Sheriff Timmons asks Trent if he's heard anything from Tina Lowe in the last few days. Trent tells him he hasn't. Timmons says there might be a reason for that, and he'd like to come meet with Trent to discuss the details that afternoon.

Trent glances at the computer on his desk, watching his mouth move in the darkened screen. "But this is Friday, Sheriff. We have a game tonight. You know, the playoff game against Harrison?"

Silence on the other end of the line.

"I might have a little time right after school," adds Trent. "Around four, if you want to stop by then?"

Timmons agrees to the time, but before hanging up, he tells Trent this could be serious, especially given Billy's current living situation. Trent wonders how the sheriff knows, but then remembers this is small-town Arkansas, not California. There's something in Sheriff Timmons's tone that makes Trent remember Bradshaw's threat. Trent imagines the sheriff wanting to come down on Billy like all the teachers who've misunderstood the boy his entire life. Trent says, "Thank *ya*, Sheriff," trying hard to sound like he was born and raised in the hills, and then he hangs up.

Sheriff Timmons slides his cell phone into his breast pocket and kneels in the dirt. His shoulders are wide, but there's no hiding his gut. He's an overgrown high school linebacker with a crew cut and swagger, built not for speed or action but paperwork and intimidation. Sweat stains blossom out from both armpits.

The Lowes' trailer stands just behind him, leaning a little with the heat. The phone is pressed back against Timmons's ear when he stands.

"And just what're you thinking I'm supposed to find out here?" says Timmons.

A bead of sweat rolls out from under his wide-brimmed campaign hat.

"I hear you, Mr. Bradshaw, but I don't see nothing."

He wipes the sweat away with the back of his hand.

"God, I can't remember it being this damn hot in November." Timmons rolls his eyes. "I'm looking, Don. I'm out here looking. What makes you think Tina and Travis didn't just run off on that boy?"

Timmons nods, scanning the trailer.

"Hell yeah, I know Jesse Lowe. Played ball with him, didn't I?"

A breeze picks up, rattling the screen door. Timmons's eyes go to the sound as he steps toward the trailer.

"Might have something here," Timmons says. "The

screen door looks like somebody damn near busted it down."

Timmons pushes his face to the window by the door. The sun reflects back in his eyes, causing him to squint. The window is filthy, covered in a thick layer of dirt and grime, obstructing the sheriff's view like foggy swimming goggles.

"Can't see nothing," says Timmons, hands pressed to the glass. "Naw, Don. Can't go inside there yet. Not without a warrant. I'm an elected official. Somebody get word about that and it'd be on the front page of the *Siftings Herald*."

Timmons moves back off the steps, back in the dirt, toeing the tire tracks again.

"Yep, sure did," says Timmons. "Saw what Billy done to Austin, but that don't mean he went and killed nobody."

Drops of sweat dot the dirt beneath the hulking sheriff, squatting again in the road.

"Travis's car's gone. Look like somebody tore out of here in a hurry," says Timmons. "I'm telling you, I bet them sorry suckers ran off on that boy. Soon as they realized he weren't gonna get to play no more—*poof*—gone."

Timmons squints, bending closer to the dirt.

"Yeah, I called Coach Powers. Gonna have a visit with him tonight before the game."

The cruiser shakes as the sheriff wedges himself inside.

"Naw, I don't mind if you come along," says Timmons, sweating against the waft of the cruiser's AC vents. "I got a hard time trusting a Californian myself."

13.

Sitting in my locker, got my jersey and jeans on, the new jeans Mrs. Powers bought me. I'm watching all the boys get ready and I can barely stand it. Jarred walking around in his underwear. Got his pads on, acting tough. Going up to some the younger guys, giving them pep talks. He don't come my way, though. Got big headphones over my ears, listening to Dr. Dre. Old stuff off *The Chronic*. Momma always say my daddy like Dre cause he sound so mean. I reach down in my backpack. Take out a book. Bet Daddy never read no books.

Think back on the school day, how I got my tray at lunch and tried to sit down with Jarred and all the other guys at the big table. They didn't even look at me, like they ain't notice me sit down. But they did. They know all about Billy Lowe. They just scared. Scared of me and trying to hide it. Cain't blame them. Austin Murphy was sitting up there by Jarred, gnawing away on some Tyson chicken his daddy probably brought him. Both Austin's eyes still black, nose swolled up thick like a cat's. All them boys at the table know why Austin nose look like that.

Tried to tell them what Coach told me about a scholarship. Jarred laughed right in my face. Told me, "You can't be suspended and get offered no damn scholarship." Said some other shit about how you had to be Black to play big-time, college ball. Made me wanna take that Big Mac Jarred was gnawing on and shove it down his throat, but I didn't get the chance.

Jarred forgot all about that scholarship when Lorna Powers walked by. He started in talking about how she don't never wear no bra, how he wouldn't mind getting some from the coach's daughter. I's thinking about doing more than just stuffing that Big Mac down his throat when Lorna walk right up to our table and asked if I wanted to eat with her. I said, "Yeah, sure," and didn't say nothing to Jarred or nobody else when I left.

Lorna was looking good, different, but good. Like them funny earrings she wear every day, shaped like a feather but made out of metal. She even had her hair down and maybe the tiniest bit of makeup on.

Followed her down the hall and into the library. Cain't tell you the last time I step foot in the library. But it was quiet, and the lunch table, the guys—all that was gone.

Lorna show me all these books she like. Only book I can remember reading in my life is *Where the Red Fern Grows*, and I didn't really read it. Teacher read it to us in fourth grade. It was alright. Liked how that boy's name was Billy. Like how it was set up in the hills. But them dogs weren't nothing like the dogs Momma keep around the trailer.

Lorna said Coach told her about me working for the scholarship. Said she wanted to help.

The Old Man and the Sea. That the book she put in my hands. Said this the sort a book they read in college.

She ask me to read the first page to her, sitting there in the library.

"I can read," I said.

"I know you can read, but it helps to read aloud."

Ever since fifth grade, when the teachers quit reading them books to us, I hated it. Kids always laughing at Billy Lowe when he stumble over the words. Never sound like it sound in my head. Words get tangled up in there somewhere, come out sounding stupid.

"It's just me, Billy," Lorna said and touch my arm. But it weren't gonna work, not when it came to this.

"I ain't reading."

"Fine."

She left me sitting there, on the library couch, alone. If the guys saw me sitting in the library, I'd never hear the end of it. I watched her walk away from me, watched her like the guys at the lunch table watched her. Lorna weren't cute. She beautiful. I could see that then. Everything moving soft and sexy under that long hippie dress. Then she gone, out the library doors, and I's alone. The bell rang and I shoved that book in my backpack.

And now, here it is game time, and what am I doing? Reaching for that damn book. Read a little last night too, on Coach leather sofa when everybody went to bed. Some old Mexican fishing. That about all I got so far. I lean back in my locker. Prop my backpack up so cain't nobody see, and I start reading.

> *He was an old man who fished alone in a skiff in the Gulf Stream and he had gone eighty-four days now without taking a fish.*

I look up and Coach standing there. I shove the book between my legs.

"Bill?"

"Yeah?"

He give me a look. I bite my bottom lip hard enough it hurts. "Yes *sir*?"

"You might want to put those shoulder pads on," he say and kinda grin.

"Why?"

"Never know what might happen tonight."

"I'm playing?"

"You never know. That's all I'm saying."

I don't say no more, just nod and stand, already pulling my jersey up over my head, taking the headphones off, Dre still talking about the struggle. The book fall out and open onto the locker room floor. Coach bend and pick it up.

"Hemingway, huh?"

"I guess."

"He caught that fish yet?"

"Ain't caught nothing."

"Well he does," say Coach. "He catches the biggest fish there ever was, and it's the saddest thing you'll ever read. But it's a good book, Bill—a great book."

I nod, but don't say nothing. Don't make no sense, anyway. If that old man catch his fish, if he get what he want, how that a bad thing? I pull my shoulder pads tight across my chest, click the buckle in the front, and it feel good. About as good as anything's felt in a long-ass time.

14.

Tina had never missed one of Billy's games. When he scored his first touchdown in third grade, she saw it. When he started as a freshman on the varsity squad, Tina drank Southern Comfort from a Coca-Cola bottle and screamed her ass off. As much as the game scared her, Tina lived to watch Billy run. It was beautiful, how fluid and in control he was, nothing like the rest of their life, nothing like the trailer and the mess she was left with now.

Today, though, she'd not thought once of football, or the fact that it was a Friday night, getting close to seven o'clock, almost time for kickoff. Day had simply turned to night, night to day, as Tina sat and stared at the dead man in her kitchen.

She couldn't quit staring at him, watching the way Travis changed. There was something peaceful about the process, the inevitability of it. Like, if Tina just sat there long enough, all of her problems would melt away.

The smell got really bad on the second day, though, around the same time Travis's body started doing weird stuff. His face turned the color of raw steak and doubled in size. Soft *puffs* leaked from his lips like he was alive. Freaked Tina out but she knew better than to touch him. So she just kept sitting there, a dishrag soaked in vinegar covering her face, listening to the knocks at the door, watching the shadows come and go, but she did not move. They wouldn't come inside. Not yet. Tyler Timmons was a lazy man; the paperwork would take him days.

Before Travis started stinking so bad, Tina had cried for him. After Jesse and Creesha took Stephen away, Tina allowed herself a fistful of tears. Travis had his problems, sure, like all men—but he'd loved Tina. She could see it in his eyes in the night and hear it in the hot whispers that came before dawn. It was Billy didn't get along with Travis. He never said it, but Tina always felt like Billy thought she could do better. That's why he didn't like her man.

Tina had loved Travis from a distance, though, knowing there'd never be another like the original Bill Lowe. He was a man to end all men, a king, but damn if he didn't have a mean streak in him. Where Travis's evil was petty and underhanded, Bill Lowe's nasty burned bright and hot: flashes of blade and fist, blood and bone. He wasn't around long enough to leave his mark on Billy. The boy still thought of his father as some different sort of man, but he was mostly the same. Like Travis, just harder. Billy had his daddy in him. Tina saw it when he ran that football. Running angry and mean, like a chain was strapped to his back and he was dragging the trailer across the field, through the end zone, all the way down to hell.

The green numbers on the microwave turn to seven and Tina stands from the chair, automatic, like her body knows it's supposed to be somewhere, even if her mind can't come to terms with the death in her kitchen. She's almost through the door when she feels the dishrag still covering her nose and mouth. Her hands go to the knot behind her head and the rag falls away. The stench hits Tina harder than Travis ever did.

"We have to play him," Trent says.

"Naw, we don't," Bull says. "Not till the second half."

"First time the Pirates make the playoffs in, what, ten years?"

"Not worth it, Hollywood."

"We need to win."

Trent drops to the floor and begins a round of push-ups.

Bull watches him, knowing all the push-ups in the world won't free him from the weight of that whistle. Bull hopes it isn't as bad as it seems, hopes the young coach isn't on the edge, way out there the way young men get when they want something too much. But then Trent rolls to his back, performs a kip-up, landing on his feet like some sort of California ninja, and Bull can only shake his head and wait for what's to come.

"I'm going to tell Bill he's playing tonight," Trent says.

"Listen now . . ."

Trent already has his hand on the door, but Bull's tone stops him.

"Sheriff Timmons called me yesterday," Bull says. "Something's up. Something nasty with Billy's momma and that boyfriend. Things might move slower around here, but they're moving, Hollywood. I guarantee it."

Trent turns the handle on the door.

"You hear me, son?"

"*Son?*"

"It stinks, that's all I'm trying to say."

"Did Sheriff Timmons tell you that?"

"More or less."

"Well, he didn't say anything to me. Actually, he called this morning and said he wanted to meet before the game, but he never showed up."

Bull's fingers drum across his desk.

"I know Bill, okay?" Trent says. "I mean, he's living with me, for Christ's sake."

"Don't mean you know the boy. Besides, it ain't Billy I'm worried about."

Trent's grip tightens around the door handle.

"They're saying Tina Lowe's boyfriend—Travis Rodney—ain't nobody seen him in the last few days," Bull says. "Hell, ain't nobody seen Tina. Timmons even said he went by a couple times. All the lights out. Couldn't see nothing. Like they just up and ran."

"So?" says Trent, checking his watch.

"*So?*" says Bull. "Do the math: Billy's knuckles look like they been run through a meat grinder and the sumbitch he hate most in the world's missing. Don't take no rocket scientist."

"Billy's been in two fights over the last week, of course his knuckles are raw."

"That ain't helping his case none either." Bull sits back in his chair, propping his feet up on the desk, thinking he's just saved the young ball coach from doing something stupid, but then, as if on cue, the man's wife walks through the door.

Marley is dressed up for the occasion, wearing a gray blouse and black dress pants like she's running for the school board. Bull can't quite get his finger on Marley Powers, but she's a firecracker. He knows that much.

First thing out her mouth: "Is Billy playing tonight?"

Going straight for it. One of the things Bull admires about her.

Trent looks from his wife back to Bull, like he wants the old man to answer her question.

"He's been such a great help around the house," Marley adds, quick and clean. Bull pictures her rehearsing this bit in the mirror. "And there have been no issues at school or practice, right? No problems."

Bull can count on one hand the number of times a woman has been inside the coaches' office. Mainly, it's instances just like this one: some upset momma coming in to fight for her boy. Except Marley isn't Billy's momma.

"Well?" Marley says, folding her arms.

"Bull?" says Trent, hand still on the door to the locker room. "What do you think?"

Bull slides his legs off the desk, standing as he says, "I think y'all better watch how involved you get with Billy Lowe. You stick your neck out for a boy like that, and you're liable to get bit."

"That's ridiculous," Trent says. "I'm going to tell Bill he's playing."

Trent stares at Bull, as if he were daring the man to say something else. Bull takes him up on it: "Don't nobody call him Bill—that's his daddy's name."

Trent says, "I know," glances at his wife, and walks out the door.

The spark in Billy's eyes—the way he already has his shoulder pads and helmet on, just like Trent told him, sitting there by his locker, ready to go—it's worth all of Bull's shit.

Trent smiles as he turns back toward the coaches' office. It'd been such a good morning, Trent's game-day routine adding a moment of clarity amidst the churn of this current storm.

His routine goes like this: the alarm buzzes at five and he jogs two miles. He comes home, takes a cold shower, reciting scripture as the freezing water burns his skin. Then he eats breakfast, alone. Oatmeal with raisins and walnuts. He drinks his coffee black. He arrives at school just before seven, goes into his office as the boys finish their workout, and locks the door until the boys come back around two in the afternoon. Most mornings he watches grainy San Diego Chargers' film to pass time, wearing his baby-blue Dan Fouts jersey out of habit and superstition.

And now the time-tested rituals have paid off.

Billy Lowe is going to play football tonight, going to get some good film that Trent can send to college scouts, maybe the local university, Arkansas Tech. Trent's even beginning to convince himself that Billy is college material, that he really could earn a scholarship—especially at a smaller school—but it won't happen unless Billy plays.

Trent cracks the office door, ready to tell Bull about his plans, but as the door swings open Trent sees Sheriff Timmons and Principal Bradshaw standing alongside Marley and Bull.

"Hidy, Coach," Timmons says, hand outstretched. "Sorry I'm late, but I figured if I waited a bit, I could kill two birds with one stone."

Trent turns to Marley, embarrassed she's having to witness this.

Timmons's fingers fold into his palm as he retracts his hand. "Uh, Coach?"

"This will have to wait," Trent says, standing up straighter. "We only have a few minutes left before kickoff."

"Won't take long," Mr. Bradshaw says, stepping forward now. "Why don't you run and go get Billy. That way we can talk to the two of y'all together. Like Sheriff Timmons said—kill two birds with one stone."

"You're serious?" Marley's voice cuts through the musty locker-room smell of the coaches' office. Principal Bradshaw and Sheriff Timmons turn to her in unison.

"Excuse me, Mrs. Powers?" Bradshaw says.

"You heard me. This is ridiculous."

Trent stares at Marley. He sees her father in her eyes, the way she's not giving either man an inch.

"Easy now," Bradshaw says. "You're a long way from home. We do things a little different around here."

"That's right," Timmons adds, the two men playing off each other. "We abide by a certain set of rules. People know when they're welcome and when they ain't."

"By people," Marley says, "do you mean *women*?"

The two men look at each other.

Bradshaw nods and Timmons says, "I'm sorry, Mrs. Powers, but we're gonna have to ask you to step out. This here's official police business."

Marley whips her head around to face Trent.

"It's official," Trent says without looking at her, "business, Mar." His voice feels strange in his throat. "I'm sorry, but you need to wait outside."

15.

Feel good to be back in my pads. Like putting on a suit. Only wore a suit once, that Easter when Momma took us to church. I'm standing in the bathroom, looking good in the mirror. Got some eye black from a freshman that didn't need it anyway. Smear it all across my cheeks. Make me look mean as hell. I just about got both cheeks covered when I hear Coach holler for me.

"Bill?" he say across the locker room. "Hey Bill, I need to see you in the office real quick."

I jog over cause I'm feeling that good. Ain't nothing bad gonna happen to me, not now that I'm getting to play. Feel damn near invincible wearing these pads and this jersey. Invincible. But when Coach open that door and I see all them men standing round the office—and this close to game time too—I know whatever they got to tell me ain't no good news.

"Billy," say Timmons. "We got a few questions. You got a sec?"

Ask me like I got a choice. I play it cool and nod.

"You seen your momma or Travis in the last week?"

"Nah. I mean—*No sir*," I say, and Coach flash me a thumbs-up, quick.

"Well, ain't nobody else seen them either," say Sheriff.

"I been over there and don't nobody come to the door. Wanted to check with you before I started working on the search warrant. God, I hate me some paperwork."

"Amen to that," say Principal. "You ain't worried, Billy?"

"This ain't the first time they run off on me."

Coach smiling now.

"What about your little brother?" say Bull.

"What about him?"

"You ain't been worried about your little brother? What's his name?"

"Stephen," I say. "And you know I been worried about him, but you know what the Bible say about worrying."

Bull lean back like I just smacked his forehead with the Good Book itself.

Coach cain't keep himself from asking. "What's it say, Bill?"

"Say don't do it. Ain't that right?"

Bull raise one eyebrow like he ain't buying my shit. Coach grinning ear to ear.

"So that's all you know?" say Principal.

"That's it."

"They just up and walk out of your life and you don't know nothing about it?" say Principal. "Your momma, your baby brother, your daddy—"

"He ain't my daddy."

"Naw, he ain't," say Principal. "I went up against your daddy back in my coaching days. Running back for the Forrest City Mustangs. Best damn player I ever seen. But boy, he was sorry as hell."

Principal talking about Daddy like that make my blood

turn to fire. Daddy left when I's young, the youngest, until Little Brother. Weren't even in school yet. What's it take to make a man walk out on his own blood? Daddy had his reasons. Now I'm guessing Momma run away too. But I don't blame her, not after what I seen.

"Yes sir," I say.

"You saying you know your own daddy sorry?" say Principal.

"I don't see what this has to do—"

"Yes *sir*," I say, cutting Coach off. He ain't got to take up for me, not this time. "That why this don't surprise me none."

Bull watching me close. He got a third eye that see straight through high school boys.

"Alright," say Bull.

Timmons say it now too. "Alright."

"Just checking on you," say Principal.

"I'm staying with Coach."

"We know," say Sheriff Timmons.

"And you remember that, Billy," say Principal, but he looking at Coach. "Remember that we know. You got me?"

I nod and Principal don't say nothing else. Just keep standing there. I can hear Coach breathing behind me, sound like he just run a mile.

"Hey, you got your pads on," say Sheriff, studying me. "You playing tonight?"

"Yes sir."

"Awful short suspension," say Principal. "That what we talk about, Coach?"

Coach put his hand on my arm. "If my memory serves me, you told me to come up with a plan for Bill, which is what I did."

"That all I told you?" say Principal.

"That's all I remember."

Principal neck and cheeks go red, ears too. Coach still squeezing my arm, squeezing it hard like he forgot he squeezing it. When he let go, I feel my blood running. Clench and unclench my fists. Bull stick his head in the locker room and tell the other boys we got five minutes till we go out. Something shift in Principal and Sheriff, like they finally remember we in the playoffs. They change, look mean and serious, got they game faces on now. Then they reaching out for me, wanting to shake my hand. I think real hard about walking out the door, but I don't.

"Good luck tonight, Billy," say Principal.

"Yeah, go get 'em," say Sheriff, then he look past me. "And Coach?" Timmons wink before he can even get a word out. "That wife of yours, she's a pistol."

Then they gone, and Coach try to say something nice as we walk into the locker room, something about being proud. Keep looking at me the whole time he giving the pregame speech, still smiling, like he so happy. For what? Cause I said "yes sir"? Cause I talked about the Bible? Coach just keep smiling, like he want me to smile back. But it close to game time and I ain't thinking about Jesus. He about the farthest thing from my mind right now. This my senior year and Principal and Sheriff in there talking about all the things I hate—making me think about Him—and by the time Coach lead the Lord's Prayer, I just about got myself seeing red, tasting blood again.

16.

Billy takes the ball on the Pirates' first possession, slices through the line of scrimmage, tears into the open field, and runs right for the free safety, plowing him over. The Denton faithful—potbellied men and women with sharecropper eyes—rise like a congregation, hands toward the sky, ringing cowbells and stomping their feet.

"You see that?" shouts Trent over the headset.

"See what?" says Bull.

"He had a straight shot at the end zone, no way that kid would have caught him, but he ran him over instead. I've never seen anything like it."

"That's a Lowe boy for you," says Bull. "Jesse would a done the same thing."

Trent alters the ten scripted plays they had practiced on Thursday, mouthing "Deuce Left, 243 Power," as he signals it in.

"You ain't sticking to the script?" says Bull.

"If it *ain't* broke."

Bull's voice crackles through the headset's tiny speakers. "You just say 'ain't'?"

Trent beams as Billy takes the ball, pushes to his right, makes a hard cut, and rumbles sixty yards for a touchdown.

"Sure did," says Trent, laughing and sprinting down the sideline after Billy. The ball soars through the goalposts, and still, Bull is chuckling over the headset.

Bradshaw's threats, Timmons's questions, Billy's missing family, any and all worries from before are absolved between the lines of the football field. It should be illegal, Trent thinks, the power the game has over men, a blinding, burning feeling—a drug—that's what football is. And for the winners there are no warning labels, no side effects or hangovers, nothing except the pure, undiluted knowledge that you are superior to your fellow man.

Billy jogs to the sideline and Trent greets him with an open hand. Billy storms past, head down, fists balled by his sides.

"Bill?"

The boy's cheeks are completely black behind his face mask, like a child who's found his mother's makeup.

"No love for your coach?"

"Love?" says Billy under his breath.

"What'd you say, Bill?"

"*Love?*"

"Yeah, you know," says Trent, signaling for the kickoff team, "a high-five, a chest bump. Something like that."

"Love about the farthest thing from it," says Billy and turns, trotting back to the field, pulling a sophomore from the kickoff team, pushing the boy toward the sideline. The sophomore nods and does as he's told. Billy sprints down the field, beating every other Pirate defender by at least ten yards and spears Harrison's kick returner in the chest with the top of his helmet. It takes the boy a full minute to stand again.

"Better get a leash on him," says Bull, his voice coming through loud and clear over the headset. "You hear me?"

Billy goes on to score three more touchdowns and by the fourth quarter the Denton Pirates have destroyed the Harrison Goblins. With a little over ten minutes remaining, the Harrison coach sends out his second-string players, offering up the white flag of surrender.

"Get the scrubs in," says Bull.

"Already?"

"Hell yeah. It's getting ugly."

"But we're only up four touchdowns. We need to be absolutely sure."

"We got it in the bag," says Bull. "Bad juju if you don't. Come back to bite us some season we got a bunch of pencil dicks running around."

Trent breathes in deep, pushing down the memory of Bradshaw's ultimatum. His eyes wander to the south end zone. Marley is there, arms folded across her chest, pacing circles around baby Ava playing in the grass, probably still upset over Timmons and Bradshaw forcing her out of the office. Trent squints. Marley's amber eyes and strong jaw are blurred across the stark white lines, the fifty or so yards that separate them. All that remains is her presence, always there, watching every move he makes, just like her father had done. Trent looks to his wife for direction, a turn of the thumb, up or down, but there is too much ground between them.

He looks past her, to the small berm that surrounds the stadium. Standing on the rise, there's another woman, a ghostly figure, barely visible beneath the towering lights of Friday night. Her shape is familiar, though, the way she stands bent against the backdrop of the small, Southern town. Trent can feel her pull, their lives woven together now like the thick white laces on a football. Bull's voice crackles over the headset. Trent calls for a time-out.

The boys gather around their coach. They're breathing heavy, pupils big and black like drops of ink, a high they'll try and return to the rest of their lives.

"Second string," says Trent, "get ready. You're going in after this time-out."

"The hell?" says a voice from the huddle.

Trent immediately recognizes it but continues. "Austin Murphy, you'll go in at running back."

"This some bullshit."

"Are you kidding me?" says Trent, turning to Billy.

Billy's eyes shine like bullet holes behind his facemask.

"They've put their second team in, Bill. It's the right thing to do."

"Putting Austin in for me?"

"It's not like that."

"Bullshit," says Billy and trots out to the field, lining up at his running back position. The ref blows the whistle. Bull barks over the headset. Trent sends the rest of the second team—except for Austin—onto the field.

On the next play, Billy rips off another long touchdown run. Even the Pirate fans boo as they exit the bleachers and head for their cars. Trent glances back to the berm but the woman is gone. The scoreboard glows orange and interminable. Ten long minutes remain in the fourth quarter. Trent makes a beeline for Billy.

17.

Thinking about love when I ram my helmet through that Harrison kick returner heart. Thinking about Him and that dog pen, that cigarette. That love? That make more sense than what Coach talking about. *Love*—what the hell is love?

This is football. This field the only place I feel right. My whole life just been hit after hit. Everything I ever learned been taught through pain. Started with Him, all those years I took His shit then couldn't take it no more. Cain't remember one thing about my daddy, beside him leaving. And then He show up. Feel His fire out on this field. The burn of that cigarette. Little Brother eyes looking through the chicken-wire dog pen. Every time I break through that line I'm running from Him, running like my daddy did. He out there somewhere and God knows he got to be better than the man that came next. He get me sometimes, when I ain't looking. He get me low around the legs and I go down. But there always another play, another chance for me to run that ball. That what football mean to me—mean I got a chance. I score three more touchdowns, and love ain't got a damn thing to do with it.

Still ten minutes left in the fourth quarter. I'm thinking I can score at least three more touchdowns—let the crowd call my name, let the band play the fight song, maybe even break brother Jesse record—but then Coach call a time-out.

Trying to put Austin in for me? Bullshit. I let him know it too. Then I go back out to the field. What Coach gonna do now? He don't do nothing but call 243 Power, and I take that ball and run it all the way to the end zone. Don't nobody even touch me. But the crowd don't cheer this time. Like they don't see me out here running for my life. It cause this team so sorry, that's what it is. Make it look too damn easy. I walk off the field, don't even jog back to the sideline. Coach waiting for me, don't got his hand up this time. Maybe he finally learn something from Billy Lowe.

"I'm taking you out."

Won't even look at me when he say it.

"This some bullshit."

"Don't do this, Bill. Not now." Coach keep looking over his shoulder, like how I was looking during the Lutherville game, like he embarrassed. "Not after all I've done."

"All that shit you talked about a scholarship, and now you trying to take me out the game?"

"I can't let you go back in."

I don't say nothing. Just turn and walk to the bench. Don't even take my helmet off. Just sit and watch Austin Murphy try and run the ball. What he running from? His daddy right up there in the stands, sitting next to Principal with his Tyson shirt on.

All those smiling faces get me thinking about Momma.

Know she proud when she up in them stands. Know she know I'm the best, and all them other mommas and daddies—they know it too. Momma ain't in the crowd tonight, though. Try not to think about where she is, what she doing, or what she did.

Scan the crowd, looking for the only other face that give a shit about me now, but Lorna ain't up there either. She don't like coming to the games. Said her momma get all crazy and her dad too far away when he down on that field. Told her she should come to this one, though, first time the Pirates made the playoffs in years. She laughed, like that didn't mean nothing to her.

Bullshit. This some bullshit.

The scoreboard buzz and the game finally over. Coach hollering for us to line up at the fifty and shake hands. We beat Harrison by thirty-five points and Coach talking about sportsmanship, talking about shaking hands.

I watch them other boys. Watch them smile. Some of them even hug a few Harrison boys. What is that? This football. Coach blowing his whistle now. He standing out on the field, blowing his whistle and waving for the team to come take a knee. What he got to say? *Billy Lowe score all our touchdowns so I take him out.* That what he gonna say? Ain't got time for that.

I stand and start heading back to the field house. Principal come down from the stands, in the end zone now with his hands on his hips. I'm headed straight for him, thinking he better move or I'll run his ass over, just like I done that free safety. But then Bull see me and start jogging my way.

"Where you going, Billy?"

Somebody holler for Principal. He look one more time at me then turn and walk away.

"You hear me?"

Bull at least look like a football coach supposed to look. Got beady blue eyes. His skin cracked and dry, like leather.

"Field house."

"Coach calling everybody up. Need to go take a knee."

I don't say nothing, just lower my head and try to walk past him. Bull put his hand on my chest.

"Don't touch me."

"Watch it now."

I look down at his hand.

"Trying to teach you a lesson."

I laugh cause I cain't think of nothing to say.

"You think this is funny?"

"Yeah, this a joke."

"That man over there," he say, pointing to Coach. "He's sticking his neck out for you. You hear me?"

"I hear you."

"And this is how you repay him? Walking off the field? Pouting?"

"Ain't pouting."

"We're trying to help you, Billy, but you're too damn ignorant to see it."

Before I can even think about it, I slap Bull hand off my chest. Don't got no reason to be touching me. But when I do his other hand shoot up fast, faster than I ever figured a old man could move, and he grab me by the facemask. I jerk hard but cain't do nothing. Bull got me good.

I scream, "Fuck!" cause I still cain't think of nothing else to say.

Bull lean into my helmet earhole, whispering. Here I am screaming, and Bull whispering. “Easy now, Billy.” His breath hot in my ear. “This the only nice thing I’m ever gonna do for you.”

18.

Tina makes it to the game in time to see Billy score the last touchdown. She stands high on the hill, alone, where she'd watched the games before, back when she couldn't afford to pay the five dollars and the nice woman who'd usually let her in for free wasn't working the gate. Billy trots across the goal line and they boo him. All of Denton boos him.

Did they know?

She should have done more, or maybe, she should have done less. Tina's mind goes to her skillet, wondering if there's some man out there hungry enough to take it.

"Whew," says Trent, plopping down in his leather desk chair. "Thought we were going to lose Bill there for a second, but he came around. I told you he'd come around."

Bull walks to the window, cracks the blinds, and checks to make sure Billy is there. The boy sits like a scolded dog in Bull's truck, still dressed in his football gear.

Bull lets go of the blinds and they pop back into place. "Yeah."

"That's it?" says Trent, rearranging papers on his desk. "He's good, Bull. He's the best we have, that's for sure. He really might have a shot at a scholarship. He runs so, so—"

"*—mean*," Bull says.

"Yes, that's it exactly. We need to work on that attitude, of course, but they can't all be milk drinkers."

Bull groans.

"Guess we better start breaking down this film. That first run—the one where Billy plows over the free safety—that was something."

Bull cracks the blinds again then turns back to Trent. He considers telling the young coach how he had to drag Billy from the field by his facemask while Trent preached to the rest of the team, unaware. Tell him how Billy had slapped his arm. Tell him about his one year as Head Pirate, that sultry summer heat. But he doesn't. He just cracks the blinds and stares again at his truck. Billy sits sulking in the front seat, barely moving.

"Sure," says Bull. "Let's get to the film."

They watch film for two hours, grading every player on every play. This is something Trent brought from California. Bull can't figure it out. What's the point of watching every play when you just beat a team by thirty-five points? It's a show, that's what it is. The same way Trent talks about Jesus, just beats everybody over the head with it all the damn time. This young coach wants everyone to think he's working hard—think he's holy—when they see his fruity little car parked at the field house late on Friday night and on into Saturday morning.

Bull thought the Californian was kidding when he'd first arrived, talking about getting the boys to come in and practice on Sunday afternoons. He'll never forget Trent's response when a few of the seniors said the Sabbath was a day of rest, quoting the Bible to their newly appointed coach. Trent's reply: "Jesus Christ performed miracles on Sunday, and, boys, we're all in the miracle business now."

They're deep into the fourth quarter, watching the second team, the scrubs, but still grading every player on every play. Bull stands to stretch, then goes back to the window. As he cracks the blinds, he hears Trent's voice.

"Bull?"

Bull isn't looking at the screen. He's looking through the window. The blood rushes from his face. His cheeks buzz. The blinds scream on their way up.

"*Bull*," says Trent. "What is this? What did you do?"

If Bull were to turn back—if he were to look at the projector screen instead of yanking open the office door—he would see that the pimple-faced boy they pay twenty bucks to film the games had not stopped recording after the final play. Like the kid thought it was funny, or at least something worth filming, the way Bull was wrenching Billy by the facemask, dragging him across the field while Trent smiled and spoke to the rest of the kneeling boys, preaching to them about hard work and sacrifice. But Bull does not turn back, keeping both eyes on the passenger-side door of his truck, open just far enough for a boy Billy's size to slip out.

19.

Been sitting in Bull truck for over two hours. Sitting here stinking in my pads. Sore too. Whole body ache like He been at me with a dowel rod. Never would use His hands. Always had to get ahold of something. But He won't never hit me or Momma or Little Brother again. If brother Jesse weren't already out in that trailer by Eden Falls Cave, he'd a done it a long time ago. But he gone, just like everybody else. Gone.

Ever once in a while, Bull look through the blinds checking on me. Coach even know I'm out here? Doubt it. Probably too busy watching me run all them touchdowns. Probably think I'm back at his house playing board games with Mrs. Powers and Lorna. But I ain't. Billy Lowe stuck out here in this truck, and for what? What'd I do? Know I run five touchdowns, got us our first playoff win. I did do that.

I reach for the door.

Bull think he can just tell me to sit like I some kind a dog? Trying to teach me a lesson? Probably want me to walk back in there and tell Coach sorry. For what? Bet Coach think I shook all them Harrison boys' hands. He ain't worried about me, and that's why I'm done waiting. Don't even know what I's waiting for.

I open the door and leave it open. Afraid they might hear it. Then start trotting across the parking lot. Almost out to the road when I turn around. Sneak back in the locker room, real quiet. Dig in my backpack for the book. By the time I get to the road again I start to run, cleats crunching on the hard black pavement.

When the rock hit her window it sound like it crack. Stupid. Billy Lowe you can be so damn stupid. I jump in the bushes. Sitting there, thinking how stupid I am, thinking I broke Coach window, when I hear her whisper.

"Hello?"

I don't say nothing.

"*Hello?*"

Stupid, stupid, *stupid*. Still got my pads on and everything. Lorna gonna think this some kind a joke, but it ain't. This about the farthest thing from a joke. Just didn't know where else to go, couldn't think a nobody else. I got that book in my hands too. Of all the damn things, a stupid book about a Mexican and a fish.

"I hear you," she say. "I can hear you down there moving in the bushes."

Close my eyes so hard I see purple and green.

"This isn't funny. Come out or I'm calling the cops."

I open my eyes and step from the bushes, feeling about as stupid as I felt in a long time. Hold the book up, like maybe it can save me, like maybe I ain't got to say nothing, just hold that little book up and let it do the talking.

"Billy?" she say. "Is that you?"

"Yeah."

"What are you wearing?"

"My pads."

"Oh, the game," Lorna say, like she forgot all about it. "That was tonight, wasn't it?"

"Yeah."

"What do you have in your hand?"

"That book, you know, the one about the Mexican."

She start laughing, and now I feel real stupid. Almost run, just take off across the yard and down the street and run like I ran all them touchdowns. But there ain't nowhere else to go.

"He's not a Mexican, Billy," she say, still laughing. "He's *Cuban*."

"Same difference."

"Have you even read the book?"

"Maybe."

"You've either read it or you haven't."

"I read some. The old man talking to the boy. The boy saying he a good fisherman. But I don't get it, he ain't even caught a fish."

"You *have* read it," she say, excited now. "Wait right there, I'm coming down."

Got blood and sweat and grass all over me. I hold my helmet in my left hand, then my right. Trying to look cool when she slide out through a crack in the front door. Lorna wearing a loose tank top, like a basketball jersey or something. She ain't got no bra on, never got one on. Cain't tell if she got shorts on or not, the jersey so long. Lorna wear these clean white Nikes don't none the other girls wear at school. Hair pulled back in a loose knot behind her head. I like that, like the way I can see her neck. She got them new clothes Mrs. Powers bought me in her hand.

"Why didn't you change?" she whisper and pass me the clothes.

"I didn't really have no—"

"Shhh," she say, and point back to the house. "They're asleep. It's almost one in the morning."

"Sorry."

She just stand there, studying me like maybe she can see past my pads to the glow and the syrup, see Bull yanking me around, see Him and all He ever done, but then she smile. And I know she don't see nothing.

"So you actually read the book?"

"A little."

"Well, come on, let's go talk about it. I know a place."

She point her keys at the car. It her momma's car. Lorna ain't got no car, and I can respect that. The car headlights flash like two eyes opening and closing. I almost get in, almost just sit my stank ass in the car like I's sitting in Bull's truck, when I realize I still got my pads on.

"I need to change."

"You can change when we get there," she say. "You can wash off, too."

"Where we going?"

"I heard about this place called Eden Falls Cave," Lorna say and my gut flip over. "If you go far enough back, there's like this secret room with a waterfall."

Lorna ain't got a damn clue what she talking about. Don't know how hard it is to get back to the big room. Don't know about the pool, the deep one that Jesse say ain't got no bottom. How you cain't see cause it so dark, all that water coming down around you. Nuh-uh. No way. Last place I wanna go is Eden Falls Cave.

"That cave ain't no place to go," I say.

Lorna plop down in the driver seat, eyes smiling when she look up at me. "Is Billy Lowe scared?"

"Ain't scared."

"Then come on. I want to see it."

"Ain't going to no damn cave."

Lorna nose scrunch up like she mad but I can tell she just playing. She drum her fingers across the top of the steering wheel a couple times. "Well," she say, "do you have any better ideas?"

"We might could go to the river." Don't really wanna go there either. Everybody go to the river after the games, but it sure as hell better than Eden Falls Cave.

"The water," she say and look up. "The moon. Yes, that's perfect."

"I guess, but I still got my pads on."

"Who cares?"

"Your momma care, bet she don't want me getting her car all nasty."

"Billy, it's just a material thing."

I don't ask her what that mean. Don't say nothing. Just stand there. I ain't getting in her momma car, not with my pads on, not smelling like I smell.

"Fine," she say. "Go change."

"Where?"

"Behind the house. I don't care, but hurry up."

"Behind the house?"

"You can't go inside. You'll wake up Mom and Ava."

I keep staring at her, sitting behind the wheel of her momma car. I take the clothes and go back behind the bushes. The moon bright, so bright I can see. I try to change quick, but it hard getting out football pads. I look at Lorna. She ain't watching, but I feel her all the same. What am I supposed to do with these stinking pads? Cain't stick them in the car. Smell too bad.

"You coming?" whisper Lorna loud enough for me to hear.

I jab the jersey and the pants and kneepads in my helmet. Stick the helmet inside my pads like I used to when I's in peewee. There a little spot in the bushes, just big enough for all of it, so that's where I put it.

I get in the car but don't say nothing. Lorna ease it out onto the road. She turn to me and smile. "I don't have a license," she say. "See, I'm a rebel, just like you."

I don't say nothing cause she ain't. She might think she is, but she about the farthest thing from Billy Lowe. Wouldn't mind getting a little closer, though. Wouldn't mind that at all.

20.

The seat of Bull's truck is still warm, smelling faintly of soured sweat.

"What is it?" Trent yells from the coaches' office door. "What's wrong?"

The engine rolls over and comes to life.

"Bull?"

The passenger door pops open. "Get in," Bull says. "It's Billy."

The truck roars, tearing out of the parking lot and down Main Street. Bull tells Trent he was just trying to let the boy cool down, trying to help him out. The truck hurtles on, one road then another, road after road, each one leading to a dead end. Bull knows every high school hangout in Denton. They come to the end of a dirt road and the Arkansas River appears. The headwaters start up in Colorado, crisp and cool like a Coors commercial. By the time the water is filtered through the Ozarks, passed through the discarded box springs, dishwashers, and the other redneck debris strewn about the hills, the river becomes the color of chocolate milk and smells like skunked beer.

On the bank, there's a bonfire with kids dancing and swaying in the shadows. They disappear into their vehicles like roaches as the headlights sweep across them. Trent rolls down the window and calls Billy's name.

Bull grabs Trent by the back of his shirt. "What the hell you think you're doing?"

"I just—"

"Need to slow down," says Bull, turning the truck back onto the dirt road. "You hear me?"

"Slow down? You just assaulted our best player. I watched the whole thing on film. You drug him off the field like he was some kind of animal."

"That's a good way to put it."

"You think he's an animal?"

"Takes one to know one."

Trent turns from Bull, staring out the window.

Bull's veiny forearms bulge as he grips the top of the wheel. "Listen, Hollywood. I was in a hurry once, hell-bent on winning, just like you."

"I've heard the story. Principal Bradshaw told me all about—"

"You trust Don Bradshaw to tell you the truth about anything?"

"Well, no."

"Then let me tell my own goddamn story."

Trent rolls his eyes but keeps his mouth shut. A minute passes before Bull speaks again.

"Pushed them too hard, too fast. It was the summer before my second season. It was hot, damn hot, but I just kept working them, and then a boy went down on the field. Never forget the way he fell."

"A concussion?"

"Heatstroke. Fried him up from the inside out. Worst

part was, I kept calling plays. Left him there, like I didn't see he was down. Didn't want the other boys getting any ideas about skipping out on practice."

"What happened?"

Bull remembers the sound his buck knife made when it cut through the jersey and the laces on the front of the boy's pads, the rush of heat that rose up off his chest, the ambulance, the hospital—the funeral.

"Don't matter now," says Bull. "All that matters is I'm here to tell you—to warn you—you need to slow down."

"This is ridiculous. I'm sure Bill just went home."

"That's where I's headed," says Bull, turning back onto Main.

"Well, you're going the wrong way."

"I know where the Lowes live. Been picking them boys up and hauling them to practice long before you ever thought of blowing a whistle."

"*His* home? That's ridiculous," says Trent. "Bill's with me now."

"I hear you."

"Turn the truck around."

"You ain't thinking like he thinks. Thinking you and him all buddy-buddy, thinking you know him—but you don't."

"What's that supposed to mean?"

"How you think Billy felt after I drug him off the field like that?"

"I'm sure he was hurt," Trent says, "embarrassed."

"That's where you're wrong. Boys like Billy don't feel nothing. They're just like fighting dogs, animals bred up in violence. They don't think, they just react."

"Bill *thinks.*"

"Right," says Bull, the truck engine whining higher. "Maybe the boy thinks. *Maybe.* But not when it comes to stuff like this. Not when he's mad. And he's mad. I can guarantee that." Bull rubs his left hand, the hand Billy slapped.

"That's human nature—" starts Trent, but stops as the truck pulls into the muck surrounding the Lowes' doublewide. The headlights reveal Shady Grove in a hard white spotlight. The trailer frowns in the night, sad angles everywhere: bent gutters, broken windows, a screen door torn from all its hinges but one.

"Look like animals live here, don't it, Hollywood?"

"Not animals," says Trent. "People live in this, and that's what makes it so horrible."

Bull gets out and starts for the trailer. Trent stays back behind the truck door, crouching, like he's preparing for a gunfight, or just scared shitless. Bull can't decide. The old man is almost to the tiny porch when he stops, coughs, and brings his arm up to cover his face.

"What?" says Trent. "What is it?"

"Stinks."

"Like what?"

"Might be them chicken houses," says Bull. "But damn, it's bad."

"I can smell it now," says Trent, coughing. "Smells like rotten meat. Garbage, maybe?"

"*Animals,*" says Bull and lifts his shirt up over his nose, pressing it there smelling only himself, a light tinge of sweat and Stetson cologne. Bull makes it to the door and knocks three times.

Silence.

Bull holds his breath until he can stand it no longer. He exhales then inhales, breathing in a long gulp of the rancid air, tasting it now. Bull knocks again, harder this time.

"Well, hell," says Bull.

"See," says Trent. "I told you Bill wouldn't come here. Let's go."

Bull steps back from the porch and away from the smell. He's nearly to Trent when a breeze picks up. The dilapidated screen door rattles, holding tight to the last remaining hinge. Bull turns to the sound, but when he does, it's not the screen door he notices; it's something inside the trailer—a glow.

Bull is back on the porch, hands pressed to the window.

"What?" Trent says, his voice small across the night. "What is it?"

The smell is all around Bull now, a physical force, a cloud of gnats fluttering in his ears, his nose, seeping into his pores. In the glow of the single kitchen light, almost completely hidden from view, Bull squints and sees a thing that makes him forget even the smell.

21.

The river run hard and fast below us. The moon in the water. The moon in the sky.

Everybody come to the river after a game. Saw them when we drove up, whole bunch of them good and drunk already. Big bonfire tearing at the low branches, lighting they drunk smiling faces.

"I've never even had a beer," Lorna say as we drive by.

"Not one?"

"Nope," she say. "Dad made me sign a pledge when I was younger."

"That said you wouldn't drink beer?"

"It was for church."

"Like sins and stuff?"

"Like drugs and alcohol," she say. "And sex."

I swallow, the bonfire only shadows behind us now. We go upstream a ways, on up to the bluffs. Get out the car and just walk a while, walk all the way down to the edge, as close as we can get.

Bluffs big and high this far upstream. Probably twenty, maybe thirty feet. So we cain't get in the water, not unless we jump. I jumped before. Everybody jump from the bluffs, but not in the night. Even with a full moon, you be stupid to jump in the night.

Lorna brought a blanket, but it ain't cold. Hottest damn November I can ever remember. The river still warm from the heat of the day, rushing up from below. But women good for that, for thinking about things like blankets. Momma good for that when she weren't drunk or stoned.

Momma.

Ain't thought about Momma in a minute. I kinda start to see her again, remembering her in broken bits and pieces. She left that night. Just up and left me there with Him cause she knew what I's gonna do. Probably been waiting for me to do it, like she had it planned.

"Sit down," say Lorna, patting a spot on the blanket beside her. I still stink. Know I do. Still smell all that sweat and football coming up through these new clean clothes.

I sit down a ways from her, hoping she cain't smell me. You think about how you smell when you got brothers and a momma who cain't keep ahead the laundry, even if she try, and she do try. Sometimes. You think about it cause them other kids smell you. They always smell you. So I sit about six feet from Lorna, wishing I had a cold beer. Something to do with my hands. Something to make me quit thinking so much. But Lorna ain't even looking at me. She looking at the river.

"What page are you on?" she say without turning to me.

I fumble with the book in the dark. The book about the farthest thing from my mind right now, but she wanna talk about the book, so I turn to the page I got bent down.

"Twenty-five."

"You read twenty-five pages today?" say Lorna. "And played an entire football game? Well, Billy Lowe, you are a Renaissance man."

I don't say nothing. Lorna probably know I ain't got a clue what she talking about cause she say, "It just means you have many talents. Like you're good at a lot of stuff."

"Yeah, I know."

She laugh and turn to me now. The moonlight come up off the river and shine behind her. Cain't really see her face, just a mess a hair piled up on her head like a halo, shining and moving when she move.

"Okay," she say. "If you're so smart, read to me."

"I told you, I don't—"

"I know what you said, but there's no one else out here. It will help with your comprehension."

I don't say nothing.

"You know, like help—"

"I know."

She smile and her teeth light up the dark.

"Please, Billy," she say and lean all the way across the blanket and take hold of my hand. "For me?"

I jerk away fast, probably too fast, and it ain't cause I don't want her touching on me. That ain't it at all. It the stink. The way she pull her hand back slow make me feel sorry for being so rough.

"Okay," I say.

She stop rubbing her hand. "Okay, what?"

"I'll read."

She bounce there on the blanket like Little Brother do when he real happy about something. The book feel huge in my hands, but it a small book. Feel heavy too, but it ain't. I feel her moving across the blanket, coming for me. I start to read before she get too close.

"*He no longer dreamed of storms, nor of women, nor of great occur-occur—*"

I stop and breathe in deep through my nose.

"Occurrences," she say.

I close the book.

"Billy, come *on*. It's just like when Dad tells you how to take a handoff. It's like being coached."

"He don't tell me nothing I don't know already."

"I bet those college coaches will teach you a thing or two," Lorna say, all teeth now. And it the way she say it—like she really believe it, like there ain't no doubt in her mind—that make me pick up the book and start again, "*nor of great occurrences.*" I see her nod out the corner of my eye.

I read for some time, and she just sit there, nodding and making sounds like she like it, like hearing me *read*. Not gonna lie, for the first time I kinda like reading. Like we having a conversation, but it ain't me talking. It's this guy, this Hemingway. He talking through me, but it making me sound smart and I like it.

I stop reading cause I'm curious.

"Who is he?"

"Who?"

"Hemingway."

"You mean, who *was* he," she say. "He's dead. Blew his head off with a shotgun."

"A shotgun?"

"Yeah, pulled the trigger with his big toe."

"Damn."

"He reminds me of you, Billy. Minus the shotgun."

"Why you say that?"

"He was a man's man. He was all about bullfighting and hunting. He even lived in Arkansas for a while, wrote one of his most famous novels over in the Delta, a town called Piggot."

"No shit?"

"No shit," Lorna say, working her way across the blanket again. She don't know what she doing. Don't got no clue about Creesha and Neesy, about what she get herself into if she let Billy Lowe get ahold of her. I pick up where I left off.

"*. . . and if she did wild or wicked things it was because she could not help them. The moon affects her as it does a woman . . .*"

She almost on top of me. I stop reading.

"Do you know what Hemingway's talking about?" she say.

"He talking about the ocean, right?"

"Yes. But he's also talking about women and the moon, and nights like this one right here."

"Yeah," I say, but she standing now, walking over to the edge of the bluff.

"The *moon* . . ." she say, but that it. She bend over the edge, looking down in the water. The light still behind her. She just a shadow standing there, but when she pull that basketball jersey up and over her head, a shadow's all I need.

I don't move, don't say nothing. Every shape a man could ever want is outlined in the dark right there in front a me. She bend and slide her shorts down around her ankles. She step out them, careful, like she stepping into cold water. But she ain't in the water yet.

I still ain't said nothing. She ain't either. She just keep bending over the bluff looking down, like the book was right, like the moon just keep calling her name.

I about to call her back from the edge when she jump. Look like the moon just went behind a cloud and took her shadow with it. But then I hear a splash and I know she really did it. My heart beating in my chest, feel the blood thudding behind my eyes, in other places too. I run to the ledge, and there she is, bobbing in the water like a sliver of just-poured milk in black coffee.

There ain't nothing good come from me jumping in that water. I jumped enough to know you got to know where you jumping, know what's below you, to even jump at all.

"The moon, Billy, can't you feel its pull?" she yell.

I sure as hell ain't thinking about the moon. But I'm damn thankful for it, thankful for how it light just enough of her bobbing up and down in the water. I keep trying not to stare.

"You crazy," I say. "*Crazy.*"

"Well, you're just chicken!" she holler.

Don't nobody call Billy Lowe a chicken. And there's just enough light from the moon to see what I need to see. Get my shorts and shirt off, and then a breeze blow in, cool, like it carry something with it. Kinda stink like chickens, like it connected to something way back in town.

"Well?" she say.

The breeze stop blowing. Just me standing there alone thinking about what at stake, thinking about a college scholarship and Lorna Powers floating down there, waiting for me. I finally let myself look at what's bobbing up and out the water, look at this girl calling for me. And the sight a her—*all* a her—is enough to make me jump.

22.

Trent is beside Bull, nose almost touching the window, face awash in the glow. He can barely make out the shape of a shoulder behind the kitchen island, DENTON WASTE MANAGEMENT printed straight across the sleeve. Trent imagines the rest of the body, hiding back there somewhere. He leans in, his breath clouding the glass.

"That's *him*," says Bull. "Billy's momma's boyfriend."

Trent whispers the man's name.

"Yeah, Travis," says Bull and spits. "Weren't no football player, I can tell you that much. *Basketball*. Probably what's wrong with him—too much air-conditioning."

Trent wipes the glass. "Is he—"

"He ain't dead, Hollywood. Just drunker than shit. Probably a good thing Billy didn't come here. Old Travis probably done had a scuffle with Tina and gone on a weeklong binge."

Trent nods, slow at first then faster.

"Come on," says Bull. "Let's see if we can't wake his drunk ass up."

Bull swats the pitiful hanging screen door and begins knocking. The final hinge breaks loose. The screen rattles as it falls. Trent watches one door give way to another, and a fear sweeps over him.

"Bull?"

"What?"

"Is he moving?"

"Naw, he ain't moving. He's drunker than shit."

"Right," says Trent, thinking of Billy's knuckles and a meat grinder, and that smell, that god-awful stench that could be rotten garbage, or something else entirely.

"We gonna have to bust it down," says Bull.

"Bust it down?"

"Yeah, Hollywood, this could be serious. Believe it or not, you can drink yourself to death. If he ain't heard me pounding by now then there's no telling how bad off he is."

"Yes," says Trent, his mind already formulating plausible explanations, just like the one Bull is providing: the man was *drunker than shit*. That makes sense.

Bull produces his buck knife, the blade long and blue against the night.

Trent studies it. "What do you plan to do with that?"

"Open the damn door, Hollywood."

"Oh."

"Come on," says Bull, jabbing the knife in the crack by the dead bolt. "Give me a hand."

Both men shoulder the door in unison, like a good double-team block by a guard and center. Bull yanks at the doorframe with his knife. The wood splinters. The door swings open and the smell envelops them. The gnats swarm. Trent swats the air and bends to his knees.

Bull stands over the body now. Trent cannot get any closer. The smell is so thick, so awful, like whatever the odor actually is—whether it's rotting garbage or death—is inside Trent now, in his lungs, his nose, stuck to the wets of his eyeballs.

"He's dead," says Bull, as if he were calling a blitz or changing a coverage. "And I don't think he drank himself to death."

The smell catches and bites inside Trent, a crimping of his lungs like the wadding of paper. Trent finally looks down at the mass of death sprawled on the floor, Travis with his mouth open, eyes closed, broken blisters bubbling across his bloated face.

The smell was rotting trash all along.

In a matter of minutes the trailer glows blue instead of orange. Sheriff Timmons struts about the place, kicking beer cans, thumbs hooked in his belt loops. "Something got him good on the forehead there. Just above his left eye."

"Didn't realize Travis had gotten so fat," says Bull. "Weren't y'all in the same class, Sheriff?"

Timmons snorts. "Yeah, but I didn't play no *basketball.*"

"Travis never had a chance: short dumpy white boy, playing a Black man's game."

"He weren't this fat when he died," says Timmons, looking toward Trent. "He already started the bloat. You know, gut gasses and all that coming out. That's what you're smelling now, like what roadkill do."

Bull nudges the body with the toe of his shoe. It moves like a waterbed, like the skin is loose and the rest is tight. The slack mouth jiggles, sliding back into place.

"What do you think happened here?" says Trent.

"What do I think?" says Timmons.

"Yeah."

Timmons turns to Bull, grinning. "I don't get paid to think, pard."

"Come on, Hollywood, best let the professionals take over." Bull puts a hand on Trent's shoulder and turns for the door.

"Are you kidding?" says Trent, jerking away. "This man is dead."

"Here we go," says Timmons. "You gonna tell us how it'd be done in California?"

"No," says Trent, "but I would like to know what happened. We walk in on a dead body, and you two just joke around? Hell, Bull kicked the damn thing."

"It's a man, Coach, or I guess it *was* a man."

"I know. I knew Travis."

"We all knew Travis," says Bull.

"Don't think Billy was a fan," says Timmons.

"Nah," says Bull. "Wouldn't say that."

Timmons squats down, leaning in close to the dead man's puffy left ear. "What the hell happened to you, Trav?" Travis's face is red and blotched like modern art, a death canvas. Sheriff Timmons looks up. "Gonna be a shit-storm coming, Coach. No doubt in my mind."

"He's right," says Bull.

"And the way I figure it—if you're asking my *professional* opinion—ain't but two people that killed Travis Rodney, either Tina or Billy Lowe."

"Bill?" says Trent. "You must be joking."

"By the looks of that bruising there," says Timmons, "I'd say Billy at least had a hand in it."

Trent looks away.

"Billy seems to've been in a punching mood lately," Timmons adds. "And them little dots right there? Them knuckle marks if I ever seen."

"Sheriff, listen—" says Trent, but Bull flashes him a look that makes him shut up.

"Now, that punch ain't what killed him," says Timmons, toeing the body. "All that there on his forehead, *that's* what killed him."

"*Nasty*," says Bull.

"You think he could have done it just from falling?" says Trent.

"Sure," says Timmons. "That's a possibility. But there's all sorts of things that could've happened to poor Travis. We'll scrounge around, see if we find a bloody corner, a weapon of some sort. Hell, when Tina shows back up, we'll check the bumper of that car. You never know."

Trent squats down, elbows on his knees. He's close to the body now, close enough to see the gash in the man's forehead, the deep reds turning purple.

"I'm sorry," says Trent.

Timmons turns to face him. "No need to apologize, Coach."

In the truck, Bull and Trent don't speak. They drive through the night, the moon hanging close and bright in the sky. This is the sort of night when there should only be darkness, no light to show the truth. Trent feels as if the moon is watching him, accusing him. But he's done nothing wrong. He's only tried to help. Billy Lowe needs all the help he can get.

As Bull turns the truck onto Trent's street, the moon

shines bright enough to light the driveway, revealing the empty place where Marley's car should be.

"Mar?" says Trent, breaking the silence.

"It's two in the morning, Hollywood."

"I know," says Trent, pulling the handle on the truck's door. "But her car, it should be right there."

"Easy now. Let me stop the damn truck."

But the door is open and Trent is already hopping out, into his front yard, running for the house. It's locked. He fumbles in his pockets, searching for his keys. Just as he finds them, the front door opens.

There's a moment—a fraction of a second before a blindside blitz—where Trent is relieved. His wife is okay. She's home. But that realization gives way to the ugly truth that there is a balance to all things in this world.

Trent whispers, "*Lorna*," and the moon shines bright, catching the pain in Marley's eyes, a long-lasting camera flash, sealing it forever.

23.

We float in the river awhile. I let Lorna get close cause the stink gone and the water feel good. There ain't no thinking in the water, just like out on a football field, and I like that. She move here, I go there, and all the while we're treading water, floating downstream.

"*Shit.*"

"What?" I say.

"My earring."

Lorna got her hand to her ear, touching one a them dangly feather earrings she wear every day.

"Dad will kill me," say Lorna. "He gave me these earrings for my birthday a few years ago. They were literally the only thing he's ever given me that I liked."

I start pawing at the river, diving under, eyes open in the dark water. Don't look like nothing down there. Water black and taste like dirt. I keep at it.

"It's gone, Billy," she say when I come up. "Forget it. The feather part is made of all these tiny wires. I'm sure it sunk straight to the bottom."

I'm still fighting, though, thinking maybe I can find it, while the river keep pushing us downstream. It ain't until I see the light from the fire I realize we gone too far.

"Lorna," I say. "Look."

"My earring?"

"We all the way back down to the bonfire."

"So?"

"The dam come after the bonfire. And the dam as far downstream as we can go. We float over that dam and we won't be floating no more."

"Let's just get out," she say, like it that simple. Like we can just come out the water, walk up to the bonfire. But she already paddling that way. Ain't got no clothes on. Her clothes up at the bluff. I ain't got no clothes, neither. Feel the water pushing me. I watch her stand near the bank, shadows playing across every curve.

"You coming?" she say, loud.

"You ain't wearing no *clothes*."

"Well," she say, not even whispering, "if it's between falling to my death over that dam or being seen naked—I'll take the latter."

"But all them guys up there."

"We can just walk along the edge of the bank, sneak all the way up to our clothes."

"Bank steep, Lorna. Gonna be a hard climb at night."

"Those are your options."

I paddle for her. Make it close enough to the bank to stand. The warm river water dripping off me feel like coming out from under a blanket. I see Lorna little ass swaying as she scurry up the bank. The boys hunkered around that fire back near the tree line. Good chance they won't never see us if we follow the bank back up to the bluffs. Keep good and quiet.

"Come on," she say over her shoulder.

I put a finger over my lips.

"Most guys would want to be seen in the nude with the new girl at school."

"I ain't most guys."

"I know."

We're almost up the bank, almost to flat ground and a easy walk back to our clothes, when somebody holler from the bonfire. "Who the fusk out there?" And already I can tell it drunk-ass Jarred.

"Shit."

"Who cares?" say Lorna.

"Shut up," I say and don't even mean to.

"No sir." She stop and spin around right there at the lip of the bank. About twenty feet up, about to the top. Buck naked. Hands on her hips. "You are not going to talk to me like that. Do you understand?"

I hear her, but I ain't listening. I know they coming through the woods, a whole mess a them, drunk as shit and rowdy. The whole lunch table stomping through the tree line.

"Lorna," I say. "Listen, this ain't California."

"Oh, my, *God*," she say. "Here we go again, another—"

"Ever one a those boys got a gun, a knife, *something*. They drunk as hell and now they hearing sounds in the woods. Them boys dream of this, being cowboys and shooting bad guys."

She go quiet. The moon bright enough I can see her eyes on me, all a me, but not like that—like she trying to figure me out.

"This is ridiculous," she say.

The boys almost to the bluff's edge. I can hear them talking—low, raspy, drunk sounds, like they think they whispering, but they ain't. I see the tip of a boot over the bluff now. Little bits of dirt fall in Lorna hair. She brush it away and make a sound that they hear if they weren't drunk.

I hear another voice, squeaky, saying he hear something down by the water. Sound like Austin Murphy.

"Yeah, I hear it too," say Jarred.

And now it here, the moment when they gonna look over the bluff and see me huddled up at the water's edge, naked with Lorna Powers, with Coach daughter. And she right—for most boys, that wouldn't be so bad. But this different. This what they expect. They expect to see Billy Lowe out on a Friday night howling at the moon, but I ain't. Not really. I's reading a damn book, that's what I was doing. Wouldn't want them to know that neither.

More dirt fall from the bluff and onto my face. I close my eyes. When I open them all I see is Lorna's ass dangling over the edge, crawling up, and then she gone.

"Howdy," she say, trying to sound like she from Denton. "Just going for a little swim."

I hear them boys breathing, just standing there, breathing.

"The water's so warm," she say. "I couldn't help myself."

She saving me, that what she doing. I can almost hear the boys' eyes blinking, trying to remember every bend and curve.

"Uh," say Jarred. "Well, uh . . ."

Try not to laugh cause that perfect. He wouldn't know what to do if he got it.

"Is that a shotgun?" Lorna say.

I hear Jarred turn the plastic stock over in his hands. "This thing?"

"Yes," say Lorna. "I've never seen such a *big* gun before."

"Uh."

"Being from California, and all—we don't see a lot of shotguns." She really playing it up, and I wish she'd just go on, just start walking back to our clothes, but she don't.

"Yeah," say Jarred. "You wanna hold it?"

"Your gun?"

"Yeah, my *gun*," he say, coming out of it now.

"You know what they say about guys with big guns?"

I can see Lorna grinning, just waiting for one of them to ask, when all she got to do is walk on. Smart people can be so damn stupid sometimes.

Jarred say, "*What?*" real loud.

"Oh, it's silly. But what they say in *California,* is guys with big guns have tiny dicks—you know, trying to overcompensate."

The boys whispering her words in the darkness, like they ain't really sure she said what she just said, but she did. Nobody saying nothing when I hear Jarred heavy boots start stomping across the ground.

"I show you what a big dick looks like," say Jarred.

The shotgun the least of Lorna worries now. I start up the bluff cause there ain't gonna be no stopping them, not without a fight.

"Come on, guys," she say. "I was *joking,* just having some fun."

I see her heels on the ledge. Hear Jarred laughing, saying, "Oh, it about to get real fun." Hear the other boys laughing like they at the lunch table again. And now it all welled up inside me good and strong.

I'm almost to her. Lorna laughing cause she tough and don't wanna show them she scared. I reach up. Just gonna touch her ankle, let her know I'm here and I'm a man's man, like Hemingway. When my fingers tap her ankle she jerk back, like she forgot I's there, toes clawing at the dirt bank, hands slapping at the sky, trying to keep her balance. And then there's only Jarred standing on the ledge, laughing, as Lorna fall down the bluff toward the river and into the moon.

24.

"*Lorna—*" Marley puts a hand to her mouth, catching her breath. "She was here, in her room, when I got back from the game."

Trent turns to see Bull bent at the waist, pushing his way into the rosemary bushes lining the front of the house.

"What is it?" Marley says. "God, what is it?"

Bull jerks at the bushes and leans back, producing what looks like the top half of a body. Marley cries out in the night, as if Lorna were scattered in pieces across her flowerbed. "Shoulder pads," yells Bull. "Helmet too. Hell, it's all here, the whole damn getup."

"Oh," says Marley.

"Number thirty-five," adds Bull.

The grass is wet on Trent's shoes as he slices through the yard and takes the helmet dangling from Bull's fingers. Trent stares down at the facemask, searching for answers in the darkness behind the bars, knuckles going white from his grip.

"Kids," says Bull and shrugs. "No telling."

Trent rolls the helmet over in his hands and feels the weight of it. Principal Bradshaw's voice echoes through his skull, mocking the Prius, citing the car as evidence Trent couldn't handle a boy like Billy Lowe.

"He must have taken her," says Marley. "Billy. He—"

Trent says, "Stop," and puts a hand to his face. "We don't know that."

"This is exactly what I was afraid of, Trent. This is just what I was talking about when you wanted to bring him into our house."

Trent looks over his shoulder to Bull. The old man hefts the shoulder pads up over his head and tosses them into the truck bed. "I remember what you said."

"Do you?"

Trent can see Billy in the trailer again, the scene cast in a dull orange glow. He hears the sound the boy's fist made when it connected with Travis's jaw, a hollow thwack, an axe sinking into a rotten log. Trent blinks and he's back in the driveway, not far from where he's standing now, Marley telling him to go in and take a shower, he needs to get ready for church.

"Yes," Trent says. "I remember."

"We should've called Daddy."

Trent tries to remember more, but everything is hazy, like the soapy water from that morning. He'd washed away the details until the story was simple and clear: Billy needed help.

"Your father has nothing to do with this."

"There's no arguing that," says Marley. "If he were here, none of this would have happened."

"I'll find them."

"God," she says. "I knew we—"

"Marley," says Trent, not shouting. "I'll find them."

Trent stares back at his wife, blinks, then starts for Bull's truck. Moments later, the engine roars to life. Bull opens the passenger-side door and slides into the seat. In the rearview mirror Marley is small, but Trent doesn't see her, a quarterback in the pocket, keeping his eyes downfield, focused on the road ahead.

Denton flies past in the night: redbrick churches and redbrick banks, the local Walmart glows blue and white then disappears. The night air is thick, rancid, a smell similar to the Lowes' trailer: manure, wastewater, nitrogen, and phosphorus.

"Smell that?" Bull says.

"Yes."

"Know what it is?"

"No."

"Chicken shit. Tons of it. Denton's damn near the chicken capital of the world."

"It smells horrible."

"Smell like money, you ask me," says Bull, chuckling at his own joke.

A Tyson chicken plant rises in the distance like some monstrous cruise ship run aground. Trent stares ahead into darkness.

"Your wife seemed pretty upset back there."

"She'll be fine."

"Don't think I ever told you about my wife."

"Not now, Bull."

"My old lady was tough, wouldn't take no shit. Not from me. Not from nobody," Bull says, turning to the window, settling in. "She and your wife'd probably get along good."

"That does sound familiar."

"Everything changed, though, when I got my shot as Head Pirate. All them hard stares she gave me got harder. I's gone most of the time. And then that boy had the heat-stroke, and I's gone even more. Felt like them boys needed me. Knew they did. But she needed me more."

Trent is silent now, nodding like maybe Bull's message is sinking in.

"I come home one day, couple weeks after the funeral, and she's gone. Didn't take nothing but her clothes. Didn't even take all of them." Bull sucks his teeth, trying not to think about the floral-print dresses still hanging in his bed-room closet. "It ain't got to be that way for you, Coach."

The road hums. The truck travels a mile before another word is spoken.

"Marley's dad . . ." Trent says and swallows. "He was my boss back at Fernando Valley. But you knew that already. Didn't you?"

"Small town. Everybody knew everything before you stepped foot on our field."

Trent squeezes the steering wheel tighter.

"Don't matter who her daddy is, don't matter what he done or she done—ain't nothing worth losing what you got. You hear me?"

Trent's jaw bulges.

"Not winning all these games, not even keeping this job. There's always another job."

Trent turns to Bull now, the tree line in smears outside the window. "Are you implying something about my job security?"

"Ain't no secret, Hollywood. Bradshaw got a mouth on him."

"He told you?"

"Don Bradshaw was Head Pirate for ten years. But then Jesse Lowe come along—the first we'd ever seen of a Lowe boy—and Don just couldn't quite handle all that crazy. Never could swallow being moved to principal, neither."

"Jesse Lowe was the reason Mr. Bradshaw lost his job?"

"You could say that."

"He threatened me, Bull. Told me I was finished if I didn't win the state championship."

Bull shakes his head, snorting. "You think he's got what it takes to make that call? The school board, the superintendent, it'd take all them to pull the plug, and they can't agree on nothing. Besides, you done good this year. We're *still* doing good."

Trent scratches his chin. The truck crosses the yellow lines but straightens up quick.

"Bradshaw's just blowing smoke," Bull says. "Even if he weren't, it ain't worth doing something stupid, like losing your wife."

"I've already lost my daughter."

Bull has no children besides the boys he's raised up on the Pirate football field. He cannot imagine the pain a daughter could bring.

"The river, that bonfire we saw," says Trent. "Our boys were there, right?"

"Yeah, but Billy weren't with them."

"Not where we could see him."

"What're you thinking?"

"I'm thinking, if I've taken a girl, *stolen* a girl . . ." Trent adjusts his weight, leaning forward over the wheel as the truck barrels down the highway. "Then I'm not going to sit by the light of the fire. I'm going where no one else can see me."

The truck picks up speed and Bull takes hold of the armrest, bony fingers clamping down tight. The way Trent is driving, the fact that Bull's riding shotgun—in his own damn truck—sets the old man's teeth on edge.

"They're at the river, Bull. You take a girl to the river. Trust me," Trent says as the truck turns down a gravel road, low-hanging branches slapping at the hood. "I know how boys like Bill think."

The trees pull back and the road opens to reveal the riverbank. The bonfire blossoms before them, filling the truck's cab. Bull glances over at Trent. The young coach's face glows red in the light.

"You remember that trailer back there?" Bull says. "That stink weren't just from Travis or them chicken houses—that trailer been stinking for years."

The headlights illuminate the bonfire, turning its orange to ash. There are only a few kids left, eyes Friday-night wide, a little drunk, a little scared. Trent leaves the lights on, the truck running, then disappears into the night. Bull watches as the boy-coach walks with his head down, his hands in his pockets, as if he were there to drink a few beers with the team and celebrate the playoff win. Now he's talking to them, nodding, maybe even smiling. Then, with the same nonchalance as before, Trent walks toward the flames, lifts a glowing limb from the pit, and waves it in their faces, a look in the kids' eyes like they've never seen true fire until now.

Bull's heart thuds, a heavy rhythm the old man hasn't

felt in years. He fumbles with the door handle, jerks it, then scrambles toward Trent and the kids.

"Damn it, Coach!" shouts Bull. "Put that stick down."

Trent turns back to him. Eyes all shadows, no light. "They say Lorna's here, Bull."

There's a scrape in Trent's voice, something Bull can't figure.

"Did you hear me?" Trent says. "She's *here*."

Bull looks past the glowing stick in Trent's hand to the kids behind him, three sets of eyes in the night, not even blinking as a tuft of smoke catches the breeze and drifts across their faces.

"Yeah, goddammit," Bull says. "I hear you."

25.

Lorna fall like she drunk or high. Like Momma fall when she been out with Him all night. But Lorna ain't Momma, she ain't drunk, and I ain't Him. When she hit the bank she make the same sound, though, the sound all people make when they fall.

Jarred still laughing. The other boys laughing too, giggling just like they at the lunch table. I'm caught there between them, between Lorna and the laughing boys.

"Shit, man. She alright?" say a voice from the crowd. Sound like Austin.

"Who gives a shit?" say Jarred.

I'm still stuck, cain't move. Feel like they got chains tied to both my arms, tugging, about to split me right down the middle when I hear Lorna make a sound. It a sound like Little Brother make—a sound like she don't know what happened, wondering why she naked and all them boys up there laughing at her.

My chain break loose and I start down the bank. Lorna ain't crying, though. She laughing. Laughing like Momma do after He hit her. Laughing worse than crying. Worse cause it don't sound right. Not now. And the way she sitting there: legs spread, wet hair stuck to her cheeks—it split me open, make me think about crying, or breaking Jarred face.

Know I should say something. Know I should lean in and say, "I'm here. I got you now." But feel like somewhere down the line somebody got to do something like that for you, somebody got to say it first. I can still see Jarred dangling over the ledge, pointing and laughing, like he want me to come up there and whoop his ass so bad, but then Lorna whisper, "*Billy*," and she ain't laughing no more. Momma always quit laughing too. At some point they wake up and see they naked. Lorna sitting curled in a ball, but she ain't hiding everything. She cain't.

I know this, I done this before. I hold her. Ain't got to say nothing, just hold her. She feel like one them ocean birds the old man talk about in the book. Too little for the big water. Thinking about telling her that when I hear Jarred start up again.

"They down there," he say, his fat finger pointing at us. He glowing too, like somebody got a light, but it ain't a flashlight, this a low dull glow, like the light in the trailer.

"Yeah, Coach," say Jarred, and I feel Lorna go tight in my arms cause she hear him too. "They down there."

The boys all got flashlights, but Coach standing at the edge of the bank holding a burning stick. His face different, like it was the day I ran from the trailer to the field, away from the glow and the syrup, away from Him. But now Coach brought that glow with him, carrying it on that stick, all Halloween and crazy clown eyes for Coach. He looking down at me and his daughter, a look like I ain't never seen before, not even from Him.

"Lorna," I say, but she just staring up at her daddy and that stick. "*Lorna*, what we gonna do?"

She don't say nothing cause she don't know. Then Coach coming down the bank with that stick. Bull behind him. All the boys behind Bull. The glow on all they faces now.

I stand.

That the only thing I know to do, the only thing I know as a fact in this world: stand up, be a man. I move in front of Lorna, like he coming for her, but I see in his eyes he coming for me, ain't even looking at his daughter.

"It ain't like that," I say, standing there, naked.

"Like what, Bill?" Coach voice sound hollow, empty, like he ain't putting on for nobody no more. Up this close, he don't look the same. His face a mix a white and orange, moon and fire.

"Like it look," I say.

"Shit," say Jarred. "Look like you was about to fuck his daughter."

Coach move fast. The stick cut through the air in a hot orange line. The dark end, the end that ain't burning, hit Jarred right in the gut. He drop the shotgun and fall down to one knee, start making a sound like a fish out a water.

"After all I've done for you," say Coach, like he don't see Jarred rolling around in the dirt or feel Bull at his side now, tugging his arm. Coach don't budge, don't stop staring at me. "Open up my house, give you a place to sleep, buy you food, buy you clothes, and all I asked in return was that you—"

"It ain't like that."

"—try and behave, but this, *this* is how you repay me?"

"It ain't like that."

Coach step at me with that stick in his hand. I don't

move. Ain't never backed down in my life. If this how he want it to go, we'll go.

"Dad," say Lorna from behind us.

He don't look at her and that's good. Maybe he don't know she naked yet. He just looking at me.

"*Dad.*"

Nothing. Coach eyes fire in the night.

"It was my idea," she say, her voice small, barely hear her over the river. "I wanted to go swimming. We didn't do anything. Billy wouldn't do anything. He didn't even try."

He take the stick in both hands now and I starting to think Lorna ain't helping none.

"It's okay, Lorna," say Coach. "I completely understand."

The way he say it come out weird, freaky cause it don't sound right. He looking through me to Lorna. Jarred still gulping air but standing now, mumbling to the other boys. They don't laugh. Don't make a sound. They might be drunk, but they ain't stupid. This ain't the lunch table.

"Lorna," say Coach, and then he start coming down the bank, coming at me. Maybe not at me, maybe he plan on going through me, taking Lorna out to the water, baptizing her, and letting that be the end of it. I get down in the hit position. Ready for him. But he don't never make it.

Lorna slide between us. The light pale on her body, enough soft skin and white moon to put out all fire. Coach feet thud to a stop. She standing there, his daughter, nothing on but beads of water. I watch Coach staring at her, staring like he remember seeing her before, but not like this. Back when she was like Little Brother, when it weren't nothing like it is now. I wonder if Coach can feel all them boys' eyes crawling over every inch a her. Know I can.

Then Coach take Lorna by the hand and leave me there. And then they gone. Everybody gone. Just like that. And I start walking backward till my feet in the water again. Keep walking till I'm neck deep. Floating on my back I see the too-bright moon. I dive under and nothing under there. No moon. Nothing. The dam ain't far, but the river like a warm blanket. Wish I was a baby. Not like Little Brother. Younger. When they tiny and just come out. Maybe even before.

26.

The sun isn't up yet, but already it's painting the sky in violets and crimsons. Marley had watched the colors appear over the tree line, watched a new day taking shape. A Saturday, her least favorite day, six days away from Friday, away from football, a day spent waiting, bored—a nap and a big lunch—on through to Sunday, the start of the game week. Her father had come to her on the Sunday before he fired Trent. She'll always remember that; how he came to her first. Marley watches the sky, not the road, and waits for what's coming.

Bull's old truck rumbles into the driveway. Trent emerges, shirtless. Lorna is in his arms, wearing the shirt, hair wet, eyes closed.

Trent says nothing as he walks into the house carrying their daughter. Bull stays in the truck, stopping just long enough for the door to open then close again. The truck's tires crunch dead leaves as he drives away.

When Marley comes inside Trent is facedown on their bed. Small tired breaths escape his lips. Down the hall, Lorna's door is closed. Marley goes to it and knocks. Nothing. Knocks again. When she doesn't get a response, she puts her back to the door and slides down.

Then comes a soft click, the lock turning. Marley

stands. The door is still closed, but the invitation remains. The knob feels cool against her palm. When she finally pushes it open, Lorna is lying in bed, facing the window.

The room is different than the rest of the house: pictures of Paris line the tan walls, books stacked neatly on their shelves, Lorna doing her best to make this new world her home. Marley studies her daughter beneath the covers, the soft curves and rounded edges, shapes she recognizes as her own.

"You want to talk about it?"

The pillow rustles as Lorna shakes her head.

Marley lifts her hand, hovering over Lorna's thigh, and then brings it back into her lap. She whispers, "Okay," and turns to leave.

Her daughter's words are muffled through the sheets and pillows, barely a murmur, but Marley hears her and stops. She'd already opened the door halfway. She shuts it and goes back to the bed.

Marley lifts the sheet and the comforter only enough to slide her way under. A rush of warmth escapes, smelling faintly of river water. Marley pauses, examining Lorna's bare back, the long run of toned skin, the ridges of her backbone like small rolling hills.

Outside, the sun shines bright, cutting its way through the open window, revealing the bed in warm yellow light. Mother and daughter. Marley closes her eyes, pressing herself against Lorna's back. It's early. There's still time. They sleep through the day and into the night.

Trent jerks awake, pulling free of his dreams. The river and the trailer and the body were dreams—nightmares—he awoke from sweating, only to close his eyes and sweat all over again.

He walks past Lorna's room, remembering the sight of her in the pale glow of the moon, dark places no father should see. He touches her closed door, hoping she has the power to dream the bad things away, hoping she has the power to forget.

In the kitchen, it's Monday morning: Pop-Tarts and one percent milk. Ava in a highchair, face painted a purplish-green, some awful concoction of peas and prunes. Marley hears Trent enter, but keeps her back to him. His hands slide in easy around her waist and she tenses, telling herself she's ready. She's waited all weekend for this moment. Got both of the girls out of the house most of the day Sunday, trying to clear her head, driving through the hills with the windows down and the heat on, watching the leaves fall one by one.

"How was practice yesterday?"

Trent's hands fall from her waist. "I canceled it."

"Your team is in the semifinals."

"It's been a long season, Mar. Everyone could use a little rest, especially after the—"

"*—river*?" Marley says. "Go ahead, Trent, tell me about the river."

Marley shovels another spoonful into the baby's mouth. Trent's head hangs like a sulking teenager's. Marley almost turns away, but then his eyes begin to rise, leveling out on her. There's no expression in them. Nothing. He reaches across the kitchen counter and grabs a Pop-Tart. The bag rips open. Trent crams half the square into his mouth.

"How about that game, huh?" he says as he chews.

Marley wipes a slimy glob from the baby's cheek.

"And Bill," says Trent, swallowing. "He might be the best running back I've ever coached."

Marley bends to feed Ava again, trying to make sense of her husband. Trent is a heart-on-the-sleeve kind of guy, but the face across from her shows no signs of anger, no explanations—a buoyant stare like the one her father wore, an expression Marley can almost admire. The eyes of a real coach.

"Is he coming back?" Marley says.

"Bill?" says Trent. "No. I doubt he'll be staying with us any longer."

Marley imagines what could have led to this, the way teenage boys and girls connect, passion and pain, ignorance on both ends, the sort of assembly that leads to shotgun weddings.

"She wasn't wearing any clothes, Trent."

"They were at the river. Big bonfire and stuff."

Ava lets out a scream, a happy shriek, the sort of sound babies make for no reason, like they see a good in the world adults cannot. Trent jumps, startled. Marley fears she'd only imagined his confidence from before.

"Is there," Marley says, dabbing Ava's cheek, "anything else you need to tell me?"

Trent is looking at her as he takes the milk jug, puts it to his lips, and pats Ava on the head. She smiles, and that in itself softens Marley for a moment, like maybe everything is fine, maybe there really isn't anything to worry about, and Ava can feel it because she's a baby and babies are like little litmus tests when it comes to people.

"I'm doing what you said," Trent says. "I'm trying to act like everything is normal. One more game, and then we're in the championship."

As much as Marley wants to agree with him, as much as she wants to win and be gone from this place—things are different now. Lorna is involved, maybe in the same way Marley was involved with Trent.

"She's not on birth control."

Trent shakes his head, examining the milk jug in his hands.

"After she signed that stupid pledge," says Marley, "you wouldn't let her."

"What's your point?"

"You're serious," says Marley. "Boys like Billy are the point."

"I was a boy once," says Trent, taking another swig of milk, swallowing it down. "Just like Bill."

"No shit." Marley puts a hand on the kitchen table, steadying herself. "And you think Billy will do what you did? Make the sacrifices you've made?"

"You're jumping to conclusions."

"It only took one time for us," says Marley, remembering how she was the one who'd come to the basement, ready to do the thing they'd only dreamed about doing, the sacred dance they'd skittered around until they could fight the rhythm no more.

"They were just swimming, Mar."

"You better pray to God that's all they were doing," says Marley, jabbing the baby's spoon back across the three-bedroom house, the kitchen with its fresh coat of red paint, ready for resale. "We've worked our asses off to make up for our mistake."

Trent whispers, "*Mistake?*" then reaches out and touches the kitchen's red wall. "I don't believe in mistakes anymore."

"What the hell is that supposed to mean?"

"All things, Mar, all things work together for the good of those that love the Lord."

Marley almost laughs but it gets caught in her throat, morphing into something else. She shovels another spoonful of peas into Ava's mouth. "What good can come of this, Trent? What is God's plan now?"

He turns to her, eyes wide, a giddy, almost hungry look.

"You're serious?" Trent says.

Marley has never used Trent's beliefs against him. She's never taken it that far, but she has to be sure. She has to know what they're really up against. "Yeah, I am," she says. "I'm asking you to tell me God's plan."

Trent's face goes slack. No more coaching stare, no more hunger. Nothing. "That is not for you, or me, to know," he says, opening the door to the garage, revealing the front end of the Prius cloaked in shadows. "Not yet. God's plan will be revealed in time."

"Damn it, Trent."

"I'll tell you this much," Trent says without turning, halfway out the door now. "You don't have anything to worry about between Lorna and Bill. She's just doing what we've been trying to do. She's trying to help him."

"The time for helping Billy Lowe is over, Trent."

"I hear you," Trent says and steps into the garage. "Loud and clear."

• • •

The man was larger than Travis. Tina can still feel the bulk of him. He's asleep now on the frayed sheets, and for that she is thankful.

A small roach smolders in a coffee cup. Tiny dying embers catch and flicker as the window unit cranks up and blows wet air across the room. Tina reaches for the joint.

What she's done has taken its toll.

Travis was heavy. She'd pulled him around behind the island in the kitchen, hoping Timmons wouldn't look too hard, knowing the phosphorus from the chicken houses could only hide his stink for so long. She'd simply locked the door behind her and walked out of the trailer.

The highway was almost blue in the night, blue like deep cold water, like Travis would be before too long. Tina could not escape the men in her life, or the boys. There was no difference; twenty-five years of motherhood had taught her that.

She was walking the highway after the game when the man pulled up alongside her in the semitruck.

"Need a ride?"

"Need something you cain't give me."

"Give you a ride you won't forget."

"Big talk."

"What you got in your hand?"

"Skillet."

"You gone cook for me too?"

"Something like that."

She'd said nothing more and gotten into the truck. It lurched forward and stopped again up the road at the Motel 6. After it was over, the man offered the joint and Tina took it.

"You gonna tell me your story?" he'd said, lazily, almost a drool. "Tell me about that skillet you was carrying?"

"Got me a bunch a kids," she'd said.

"Got me some too."

"Mine all boys."

"How many?"

"Three."

"Could a fooled me."

"Been fooling men my whole life."

He'd laughed and asked for the joint. Tina held it out for him. He sucked from it like her boys had sucked from her, eyes closed and smiling. Then he rolled away, like they always do, and soon began to snore.

The man is breathing steady and deep now. Tina says: "Men don't think about nobody but theyselves."

There's a tattoo on his spine: a cross with barbwire, a Bible verse caught in the spikes.

"But mommas? We carry you boys with us all our lives."

The sheets crinkle as Tina rises from the bed. She takes the man's keys and the skillet. Outside, the sky is still dark. She opens the semitruck's passenger door, pushes the skillet under the seat, and studies it for a moment. It was a small good thing. Not much to look at, but it had provided. Maybe it will continue to provide. Maybe it will save them. Tina closes the door softly and goes back to the motel room. Inside, the man is still asleep.

The nightstand drawer makes a sad sound as she opens it and takes the little green Bible in her hand. Tina hasn't read much of it, just the regular stuff a person raised in Arkansas can't help but read on billboards and church signs. She thumbs through the pages before placing the truck keys neatly atop the faux leather.

Tina is almost to the door when the man rolls over.

"You sneaking out on me?"

Tina's mouth cracks into something like a grin.

"Thought you said you were gonna cook?"

"Gotta run across the road, get some bacon."

"Cain't remember the last time I had a woman make me breakfast."

"Got me a lot a boys," Tina says. "Some habits hard to break."

The man grunts then rolls again in the bed. Tina shuts the door behind her. The sky is still dark, the new day yet to dawn, but there is hope now, a small glimmer of it, like an egg before it's cracked, the promise of food to the ravenous, starving boys of the world. The sheriff's office is a few miles down the road. Tyler Timmons is a boy like all the rest, and Tina bets he's hungry for her story.

27.

My clothes, Lorna clothes—they all still piled up at the high bluffs. Been out here three nights. Three damn nights, and I ain't said a word to nobody. Feel weird, like something changed inside me when I come up out that water.

Made a fire the first night, kept it burning all the way through.

He taught me how to make fire. There weren't no gasoline, no matches like He like. He like to pour a whole can a gas on stuff and drop the match. He like that big poof, that moment when all you think about is fire, not getting burnt. He like that. He *liked* that. Guess He don't like nothing no more.

I made a fire, though. All sticks and leaves. You can make fire you got enough time, and I had time. Where Billy Lowe supposed to go? Thought about Momma and Little Brother, wondered if they's warm while I spun those sticks in my hands, spun them so fast, so long, my hands ripped open and blood dripped on the twigs I's trying to light. Blood ain't gasoline, but it'll burn.

Just when I's about to stop, just when my hands couldn't take it no more, I remembered Coach and that stick he was carrying. I went back to the water's edge, back to where he dropped it, and it was there, small bits of hot orange still glowing on the bank.

Fire warm against the night.

Just kept waiting. Don't even know what I's waiting for. Sat and let a squirrel get so close I could touch it. Big fox squirrel. Drank water from the river and it tasted like dirt. Watched a few college kids drive down to the dam, Hank Williams and Travis Tritt blaring out from them speakers. Nobody looking for Billy Lowe.

Put my clothes back on. Used Lorna's clothes as covers, wrapping them over my shoulders when the nights got cold. And then I found the book. Thought about throwing it in the fire, see if it burned better than the leaves and sticks. But I didn't.

Read every page.

That old man catch his big fish, finally get what he want so bad. But when he get ahold of it—or it get ahold of him—it don't matter. Not like out on a football field. There weren't no scoreboard for that old man and his big fish. It was just them. And then the sharks. And after that, bones—a skinny old man and a dead fish. Dumb shit, you ask me.

Could still smell Lorna on her clothes. Strawberries. The way she float in the water like she weren't scared of nothing: not Coach, not me, not them boys and the big fire they lit with gas and a match, not even the dam. She might a been scared when Coach stood there with that stick and a look in his eye like he planned to use it, maybe, but she didn't show it. Stood right up to him, like that old man holding on to that fish. Every inch of her under the moonlight for all them boys and Bull and Coach to see, and then they gone.

Guess it Monday now, following the sun. But I don't have to follow the sun. It like my body know, like I been sitting too long. Feel my muscles twitching, aching for a bar and some weights. Need to lift something, to hit something—need Coach and football. That what my body say, but my brain say fuck them. Billy Lowe don't need *nobody*. Wonder what that old man brain was telling him after he hooked that fish? Was it his body that kept holding on? Had to be. The mind weak, tell you all kinds of things, but the body—bone and blood and muscle—them things don't lie.

Left the fire burning. Wanted somebody to come up to that spot on the high bluffs, see that fire still going and know something happened there. Wanted them to see Coach fire, my fire, the blood from my hands. Sooner or later that fire'll go out. I know that. Won't be nothing but a few burnt up sticks, some ash, just like the bones that old man lugged back in his boat.

I rise from the fire and start walking, then I run. Feel good to run. Got Lorna clothes and that book in my hand, holding them tight like they the only things I got left.

28.

The Monday morning workout is good and clean, just what the team needs. Trent can feel himself coming back to form, the horrible weekend fading away. He's relied heavily on his routine to clear his mind and help him forget, staying focused on their next opponent, the Bearden Bears, a football powerhouse down in south Arkansas.

Trent keeps his eye on the boys as they lift the bars and dumbbells. Three boys stand at a rack where there should be four. Billy's workout group. Heavy metal music blares from dingy speakers. The weights clang like kick drums.

When Principal Bradshaw enters the field house, it all comes rushing back: rotten trash, the fire and the river, Lorna's pale skin in the light of the moon. Bradshaw saunters about like he's the one running the workout. Trent keeps his distance, waiting for Bradshaw to come to him, and he does, eventually, but not before he's talked to Jarred and Austin, along with any other Pirate whose daddy pays their dues to the Booster Club.

"Morning, Coach."

Bradshaw keeps his eyes on the boys as he speaks. Trent can't be certain, but he thinks the man is watching Austin Murphy, on the floor now, doing push-ups.

"Hello, Mr. Bradshaw."

"Who says hello? Not nobody from Denton, tell you that much."

"Yes, you know I'm from—"

"—*Mississippi.* That right, Coach?" says Bradshaw, turning his eyes to Trent. "Hell, first time the Pirates make it to the semifinals since I can't remember, and we got a coach from California? Knew that couldn't be right. Did a little googling. Born in Pearl, Mississippi. That's more like it."

Trent watches Austin, his face almost healed now. The boy must have done a hundred push-ups, maybe more. Sweat drips off the tip of his nose and gathers in small puddles beneath him.

"I was just born in Mississippi. I didn't live there."

"Counts," says Bradshaw. "Kinda like being Black. You got any Black in you, even the tiniest bit—then you're Black. Same goes for the South. You're born in Mississippi, you're one of us."

"I've lived all over the country."

"Seven different foster homes, that right?"

Austin stands. Trent can almost see the boy's pulse throbbing behind his puffed-up chest. Trent feels his own heart beating.

"Six," says Trent.

"Pardon?"

"Six foster homes, then I was adopted."

"Didn't see that."

"I doubt very much you did."

"There you go again, sounding like a Yankee, or a hippie—not really sure what we call Californians."

"People," says Trent.

He watches Bradshaw's grin, a small, crooked thing. The principal is still smiling when he says, "How about Billy?"

Trent's heart thuds like the weights. "What about him?"

"Y'all got boys like that in Cali?"

Trent measures his words, trying to decide Bradshaw's angle before saying, "Yes."

Austin starts a set of sit-ups, his back slicking the rubber floor with sweat. Trent watches, knowing the boy could do all the push-ups, all the sit-ups in the world, and he still wouldn't stand a chance against Billy Lowe in the Blood Alley drill.

"Do you have something you need to tell me?" Trent says.

"You planning on playing Billy next week?"

Trent does not hesitate. "Why wouldn't I?"

"Oh, don't know, thought maybe a dead body in the Lowes' trailer might give you some pause."

"Are you implying—"

"I ain't implying nothing."

"Good, because I have a plan for Bill, and I'm following it."

Both men watch Austin now. The boy's eyes are closed as he slams his body back then springs forward, again and again.

"Got word this morning," says Bradshaw, "about somebody camping up around the high bluffs over the weekend."

Trent tries to remember the river, the boy. *Dreams*. Trent remembers dreaming of Billy, the bedsheets wet from his sweat, the sound of footsteps in the halls, Marley creeping through their house, through Trent's mind. The words she'd said to him the morning after the night that led to the river. Trent has faith in his wife, the way an athlete must have faith in his coach. How many times had Trent told his own players that classic coaching line—"The best athletes have the shortest memories"—after they made a mistake on the field? Forget and move on. That was the name of the game.

"What you think kept old Billy from coming on home?" says Bradshaw. "What'd make a boy camp out down by the river for three straight nights?"

"How about a horrible family situation like the Lowes'?"

"That ain't quite what I had in mind."

"Well," says Trent, "there was an altercation involving Bill and my daughter early Saturday morning."

"That so?"

"Yes."

"And that sits right with you?" says Bradshaw. "You just gonna let that one slide, get Billy back out there and let him score some more touchdowns?"

Trent rolls his head in a quick, short circle. His neck crackles and pops. "What is it, Mr. Bradshaw? *What* do you want me to do?"

Austin rolls forward from the floor as Bull blows his whistle. A wet spot marks the floor behind the boy, an outline like at a crime scene.

"Guess you really didn't spend no time in Mississippi," says Bradshaw, eyeing the floor. "But you don't got to be from the South to know why I'm here, Coach."

"Same reason you came to see me last time?"

"Didn't look too good after the Harrison game, Billy

going crazy like that, storming off the field. Who knows what he would've done if he'd made it back to that field house."

The heavy metal music works its way into Trent's head, a soundtrack to the memory

"Thank God for Bull," says Bradshaw.

Trent watches Austin, standing now, stronger, maybe, than he was before. Trent notices for the first time how the boy's jersey hangs loose in the shoulders, much like his once had.

"I heard another story," says Trent, but Bradshaw is focused on Austin, smiling at the boy. "One you told me."

"I've been telling you all sorts of stories, Coach, ever since you got here."

"I remember," says Trent. "Especially the one about Jesse Lowe. How he stormed off the field, just like Bill. How that coach couldn't handle him." Trent pauses, watching as Bradshaw finally turns to face him. "And how that coach lost his job."

"So you been doing a little recon of your own?" says Bradshaw. "Maybe you're finally learning something."

Trent's right hand drops into his pocket, taking hold of his keys. "If you want to talk to Bill," says Trent, scraping at the Prius key with his thumbnail, "I'll let you know when he shows up."

"You do that," says Bradshaw. "But I didn't come here to talk about Billy."

Bradshaw takes a quick step, coming face to face with Trent.

"Came here to talk about Billy's momma," says Bradshaw. "Tina Lowe showed up at the sheriff's office today.

Timmons called and said she's ready to spill the beans—but she ain't talking, not until she sees Billy."

The keys jingle as Trent withdraws his hand from his pocket, folding his arms across his chest.

"She's up at the school," Bradshaw adds, "waiting in my office."

"But Bill's not here," says Trent.

"Kinda figured you needed to explain that to her," says Bradshaw. "Since you're the one that saw her boy last."

Austin Murphy drops down for another round of push-ups. His soft pink belly smacks the floor, a sharp, crisp sound, something like a slap in the face.

29.

Cars in lines, moving slow. Parents dropping off sleepy-eyed kids, boys like Austin Murphy, after they kiss them on the cheek, tell their babies bye-bye. I run past the cars, looking crazy. Know I'm looking crazy carrying girl clothes and a book in my hand.

Don't even slow down none when I get to the field house. All them fancy trucks parked in the grass, mud tires looking mean, tires big enough to climb up and over the bluffs down by the river, but they ain't climbing nothing, just sitting there. Tires probably hate them soft-ass boys that drive them.

When I get inside the field house, everybody gone. Don't have to lock no doors in Denton. Water in the showers cold, nothing like the warm river water. Let the water wash me clean. Find some old workout clothes stuffed down in my locker. Feel better than wearing them new clothes Mrs. Powers got me.

Feel good when I head up to school. Didn't realize how long I's in the shower, letting the water wash the river off, wash everything away. Almost lunchtime when I get up there. Ain't nothing better than coming back to school after you won big on Friday. Everybody talking to you, telling you good game, proud.

But when I get in there, ain't nobody talking to Billy Lowe.

Don't even look at me, like I didn't score five touchdowns in our first playoff game. Walk down the hall and don't nobody say a word. Everybody look the other way. Then the lunch bell ring and I thinking at least the big table gonna say something, anything, talk about the bonfire, about Lorna, how Coach went all crazy. But when I get my tray of chicken spaghetti and make my way for that table, don't nobody even look at me.

Jarred talking and everybody laughing with lunches packed by they mommas or fast food brought by they daddies, not a single one with a tray like I got. A seat next to Jarred open. I stand behind it, waiting for one a them to say something. I pull the chair back. It groan when I do, like it don't want me to sit down either.

"Seat taken," say Jarred, not looking at me, looking at all the other boys. "Shit, Billy, I'm surprised they even let your ass back in school."

"What the hell? I score all them—"

"Ain't nobody talking about football."

I turn from the table cause I don't wanna hear it, and I see Lorna. She standing over by the hallway. I cain't help but see her like I saw her that night. I try not to but I cain't help it. She look me in the eyes, like she know what I'm seeing, like she feel it. But then she smile, a sad smile, and raise her chin, like she want me to come over.

"Alright then," I say to the boys at the table. "I see how it is."

"Best go check on your girlfriend," say Jarred.

"Fuck you."

"What'd you say to me?" say Jarred and stick half a Taco Bell burrito in his mouth.

I don't say nothing else, just turn from the table, and Jarred don't say nothing cause he just like Him. All talk. But He ain't talking no more. And maybe that's why nobody talking to me. Maybe they already heard about His busted head and now they figuring Billy Lowe done went full crazy.

Lorna waiting for me. She turn and start walking down the hall. I follow her. She carrying a little brown bag, got that organic peanut butter in it, the kind Mrs. Powers say ain't got no preservatives. What the hell a preservative? Taste like Play-Doh, you ask me. Happy for my tray and chicken spaghetti. I follow her all the way to the library, watching her little ass bounce under another long hippie dress. Cain't help it. Once you seen it, don't mean you stop looking.

We sit at the same spot we sat before, back on the couch in the library. She take her sandwich out and don't say nothing. We both sit and don't say nothing. I'm about sick of people not saying nothing.

"You alright?" I say.

She push the sandwich back inside that little brown bag and crumple it up like she mad now. Then she breathe in deep. Her shoulders rise and fall.

"I don't know," she say. "Dad barely came out of his room all weekend."

Now I'm the one that don't say nothing.

"I mean, the look in his eyes, and that stick—what was he planning to do with that stick?"

"Probably nothing."

"I've never seen him like that."

My mind rush back to the river. I see Coach again, the way he hit Jarred.

"Everyone is talking, Billy."

The librarian watching us now. Mrs. Marshal a big woman, heavy and soft like women get who sit for a living. She been watching us ever since we come in. Ain't no talking in the library, ain't supposed to be no eating in the library, neither. I ain't took a bite, though, and I'm starving. Ain't ate nothing in two days, but now my chicken spaghetti already cold. And Lorna sandwich all crumpled up. Mrs. Marshal don't say nothing, just like everybody else, and Lorna sitting there telling me everybody talking.

"Nobody say nothing to me."

"They're scared, Billy. People are scared—that's why they're not talking to you."

"*Scared?*"

"They found a dead man in your trailer. Travis Rodney. Wasn't he like your mom's boyfriend or something?"

"Or something."

"What the hell does—" Lorna say it too loud and Mrs. Marshal look up over her computer screen, finger to her mouth. Lorna say it again, whispering now. "What the hell does that even mean?"

"It mean He weren't nothing to me."

"A week, Billy, that man had been dead in your trailer for a week. And now people are talking about how you started staying with us—"

"Don't mean a goddamn thing," I say, loud. Too loud. Mrs. Marshal rise up out her chair and she coming for us now, stumbling through the bookshelves like she ain't stood once all day. I nod in her direction. Lorna pull a book out her backpack.

"*Pour soul, the centre of my sinful earth,*" say Lorna, just as Mrs. Marshal walk up.

"Are you eating in the library?" say Mrs. Marshal, looking straight at me.

I'm looking down at the tray in my lap when Lorna say, "No ma'am."

"It sure looks that way."

"No ma'am," say Lorna again.

"And Billy," she say. "Did I hear you swearing?"

"No ma'am," say Lorna before I can say anything. "We were just reciting these sonnets for Ms. Miller's English project. We have to memorize five of these things. Fourteen lines apiece. That's seventy lines of poetry, Mrs. Marshal. That's a lot."

"From where I was sitting, it sounded as if Billy took the Lord's name in vain," say Mrs. Marshal. She breathing hard now too, like the walk over about done her in.

"No ma'am," say Lorna. "It was probably just this Shakespeare. He was so scandalous."

Lorna try and laugh, but Mrs. Marshal ain't buying it. Mrs. Marshal studying me now. I don't look at her. She see the lunch tray in my lap and it don't matter what book Lorna's reading, or how many times she say "ma'am," she know what she heard. This ain't Mrs. Marshal first rodeo.

"Swearing will earn you three days of in-school suspension, Mr. Lowe," she say. "And I don't care how many touchdowns you scored last Friday."

Of all the damn people in school, Mrs. Marshal the

one that finally say something about me scoring all them touchdowns. She don't care, not one bit, probably don't even know if we won the game or not, but still, it good to hear somebody talk about it. Been waiting all day.

"Five," I say, and look up at her.

"Excuse me?"

"Five touchdowns—that's how many I score last Friday."

Mrs. Marshal breathing hard now, really huffing like she the Big Bad Wolf and she about to blow Billy Lowe down. I just stare at her, though, let her see what she getting herself into if she wanna come at me. Lorna feel it too, like she always do, and now she standing, waving that book in Mrs. Marshal face like she fanning a flame.

"Are you familiar with Sonnet 146, Mrs. Marshal?" say Lorna.

She ain't buying it. Her little eyes—eyes like a possum got—boring holes into me now.

"No, Ms. Powers, I am not familiar with Sonnet 146. I don't much care for Shakespeare."

Lorna look lost, trying to figure why the hell this librarian talking shit about her Shakespeare. But then it come to me. I know what to say.

"What about Hemingway?"

Mrs. Marshal face turn soft. I go for it.

"*The Old Man and the Sea*? That one's my favorite."

"You've read Hemingway?" She say it like she don't believe me.

"Yeah."

Lorna stomp hard on my toe.

"I mean, yes *ma'am*."

Mrs. Marshal ain't budging. I can see it in her face. "What happens then, Billy? You tell me what happens at the end of that book and I won't write you up. How about that?"

I nod and bow my head, really playing it out cause I want her to think she got me. I hear Lorna exhale like she don't believe I read the book either. I look up, staring only at Lorna cause I want her to see, see all the way through to my heart and know that she can trust me, know that I might be a lot a things—but I ain't a liar.

"That old man catch his fish," I say, and Mrs. Marshal nod like I ain't told her nothing.

"You could get that from the back of the book, Billy. I'm sorry, but I'm going to have to—"

"And then he kill it. Not like he wanted to kill it, not with a knife so he can cut meat off it and feed himself and that little boy who always fishing with him. He kill it just by hanging on. Kill it cause he won't let go. That fish drag him all around the ocean, wear itself completely out, and then it dies. The old man so beat, so tired, he cain't do nothing with it. Cain't even row hisself back home before the sharks come. And all he got to take back to that little boy, all he got to show for all that, is bones."

I'm still looking at Lorna when I stop talking. She look like she about to cry or smile, something. Then I hear Mrs. Marshal huff, and when I turn, she gone, already sitting back at her computer. Bet she won't get up again all day.

"Billy," say Lorna, and we both sitting there, close, like we were at the river. "You *read* it. You really read the book."

"Told you I would."

She take my hand. I look straight at her. Want her to see what I seen: the trailer and the glow and His body lying there. Want her to know I ain't done nothing. I hit Him. I did that. Knocked his ass out, but it wasn't enough to kill him. Want Lorna to trust me. But that sort of thing take time, and time ain't something we got, cause the library door swing open and there stand Coach, huffing like he ran down the hall, huffing like Mrs. Marshal just got done huffing.

"Bill?" say Coach, and Lorna slap her hand back to her side real fast. "Where have you been?"

"You worried about me now?"

"It doesn't matter," say Coach. "There's someone here that wants to talk with you."

I can almost hear Mrs. Marshal panting from back behind her computer, like she happy now that Coach coming to take me away.

"Who?"

"You need to come with me."

I don't say nothing.

"Do you hear me?"

"Yeah," I say, and look at him, hard.

Coach nod slow then quick, like he working himself up for whatever it is he about to say. Then he stop moving altogether, just staring at me. The look from the river all over his face now. Eyes red and tired.

"You need to start using your manners, Bill, or you'll stay in the same stinking pile of crap you were born into. Is that what you want? Do you want to stink like trash the rest of your life?"

Mrs. Marshal start to rise from her chair, like she

thinking about writing Coach up now too. But Lorna beat her to it. She standing between Coach and me like she did at the river, little hands balled into fists.

"Don't you dare talk to him like that."

"Bill," say Coach, not even looking at his daughter. "I need you to come with me."

"*Dad.*"

Coach look through her, still got his eyes on me. I can almost feel the heat coming off Lorna as her fingernails dig into her palms. I figure she done saved me once, about time I return the favor.

"No *sir*," I say, standing, looking straight at Lorna, her eyes red like her daddy's but wet. "I don't wanna stink like trash the rest of my life."

Coach smile, like maybe he proud, or maybe it something else. He reach around Lorna and take me by the shoulder. His hand feel like a cop hand as he lead me out the door, down the hall, taking me somewhere I don't want to go.

30.

Tina Lowe stands outside the school's front office, hair pulled back in a greasy bun. Don Bradshaw is propped against the wall like a cutout cowboy silhouette, pushing a McDonald's coffee cup into his mustache, keeping his distance. Tina fidgets, tugging at a stained Denton sweatshirt hanging from her like a black trash bag. Her hands are empty.

Trent feels Billy's shoulders tense as the boy breaks free of his grip, stepping toward his mother.

"Where Little Brother?" Billy says.

Tina doesn't answer, but instead flings herself at her son, hair falling loose of the bun, cutting slick wet lines across Billy's face.

Trent steps back, giving them some space and nearly bumps into Principal Bradshaw.

"Where Little Brother?" says Billy again.

"You look good, baby, so good," says Tina. "I been worried."

"*Worried?*" says Billy. "You ain't even called or nothing."

"You ain't got no phone, baby. How's I gonna call you?"

"I been staying with Coach."

"Oh," says Tina. "That right?"

"Yeah, that's right," says Bradshaw, cutting in. "You didn't know?"

Tina scowls at the man.

Bradshaw grins. "Way I figure it, y'all about to be out of my hair for good."

"Damn straight," snarls Tina. "Sheriff Timmons the only one we need to talk to now."

"I can give you a ride," says Trent, reaching out, touching Tina's shoulder, trying to usher her toward the door. She jerks away, eyes slicing back to him. Trent feels, for the first time, the raw kind of crazy that lies dormant in Tina Lowe, enough crazy to produce a lineage of crazy, enough to make Trent remove his hand.

"Nope," says Bradshaw. "I'll be escorting the Lowes over to the sheriff's office. You got a big game coming up, Coach." Bradshaw pushes open the school's glass doors. "Bearden Bears a fine little football program."

A chill rushes in as Billy and Tina brush past Trent on their way through the door, the first blast of winter descending into the Ozark hills. The door shuts and Trent watches through the glass as the three walk against the cold. Trent half expects Billy to turn and run. But the boy walks on, staying a few steps ahead of his mother.

The heat is on in the coaches' office. A wall-unit churns, pumping in hot air. Trent takes hold of his shirt, wafting it, and within seconds he is hot. A perfect metaphor for Arkansas: hot or cold—nothing in between.

Bull sits, legs propped up on his desk, hat pulled down over his eyes. He jerks when Trent enters, peeking out from under the brim.

"Been looking at this Bearden film," says Bull.

"I haven't," says Trent.

"I know."

Trent rearranges the papers on his desk, sits, then stands again. The whole time Bull's eyes follow him. Trent finally plops down in his leather chair, throws up both hands, and says, "*What?*"

"How much you trust your wife?"

"You're serious?" Trent's fingers tingle, remembering the conversation with Marley from earlier, how she'd asked him if there was anything else he needed to tell her.

"She's . . ." says Trent, pausing a beat too long, "my wife."

"Timmons came by just a minute ago, while you were up at the school," Bull says. "Thought you should know."

Trent turns away, eyes going to the crucifix hanging on the wall. "Timmons is about to have his hands full with Tina and Bill. What's he doing sniffing around here?"

"A bunch of our boys saw you with that stick in your hands at the river. They get to telling their mommas a story like that, and well . . . Word travels quick around here, Hollywood."

"What are you saying?"

Bull stands, lifting a whistle from a hook behind his desk. "*What would Jesus do?*" He drapes the lanyard around his neck. "Ain't that how it goes?"

"What on earth are you talking about?"

"Jesus'd go talk to his wife," Bull says. "That's what Jesus would do."

31.

Principal Bradshaw talked the whole time. I didn't say nothing. Momma didn't neither. Principal still talking when he stop his truck and we get out. I slam the door hard enough to answer all his questions.

Me and Momma start walking up to the sheriff office. Colder than hell now. Maybe this is hell. Cain't imagine it getting much worse. Whole time we walking I can only think about one thing.

"Where Little Brother?"

"Stephen?" she say, like she don't remember having no baby in her arms for the last two years.

"Yeah, Little Brother."

She walking faster now, hugging her shoulders, cold, probably thinking about leaving me standing here in the parking lot, and that when it hit me.

"What you done with him?"

"Watch it, Billy."

"What you done with him?"

"Ain't done nothing. He with Jesse and Creesha now."

Momma know Little Brother better off dead than get left with Jesse Lowe. Wouldn't put nobody under Jesse care, not even Jarred. After Jesse start drinking, he slice bacon off Jarred fat ass for breakfast.

"Come on, Momma. You ain't that stupid."

She stop, turn, and come at me fast. "That what that fancy coach taught you while I's gone? Taught you Tina Lowe just some dumb bitch?"

She raise her hand like she gonna hit me, raise it high and block out the sun. The shadow on my face feel like nothing. Just gonna let her hit me. Won't hurt none.

But she don't. She move her hand and the shadow gone.

"Like you one to talk," she say.

I raise one eyebrow.

"Leaving Creesha and Neesy out there with Jesse. That ain't no place for women, Billy. Little Stephen can handle hisself. Jesse teach him a thing or two, but it ain't no place for women."

"Don't care what Creesha say, Neesy Jesse baby."

She lift both hands out to her side. "Either way that little girl mine. Don't you see that? And it take a lot out a woman to try and care for all these kids."

"Like how you didn't even call me the whole time you been gone, wouldn't even answer your phone?"

"You ain't got no clue," she say and start walking again, "what I done for you."

"I-I—" It won't come out, the words tasting funny in my mouth.

"You what?"

"I'm sorry."

"I know, Billy. Know you are," she say over her shoulder, not slowing down none.

I jog to catch up but she don't stop. We almost to the front doors now.

"And now you gone and brought all this on us," say

Momma. "I know Travis weren't your daddy, but he's the best I could do. And now he gone too. Just you and me, baby. Guess that what you always wanted."

Her words stop me walking, sharp like the cold.

"I didn't do nothing, Momma."

She stop now too, looking past me to Sheriff Timmons. His big dumb ass already waving from the front door.

"Don't matter if you did."

32.

"Trucker, huh?" says Timmons. "You got his plates?"

"Plates?" says Tina. "Nah, but he come through here about once a week."

A flickering fluorescent bulb lights the cramped room. A patchwork of pain, a timeline, is exposed across Tina's face: wrinkles from the worry of her boys, scars from the fists of their fathers.

"This trucker got a name?"

"Chuck."

"Chuck what?"

Tina's eyes go up, searching for an answer. "Just Chuck."

"So you was sleeping with this man for"—Timmons checks his notes—"three months, and don't even know his last name?"

Tina had it all figured before she'd sat down, a simple story, as old as the hills and the Ozark streams. But now, with Timmons sitting there before her—a large man like the trucker, his pen scribbling her every word—the story begins to fade.

"He's paying me."

"That ain't legal neither, Tina."

"Want you to know I'm serious."

"So this man's paying you for your services, dropping in

once a week off his trucking route, and you trying to tell me he got jealous or something?" says Timmons. "Mad enough to come in and beat poor Travis to death with a skillet?"

Tina nods but feels the light on her face. It's not like it was before. Time has taken from her all power she once held over men.

"Yeah," says Tina. "That's what I was saying."

Despite Bull's warning, Trent stays for practice. He can't quit staring at the old man, though, unable to forget what Bull had said, *how* he'd said it. As a result, the boys are sloppy and wild. If Larry Dommers had witnessed such disorder, Trent would've never heard the end of it, especially with the semifinal game fast approaching, especially after canceling the practice on Sunday. When the messy ordeal is finally over, Trent goes back and sits in his office with the lights out, game film of the Bearden Bears playing on repeat across his computer screen. Trent's eyes flicker in the dim light, unable to focus, lost in his own game now. *Marley's* game. All the choices she's made for him, the details he's chosen to forget, that's what's playing through his mind, a highlight reel of broken memories and fractured faith. Two hours later, Trent decides he's seen enough and leaves for home.

As the garage door clanks shut behind him, Trent kills the Prius's engine and closes his eyes. He doesn't realize what he's doing, doesn't even feel his head on the steering wheel, until he hears the sharp burst of the car's horn, a sound like a small dog yipping.

Trent opens his eyes and Marley is standing in the

doorway. She puts a finger to her lips, staring at her husband.

"Ava is sleeping."

"Sorry."

Marley's jaw pulses as Trent walks past her and into the house. He takes a seat at the kitchen table as she closes the door.

"We need to talk," says Trent.

There's a sound from the living room. Marley turns the dead bolt and stands on her tiptoes, peering over the swinging doors.

"Lorna?" says Trent.

Marley shakes her head. "She's at play practice."

Sunlight pours in through the window above the sink, illuminating Marley's face. She is beautiful but weathered, worn down like women who carry their men.

Trent says, "I want to tell you about what I saw," and reaches across the table, his palm open and up.

Marley stares down at her husband's hand.

"At the trailer that night," Trent adds. "I need to tell you everything."

Lorna hears her parents talking as she unlocks the front door, low, hushed tones, words not meant for her ears. She eases the door shut, not even closing it all the way, and creeps into the living room.

All day it'd been the same thing: Billy Lowe. She hasn't seen him again since her father took him away at lunch. But everyone has been talking. It's all over social media, conspiracies spreading like the wildfires they left in California.

Lorna creeps up the living room steps and stops halfway to the top, far enough that the kitchen's swinging doors are hidden from sight.

She couldn't even go to play practice, not after Jarred Trotter had tagged her in a post, calling her Billy's "fuck-toy." Then there were the comments, the other girls citing the fact that she does not wear a bra as evidence of her debauchery.

Lorna lets the day settle as she sits atop the stairs, feeling like maybe, sitting up this high, with her parents down below, she is above it all. She knows people talk. People always talk. Especially when you're the new girl at school, your dad's the head football coach, and you don't wear a bra. Not because you're a slut, but because bras are confining, all part of the patriarchal, chest-beating world in which Lorna exists.

She hears her mother's voice, sharp tones drifting all the way up the stairs. Lorna leans toward the whispers, pressing her ear to the stairway's metal railing, and listens.

"It's almost been a week," says Marley, staring at Trent's open hand on the table. "Why didn't you say something before?"

"You remember when we left the Valley?"

"Of course I remember."

"All the gossip, all the nasty things people were saying about our family?"

"I remember."

"And we didn't talk about it. We just left."

"We both know what happened." She swallows and

grimaces, as if she were stomaching everything that had led them here. "We lost."

"I know."

"But this is different. This isn't just football." Marley reaches over, bypassing Trent's hand, touching his chest, the side opposite his heart. "What you said you saw at that trailer, Trent. If you didn't tell me everything, then—"

Trent jerks his hand back, eyes moving slowly up the length of his wife. "Principal Bradshaw threatened to fire me."

Marley's mouth falls open, that old flame burning again. "*Fire* you?"

"About a week ago. Right after Billy went ballistic on the sideline of the Lutherville game." Trent pauses, remembering the look in Billy's eyes, the blood on his hands. "Bradshaw wasn't pleased with the job I was doing."

"But you're in the second round of the playoffs."

"He didn't like the way I was handling Bill."

"*Handling* him?" says Marley.

"He didn't think I was giving the wealthy players, boys like Austin Murphy, the proper spotlight."

"And he still expected you to win?"

"Well, not exactly."

Marley raises both eyebrows.

"He said a state championship was hard to argue with."

"A state championship?" says Marley. "Without Billy?"

"That's why I've been so distracted." Trent folds his arms, pushing his fists up under his chest. He feels weak, deflated. He fights the urge to drop down onto the floor and start a round of push-ups, a quick set. Instead, he places his palms on the kitchen table again, both of them this time. "And the way Bill beat on my desk that day, the look in his eyes, it was bad, Mar. I could feel it."

"That's why you brought him to our house?"

"I was about to lose another job. I was afraid we'd have to move again." Trent waits, looking past Marley to the door. "And I knew we didn't have anywhere else to go."

"You should have called Dad, or let me call him."

"*No*," Trent says, slapping the tabletop with enough force it rattles the few pictures hanging on the walls.

Marley jerks up and out of her chair. It falls behind her, a harsh crash to match Trent's table slap from a moment before. She's almost through the swinging doors, into the living room, but then she stops.

"God, Trent. I hope you know how to handle this."

Marley waits, the doors flapping out a heartbeat's rhythm behind her.

"I've already handled it," Trent says, and the swinging doors snap to a stop.

33.

Been in the sheriff office before, been here a whole bunch a times. Always the same though, just like sitting outside principal office, it a waiting game. You wait on them to call you in. They wait on you to tell them what they wanna hear. Everybody waiting, and it don't matter if you done it or not, they just keep on waiting, asking the same questions again and again.

Momma in there with Sheriff now. Usually I ain't got to worry about Momma. Hell, she the one taught me how to wait. "Deny till you die." That what Momma always said. Say it harder to catch you than you know, and if they asking questions, then they ain't got you pinned.

But something different about Momma now, see it in her eyes, like she finally just broke. Like she could only wait so long for her boys to grow up and move on, maybe give her something back. Momma all used up. Sucked dry. Little Brother probably ain't had nothing to suck on for the last two years.

Little Brother the only boy she had by Him. Guess there weren't no guaranteeing it was His baby, but he sure weren't Daddy's boy. Little Brother ain't got it like we got it. Don't look nothing like a Lowe, look just like Him. Kinda soft. Kinda round. Like a marshmallow. Little

Brother never even got the cigarette, just the pen. Maybe He knew His boy couldn't handle the heat. Or maybe it just the fact that there weren't no milk left for Little Brother. Maybe that why he so small and weak. Maybe that why Momma took him to Jesse. Maybe now that He gone, she just cain't carry that baby around no more. But if she did, if she really took Little Brother out to Jesse, then there no telling what she saying to Sheriff in there.

One of the deputies, a Black dude named Rome Montgomery, just come out the room where they got Momma. Rome played strong safety for the Pirates. Tall and skinny, not that strong. Always forget he Creesha brother. Don't know why. Montgomerys really the only Black family we got in Denton. Ain't even really Black. Light skinned. Got traces of Indian blood and God knows what else, but damn sure dark enough to be Black around here. Rome was smart and would knock you out, especially if you weren't looking. They grew up two trailers down from us in Shady Grove, Momma Montgomery raising up all them kids by herself. Couldn't find no Black man, and all the white guys knew better. Maybe that's why Rome wearing that uniform and I'm sitting here waiting—didn't have no dumbass doing dumb shit all the time. Used to have a lot of respect for Rome, till me and Creesha got together.

"Billy," he say and nod at me.

I don't say nothing.

"So that's how it is?"

"I ain't the one wearing no damn badge."

"Right, right," he say, his voice already sounding like a cop. "Now you gonna tell me how stupid I am for making something of myself."

"Making something of yourself?" I say and spit right there on the sheriff office floor. "Don't look like you made nothing of yourself. Look like bullshit, you ask me."

"Nobody asking you," he say, and hitch at his belt, sliding his hand across his gun.

"Ain't that what I here for? Somebody supposed to ask me some questions?"

He don't say nothing.

"That right," I say and wipe my lips. "I ain't here for *you* to ask me nothing."

I see it flash in his eyes, see Shady Grove burn hot in his blood, see how pissed he still is about Cree getting pregnant and dropping out of high school. Rome look like he about to spit too, but he don't, just suck his teeth and keep staring at me. That badge, that belt and that gun, them things you earn by holding it back. Being Black in Denton, Rome probably know all about holding it back. People always think my daddy got Black blood in him, and that been tough enough.

"Alright," he say. "I'll shut up, Billy, but somebody should a told your Momma that before she went back there. She telling Sheriff everything he need to know."

Almost get up out the chair, almost take off after Rome, fast and low, but then the door open. Momma come out crying. Of course she crying. Sheriff behind her. He look worn out.

"Come on, Billy," say Timmons. "Your turn."

The little room don't look nothing like the rooms they got on TV. Ain't dark. Ain't got no hanging light. This room like a room at school. Some place where they make you sit and write, "I will not cuss in class," over and over until your hand start to lock up. Then you got to write some more.

"Where you been at the last few days, Billy?"

Keep my mouth shut.

"Silent treatment, huh?" Sheriff say. "Let me put it a different way."

There ain't no handcuffs, nobody else but me and Timmons. He open a folder he got lying on the desk. See Him all sprawled out, looking like shit.

"Got some things I need you to look at. See if they ring a bell," say Timmons and slide one them pictures across the table to me.

Don't look nothing like I remember. The picture's in black-and-white, the glow gone, and I wouldn't recognize Him if I didn't know. Don't look like a clown no more, don't look like a man either. He weren't no man, about the farthest thing from it. Look like a swolled up rotten tomato, a busted pimple, something like that. I don't say nothing. Slide the picture back to Sheriff.

He look down at it, then back up at me. "You know that man?"

I click my teeth, look straight through Sheriff.

"Of course you do. Guess the better question is—you gonna tell me what happened to him?"

I don't say nothing.

"So this how it gonna be, Billy?"

"Guess so."

"Don't matter. Pretty sure Tina done told me everything I need to know."

"What she tell you?"

He smiling now. "You tell me. I tell you."

"I ain't stupid."

"Naw, Billy, you ain't stupid, but you sure are something. What exactly, I ain't figured out just yet. But I will. Guarantee that. Denton a small town, not many homicides on our books. I got all the time in the world."

That the first thing he say that make sense. Make sense cause it true. He got time on his side. I got Bearden coming up, the semifinals. Good chance a college coach be at that game.

"You gonna tell me what she said?" I say.

"Hell, Billy, I'll show you what she said," say Sheriff, and turn his laptop screen around so I can see it. Momma looking back at me, frozen in black-and-white, frozen like He frozen in that picture, but different. I know if Sheriff push a button, Momma come back to life, start talking, saying whatever it was she say to him when she in here crying.

"Alright," I say, and Sheriff eyes go wide. "This all I know."

I tell Timmons about how I hit Him, knocked His ass out with one punch. Tell him about drinking all that whiskey after it was over. I don't tell him about the glow, though, and how it made me think a Halloween. How I thought Momma had spilt some syrup, or something, all around Him, maybe making pancakes for breakfast cause she do that sometimes. But then I remembered Momma weren't home and it weren't syrup, and I knew He was dead. So I took off running. Don't tell Sheriff none a that. I ain't stupid. Rome probably watching on some camera, calling bullshit.

"So you did hit him?" say Timmons. "Tina weren't too sure about that. Said she'd already up and left."

"Yeah, one punch, but He's still talking when I left the trailer."

"What'd he say?"

I remember how it'd come out so weak, remember thinking maybe something was bad wrong, but I just took that whiskey bottle down and stood there over Him while He squirmed around, asking me for help.

"Nothing."

"Alright, Billy," say Sheriff, shaking his head. "There weren't nobody else at the trailer?"

"Momma already told you she left."

"Right," say Timmons. "But there weren't nobody else?"

"Jesse weren't there, if that's what you asking."

"And you hit him with your fist. That's it?"

"You wanna see my hand?"

"I see the swelling there," he say. "But that gash on his forehead, that's what killed him, and I'm starting to think I might know what done it."

Feel my nose twitch.

"And I'll tell you," Sheriff say, "but first I'm gonna need you to answer a few more questions."

I don't say nothing. Just watch Timmons open that folder again.

"Who's the man in the picture, Billy? What's his name?"

"What I got to say His name for?"

"Records, you know, keep everything nice and neat."

I ain't said His name, not once since the dog pen, the cigarette. Told myself I'd never say His name again. He ain't got no name when it come to me.

"Billy, if you want to see what your momma said—everything she told me about what happened after you left—you're gonna have to say his name."

"He ain't got no name. He ain't nothing no more."

"So you weren't a big fan of Travis Rodney?" Sheriff say, and just him saying His name send red crawling up my spine.

"Nah, I weren't no *fan*."

He scribble something on his paper and look up to the back corner of the room. I follow his eyes, and there it is, the little red light, the camera. Rome sitting somewhere on the other side, probably laughing at how stupid Billy Lowe is.

"What you writing?"

"Just keeping the record."

Sheriff put his pen down and push his computer at me. Momma look bad, even worse than real life.

"Shit, Billy," say Timmons, and the fact Sheriff went to cussing make me think he ain't worried about nothing no more, make me think he got it all figured now. "I'm gonna show you the damn video, and after it's over, we'll see what you got to say."

He push the button.

Momma talking now, start off saying my name. She going on about how me and Him ain't never got along. Say some other bullshit about my daddy. Then she get to the glow and the syrup, back before that, talking about that night. Say He was poking at me, and that's true, but He was poking at Momma too. She leave that part out. Then she stop talking. Cain't talk no more cause she crying so hard. Her cry sound different coming out that computer, sound like something you see on TV. Sound fake. And I know, right then, whatever she say next—whatever she told Sheriff—won't be nothing but bullshit.

I ball my hands into fists. Wishing for the handcuffs now, keep me from doing something stupid when Momma say whatever dumbass thing she about to say on that computer screen, but then it hit me.

There ain't no handcuffs.

The little table catch on my legs as I stand.

"Easy now, Billy," say Sheriff, standing now too.

"Ain't got shit on me!" I yell, over my shoulder, already out the door.

Sheriff yell something else, but I barely hear him. I'm gone. Running. Should a used them handcuffs. Rome Montgomery waiting for me at the door, just like out on the field, some skinny-ass safety trying to keep me from the end zone. He got his gun in his hand, but I know he won't pull the trigger. Don't matter if Cree his sister. Don't matter if she stuck out in Jesse trailer forever. Rome got that gun by holding it down. I lower my shoulder, aim straight for his chin, and blow right through him.

I'm running, free now, away from all them questions that ain't got no answers. Momma the last thing I see before I hear it. The way she was just standing there, crying, like she know she cain't save me now. I hear it before I feel it. Don't sound like nothing, just a pop. And then my shoulder burning, like when He stuck me with that cigarette, except now the burn's leaking out. The fire that started everything. I look over and see blood on my shirt, wet and warm. Think about Rome, and what he must a been thinking. Did he pull that trigger for his sister, or did he pull it for the Law? That's another question that ain't got no answer, so I just keep running, down the same road that brought me here. Running, and there ain't but one place I can think to go.

34.

Lorna doesn't understand why her parents are whispering. Down the hall, she can hear the baby's sound machine, a rush of electric waves rolling out from under the nursery door. Maybe it's Ava, Lorna thinks. Maybe that's why they're whispering, but that can't be it. Ava sleeps through thunderstorms, even football games.

Maybe they're talking about her. There were so few words after the night at the river. Lorna remembers the warmth of her mother, curled up beside her in the bed. It was as close as they'd ever been. But when she awoke, her mother was gone. No questions. No answers. And then their lives just kept hurtling along toward Friday, the next practice, another game.

A chair falls in the kitchen. Their voices grow louder.

Lorna hears her mother coming, sees the saloon doors part, and jerks her head back from the railing. The single remaining feather earring—the gift from Trent on her sixteenth birthday—catches on a metal spindle and rips free of her ear, falling to the hardwood below.

Both of Lorna's hands jerk to her ear, feeling the tear in the lobe, warm blood on her fingers. She whispers, "*Shit*," and leans through the metal rails again, staring at the feather's warped wires lying mangled on the living room floor.

Lorna is still holding her ear, waiting for her mother to enter the den, see the earring, and face the grounding that will ensue, but Marley never comes. Lorna hears the swinging doors flap to a stop, and then her father begins to speak, louder than before.

"Like I said, I went to their trailer." Trent bends to the fallen chair, lifting it from the floor. "I drove around behind it. I was in the Prius. I know they didn't hear me. Not even Tina, when she came running out."

Marley paces, her toned arms cutting lines against the kitchen's red walls. "You told me this already."

"I'm trying to get everything right this time," Trent says, holding tight to the chair, hoping maybe she'll put the pieces together.

"So you were doing what? Watching them through the window?" Marley says, gnawing at her fingernails now. "Trent?"

"I was there to help." He reaches across the table, taking her hand from her mouth. "Just like you said. But then Bill hit him and took off running. I let him get pretty far down the road. I waited. There's no way Bill saw what happened next."

Marley jerks free of his hold. "*Next?*"

Trent's back in Shady Grove, watching Billy disappear over the dark horizon, the look on Travis's face, exposed in the headlights, like he never saw it coming.

"I was so focused on Bill. So worried about him, like nobody ever worried about me. I didn't see the guy. He was down on all fours, crawling in the road. It was dark. So dark, I—"

"*Trent*," Marley gasps, both hands to her mouth now.

Trent closes his eyes, trying to make sense of what had happened that night, waiting for the words to come. He can feel the wheel jerk in his hands again, the hard bump beneath the Prius's tires rattling in his chest, rising up from his heart to his throat. A bitter taste like blood floods Trent's mouth, coating his tongue as his eyes open and the truth flows from his lips.

In the stairwell, Lorna holds tight to her ear. It's bleeding, dripping onto the carpeted steps, but she doesn't feel it. Her parents just keep talking, louder and louder, their words burning brighter than the blood. The confessions. The truth. She hears everything.

What shakes Lorna most—the thing that makes her scamper down the steps and out the front door into the sinking November sun—is not her father's confession, but what comes after. The questions her mother asks. The answers her father has forged in the depths of that trailer.

Lorna's running, down their road and onto Main Street, running as the sun finally disappears over one of the distant hills leaving only the coming darkness, a new cold settling in, the knowledge of everything she was never meant to know.

35.

When I get to the river the sun down and I cain't feel my face. The blood's warm, dripping off my pinky like water in the shower, but everything else is cold. Colder than it been all year. Storm blew up out a nowhere, just opened up and dumped on me the whole time I's running. I go back to the same spot as before, the high bluffs. The river swolled up below me like it know, like it feel me up here above it. I go to work tearing my shirtsleeve away, trying to get it tied tight around the hole in my shoulder, when I hear somebody coming up the tree line.

I crouch there, ready for the end, ready for Sheriff and Rome and maybe all the Denton marshals to be creeping their way to me, vests on, guns shouldered. I get skinny behind a pine tree and steady my heart. Slide down. Pick up a fist-sized rock with my good hand. Feel heavy enough to do some damage.

I listen to them coming. Footsteps light, like they trying to be sneaky. Then a stick crack. They stop cause they know they messed up now, know I heard it. They standing there, not ten feet away. I can hear them breathing. Sound quick. Sound scared. I rub my thumb across the top a my rock and feel the blood leaking out my shoulder.

They start walking again. I close my eyes and raise

the rock up high, ready. But something hold me, just one extra second, just long enough to let them walk on past. It dark, but I can already see her hair, smell it too. Strawberries. I wait to see if Timmons sending her out front like bait. But it just Lorna. She walk out to the edge of the high bluffs, looking down in the water when I come up behind her.

She don't hear me. I keep back a ways, just standing there when finally she turn, like she seen all she need to see of that hard and fast water. I see her ear first. Tore up and red. She don't say nothing, but still, she startle, kinda stumble back. The bluff close and wet, slippery from the rain. Lorna the sort of girl that don't think about falling, even if she already fell once.

"Your ear?" I say. "That blood?"

"Get back," she say, like I some kind a dog. "Get *back*."

I feel her eyes, even in the shadows, taking in the mess a me. I turn my bad shoulder away and she see what I got in my other hand. The rock. I drop it.

"And just what were you planning to do with that?"

"Didn't know . . ." I say but the words hard to get out. "Didn't know who was coming."

"So you were just going to hit me? Is that your answer for everything?"

"Weren't like that," I say and step toward her. She scoot back a little. I'm watching her feet the whole time, watching cause she ain't watching.

"It was *just* like that. Violence is your only answer." She pause and don't say nothing for a second. Then she ask me a question I ain't never thought of before: "Why do you hit things, Billy?"

The way she say it, the way she put it so simple like that, really make me think about it. And then I wanna tell her cause a girl like Lorna—*especially* a girl like Lorna—need to know.

"I hit things cause that the only thing ever worked in my life."

"And all of those hits," she say, quiet, almost a whisper, "have led you here."

"Only hit people need hitting."

"Like Travis Rodney?" she say, and my skin crawl, my shoulder burn. "Was he the sort of man that needed hitting?"

"Yeah. He was."

Lorna keep looking at me, like she trying to figure me out, trying to see all the way back into the trailer, make sense of something she don't know nothing about.

"And now he's dead," she whisper.

The way her eyes dance make pieces of that night start coming back, or maybe it just the blood, how much I lost already. Flashes come and go, like hard shots to the head, like running over somebody, tackling somebody.

"I heard Mom and Dad talking."

I blink and the memory die. I almost saw it all. Like I could almost feel just how hard He fell.

"Talking about what?"

She lift one foot out over the water, hovering there while the river churn. "I want to get away from this place."

"The river?"

"This town. Football. The Denton fucking Pirates, Billy. I want to forget everything."

"What about me?" I say, and the words surprise me.

I can barely even feel the burn in my shoulder, not with Lorna foot still dangling out there, a little farther now. I can see her other leg start shaking. She turn her eyes back to me, just her eyes.

"I don't know about you," she say and bring the leg down.

She right. Lorna Powers ain't never gonna know nothing about me, not really. Make me wonder why she ever started talking to me in the first place, showed me that picture, told me about Theogenes.

"Acted like you wanted to know me," I say. "You was acting like you wanted to get to know me real good."

"It wasn't about you, Billy. It was never about you. It was about my parents."

"So you was what? *Using* me?"

"Kinda. I mean . . ." She reach up and touch that busted ear she ain't said nothing about. "I guess I wanted to hurt Mom, and I knew if she saw me getting close to you . . ." Lorna pause and look down in the water. "She'd think I was going to make the same mistake she did."

"Mistake?" I say. "You calling me a mistake?"

Lorna shake her head. "I'm the mistake."

I don't say nothing. She don't neither. Nobody saying nothing about the hole in my arm or the blood on her ear. The water rush and roll.

"I just want to get away," say Lorna. "I need to disappear for a while, go somewhere that'll make me forget."

There only one place I can think to go, and it ain't the sort a place I wanna take her. But it far, far from anything she ever known. And my shoulder. Know I need to do something about that too.

"I might could take you somewhere."

"Yeah?" she say and turn to me. "Where could you take me, Billy Lowe?"

"I got a brother. He don't live that far from here."

"A brother?"

"Yeah. Jesse." Even just saying his name don't sound right. Know better than to take Lorna out to see my brother, but sometime there ain't nowhere else to go. "He stay in a trailer about a mile up the road."

"And what makes you think I'd want to go to some trailer?"

I'm standing there, trying to come up with the right words, some reason that would make a girl like Lorna Powers wanna step into my world, when the river rise up to meet me. That what it feel like, like going too fast over a hill, like floating before you fall.

My knees buckle and I go down, hard.

In the darkness I see Momma with all them animals she took in over the years—stray dogs, cats, some squirrels and baby birds—chewing everything, shitting everywhere. At one point we had eleven animals in our trailer. But then it was like Momma could only put up with so much. Like she broke. Lying there, I see the rock I dropped, the one Lorna saw in my hand. Then I see Momma again, out one morning, take number twelve—a fiery little pup that wandered up the night before—Momma put him in a plastic Walmart sack, slap him up against the trailer, slam him again and again till the sack weren't white no more. She take that red sack, drop it in the garbage with the beer bottles, cigarettes, and all the other things we'd already used up, and then she shut the lid.

"*Billy.*" Lorna bring me back, enough fear in her voice to get me to my knees again. "My God, your shoulder, it's—"

"Yeah," I say, "it is." Lift my good arm and point. "Brother Jesse live about a mile down that way. Let's go."

36.

Silence hangs thick in the kitchen. Marley plays it all back in her mind, the story her husband just told her. It makes too much sense not to be true. The way Trent had fallen for Billy as soon as they arrived in Denton, bending the rules for the boy, seeing himself in Billy's black eyes—Trent was blinded. But Marley can see clearly now, running over her options like a veteran coach calling an audible.

"This changes everything," Marley says, breaking the silence as she stands.

Trent nods, still sitting, staring out the kitchen window.

"As soon as Lorna gets home, we pack the car up—the Prius—we have to take the Prius." Marley's at the saloon doors now, peering into the living room without really seeing it. She turns back to Trent. "Are you listening to me?"

He whispers, "*Yes*," and his voice sounds like a dry leaf, rustling over concrete.

"We leave. Tonight. Take just what we can fit in the car."

"That won't be much."

"God, Trent. Who cares?"

He lifts both hands and lets his head fall into his palms.

"We can make it back home by tomorrow. Drive straight through the night. We'll be so far from this shithole town, so far away from dumbass Timmons, he won't come looking for us. I'd be surprised if Timmons could even find California on a map." The more Marley says, the more the plan makes sense in her head. "These are the Denton *marshals* we're talking about. This is too big for them. Too much trouble. And for what? Some scumbag child abuser?"

The heels of Trent's palms work in deep around his eyes, and then he pulls back. "When Bull and I were in that trailer, when we found the—" He pauses, shaking his head. "When we found *Travis*, Sheriff Timmons checked the body, Mar. He saw the gash on his forehead. He knew it wasn't a fist that had done it."

"That's why we're taking the Prius." Marley pushes the swinging door open, just a bit, and lets it flap closed again. "You said you left the skillet out? That was smart. Did Timmons see it? Did he say anything about Tina?"

Trent closes his eyes. Wrinkles Marley can't remember form in his forehead. The one small scar her husband shows her every time he brings up the foster homes is hidden beneath the folds. "It wasn't there," Trent says and opens his eyes. The wrinkles are gone but the scar, small and white, remains. "The skillet. It wasn't in the kitchen when we found him. It was—"

"It doesn't matter," Marley says. "By the time Timmons gets around to asking questions, we'll be gone."

"Maybe."

"Maybe? *Maybe?*" In three quick steps Marley is back across the kitchen, squatting before her husband. "The time for maybe is over, Trent. Do you hear me?"

He lifts his eyes and nods.

"Good," Marley says, patting him on the thighs. "I'll call Daddy as soon as we get on the road. He'll think of something, a reason why we had to come back home."

Trent's left knee starts jerking up and down. "You don't have to do that."

"Yes, Trent, I do. That way, when the Pirates wake up on Tuesday morning and realize their head coach has skipped town a few days before the semifinal game, there's an explanation. Daddy will know just what to say. He'll think of something."

Trent's leg stops all at once. He stands from the kitchen table, brushing past Marley on his way to the saloon doors. "What time is it?"

"What?" Marley says. "Why?"

"Lorna. It's almost nine, on a school night. There's no way they're still rehearsing for that play. Not this late."

"Yes, Trent, they rehearse late almost—"

"Lorna?" he says, pushing through the swinging doors and turning on the lights in the living room. "*Lorna?*"

Marley moves to the doors, catching one and holding it open. Across the living room Trent is bent at the waist, inspecting something lying beneath the stairs when his cell phone rings. Ava's wails rise from the baby monitor, but Marley keeps both eyes on her husband as he lifts the earring from the floor.

"*Sheriff?*" whispers Trent, hand shaking as he presses the phone to his ear. "Y-yes, we're home."

Marley stays back, not wanting to hear whatever it is Trent's about to stay next.

"Bill?" Trent puts a hand to his mouth. "He's gone? *Where* . . . What happened?"

Marley remembers the birthday party where Lorna received the earrings, the way she'd smiled when she'd opened the gift from her father. The feather disappears as Trent clenches his fist and falls to his knees.

"He's been shot?" Trent straightens, glancing over his shoulder. "Wait . . . There's blood here, on the steps. No, not much, but—"

Marley runs to her husband and puts both hands on his back. The phone falls, landing screen up on the hardwood floors, the place where the earring had been only moments before. Timmons's voice crackles on the other line, loud enough Marley can hear it: "Stay put, Coach. I'm headed your way."

37.

The door give a little when Lorna hit it. Orange light shine through. Always orange light from a trailer, never clean white light like back at Coach house. Lorna standing there, looking so different than anything out here by the river. Almost turn around, take off back down the road again, but then Creesha open the door looking like microwaved hell. Hair grown out, titties hanging low in a white tank top.

"Don't be bringing no shit here," say Creesha, still halfway behind the door, like she don't see the blood all over my shirt, don't see the way Lorna holding me up.

I don't say nothing.

"Your momma already brought enough."

Creesha open the door all the way. Little Brother holding tight to her left arm. Her baby girl Neesy, all eye-balls and blue veins, hanging from the other side.

"Don't got nowhere else to go," I say and the words taste like rust in my mouth.

"No shit."

"Where Jesse?"

"Where the fuck you think?"

"Already?"

"Already my ass. Time don't matter, Billy, not no more."

She move back. It the closest thing we gonna get to an invitation. Lorna step through first and I follow her in. All that blood I lost, the blood I'm still losing, scream in my veins as the trailer close in around us.

Mounted head of a ten-point buck Jesse shot when he's fourteen hang over the TV. Something been at it, though. Missing fur on one side, pink plastic shining through. Beer cans thick on the floor. Stink too, like it always do. Like somebody pissed in the air duct. But this a different stink, even I can smell it. Smell like a drunk bear sleeping back there somewhere. You ain't never seen a man turn evil like my brother Jesse when he get bad into his drinking. I know he back there, passed out, and it ain't even ten o'clock yet.

Forget about Lorna for a second. That how bad it is. Forget how she had to hold me up as we made the walk over.

"Who's the bitch?" say Creesha.

"Excuse me?" say Lorna.

"Ain't no bitch," I say.

"What you bring her here for?"

"Told you already."

"Know why you come out here."

Starting to think Cree must be blind. No way she don't see the blood on my arm. But then Lorna step forward a little, like she trying to make sense of the trailer and that deer mount. And I realize Creesha probably ain't even looked at me once, too worried about Lorna.

"You do it?" Cree say, and still don't look at me, bouncing Neesy up and down.

Something stir in me. Lorna take a step at Creesha, probably just wanting to talk, but Creesha like me. She ain't never been one for talking.

"You got something to say to me?" say Creesha and toss both babies on the couch. Little Brother eyes don't change, a flat stare, like he seen it all before. And then Creesha start popping her neck, coming at Lorna, a look on her face like she all talked out.

I move fast, as fast as I can with that hole in my shoulder, and grab Creesha by the arm before she do something stupid. That it, nothing else. She don't need to be getting all her nasty on Lorna. But the way Creesha start screaming, you think I hit her.

"Don't you touch me!"

"*Creesha*," I say, but it don't matter.

Neesy crying now.

Little Brother silent as stone.

"No fucking way," say Creesha. "Not after what you done to me already. Big-time Billy, first time you seen Neesy, in what, two months?"

"Football," I say and the word catch in my throat. "It's football season."

"Look to me like your season's *done.*"

"Ain't like that, Cree."

"That hit a nerve? Don't matter I'm living out in this shit-pile with your fuck-tard brother? But Creesha go to talking about football and now big-time Billy got his panties in a wad."

I stare hard into Creesha eyes. I can still see her—what's left a her—in them eyes. See her in her cheerleading suit, back before Neesy come along. Creesha weren't cheer captain, but she could still put on a show. This'd be her senior year if she ain't dropped out when she had that baby. Neesy Jesse baby, though. Tell by her ears. Got ears look like car doors standing wide open. Jesse ears. All that left of old Creesha in her eyes, everything else been sucked away by Neesy, run over by Jesse and the trailer.

"Creesha," I say, holding it down, "*don't.*"

"Creesha, don't?" she say. "Don't what? Just like you momma—sorry as shit. Bringing your little brother out here when shit get real cause she don't know how else to handle it."

"Creesha," I say, looking at Lorna now. She just standing there, mouth open like she wanna talk but she starting to realize them fancy books don't got the answer for everything. This all a mistake, anyway. The river, the bluffs—they better than this. Anything better than this.

"What?" say Creesha.

I'm about to tell her, just shoot her straight, when Lorna step forward and say, "Billy's hurt. He's been—"

"No shit," Creesha say. "You think I ain't seen that blood?"

Lorna mouth move but no words come out.

"You think I ain't heard what everybody been saying? What they think Billy done? And if you don't think I know what kinda shit gonna follow him out to this trailer, well, you just as dumb as you look."

Everything Creesha say make sense. You don't stir your own shit. I get that. That's why I don't say nothing about how it was Rome that shot me. Her own brother, her own blood. It don't matter, I know that much. But Lorna, the way her fists balling up, the way her nose crinkling—she don't got a clue.

"We gone, alright?" I say before Lorna say something stupid. "That what you want, Cree? We'll go."

"You can take you little retard brother too."

I bite my cheek. Hold it down, Billy Lowe. LaCreesha Montgomery ain't never been worth your time.

"Cain't take Little Brother," I say and grab Lorna hand.

Lorna squeeze my fingers and say, "What about your shoulder?"

"It alright," I whisper. "Let's go."

And that the thing that start Creesha hollering again, of all the damn things, a whisper.

"Talking sweet to this bitch? Talking like you should be talking to Neesy. She right there, Billy," say Creesha, pointing to her baby girl but she really pointing at herself. "She right there. Talk to her. Talk to you daughter."

"She ain't mine, Cree," I say, still holding Lorna finger, and then she pull away.

"Your *daughter*?" say Lorna and cock her head to the side, just like Creesha's.

"Shit," say Creesha, smiling. "He ain't told you? Look at Neesy's ears, got big-time Billy ears."

I'm almost to the door, almost out, and Lorna still standing back there, like she don't wanna go now, but then she see what we leaving behind, see Creesha and bug-eyed Neesy with that little ponytail sticking straight off the top her head, and Lorna don't say nothing cause there ain't no words. She turn to follow me out when Creesha start screaming.

"*Jesse!* Jesse, wake you ass up. Get in here!"

Just about to run again, just about to tear off into the night, back to the river hard and fast, when I hear Jesse—oldest of the Lowe boys, the one Momma actually tried to get right and that been his problem all along.

"Bill Junior?" he say, his voice like bone on bone.

I stop. Don't wanna see what's become a Jesse, what the trailer and the drink turned him into tonight. Feel the blood screaming again, screaming cause it know we back close to where it all started. I try to close the door but a empty bottle wedged in there. Don't matter if the door closed or not, we stuck here now. I reach out for Lorna with my good hand, but she standing on her own, straightening her dress. Don't got to turn to know Jesse eyes on her, scanning every inch a Lorna, everything that Creesha was but ain't no more.

38.

There's a window of time before Timmons arrives where Trent and Marley wait. Trent never leaves the living room, staying close to the blood, still holding tight to his oldest daughter's earring. Marley stands behind her husband. She doesn't want to see his face. It might make her think the same things he's thinking, and Marley must remain calm, focused. There is no need to become frantic. No need to worry, yet.

Ava's cries echo across the void. Marley pictures herself going to get her. She can almost feel her daughter's warmth, the softness of her skin, but Marley fears what Ava would feel in her mother's touch and turns away, heading for the kitchen instead.

Standing at the sink, Marley looks out the window and into the backyard. The fiery-leaved maples are cast a dull gray in the streetlights, hanging like afterthoughts in the dark of the night. A swing set that was there when they bought the house cuts through the shadows, bent and wobbly. The chains catch and drift in the breeze. The movement draws Marley's eye. She blinks, and then she sees her.

A woman stands at the edge of the tree line, her face hidden beneath the dim-lit maple limbs. Marley knows who it is, despite the distance and the dark. The kitchen door creaks as it opens.

Dead leaves crunch underfoot as Marley takes slow steps toward the woman. The shadows peel away. Marley has seen Tina at the games, but she's never talked to her. She looks different up close. Worse.

"Give me one reason I shouldn't call the cops," Marley says, knowing Timmons is already on his way.

"I'm Billy's momma."

"I know. What are you doing here?"

Tina says nothing, just stands there, holding one arm at her elbow, swaying side to side.

"Why did you come to my house?"

"Had a talk with Timmons earlier. Billy did too, but then he ran. I's standing right there when—"

Tina stops and gazes up to the sky. The underside of her neck looks younger than the rest of her face. Marley tries to assign her an age, but there are no numbers that can describe the years Tina Lowe has endured.

"When Billy ran . . ." Tina says, still with her eyes to the sky. "When that Black cop shot my boy in the back, I's standing right there. It didn't stop him, though. Didn't stop my Billy."

"You think he came here?" Marley says. "That's what you're saying?"

"Naw, Billy too smart for that. I just couldn't figure out where I needed to go. Started walking down the road, following the sidewalks without really thinking. Guess my feet brought me here. You know? Then I saw Coach funny car in the driveway. You don't see many them little electric cars around Denton."

"You've already spoken to the sheriff?" Marley says, and Tina looks down from the sky, past Marley to the house, ear cocked like she's listening for something.

"Your baby crying in there?"

Marley doesn't turn from Tina's eyes, staring straight back at her.

"Sometime it good to just let them cry," Tina says. "How old is it?"

"She's almost two."

"Got me one a little older than that. Another boy."

A breeze picks up and blows Tina's stringy hair across her cheeks. It's cold, but she wears only a ratty sweatshirt, jeans. Marley notices a small scar beneath her left eye, the skin waxy and white, almost a perfect circle.

"Didn't really tell Timmons the whole story when I's in there," Tina says, pushing her hair behind her ear. "Don't trust no cops."

"The whole story?"

"Billy a good kid. In his heart he really is. He just don't take no shit. Cain't blame him for that."

The urge to reach out and touch the woman tugs at Marley, but instead she says, "Trent thinks Billy might be able to get a football scholarship."

Tina laughs as a semitruck downshifts somewhere out on a highway in the dark, a low, grating sound. "Ain't nobody talking about no scholarship, Mrs. Powers. We just trying to survive."

"Survive?"

"Yeah, me and my boys. Sometime it ain't even death you got to worry about."

"What could be worse than death?"

"If you don't know already," Tina's lips barely move, "then don't go asking."

For a while the women are silent. Tina leans forward, putting her left hand on the rusted bars of the swing set. Her thumb dangles out around it, tomato-red paint cracking along the smoke-yellowed nail.

"Just trying to help my Billy," Tina says and lets go of the bar.

"Help him? What do you mean?"

"Don't make it more than it got to be."

Marley waits a few moments, hand going to her chin, like she's actually considering the warning, before she says, "You mentioned Trent's 'funny' car earlier?"

Tina shoots Marley a look she's honed over the years, sharp enough to cut most women.

"Please," Marley says, unfazed. "You can talk to me."

"Just worried about my Billy."

"I would be too."

Tina stiffens.

"We know," Marley says. "We know what Billy did."

Tina's eyes narrow. She takes a breath before she says, "And you ain't said nothing?"

Marley gives only the slightest shake of her head.

Tina pulls a greasy strand of hair down from her ear and begins gnawing on it. "Well, I got me a story, too," she says, voice cracking, the harsh look from before replaced now with uncertainty.

"Your story," Marley says, just as Ava lets out a scream from inside the house, so deep, so guttural, it's as if the child knows what her mother is about to say. "How does it end?"

A siren wails in the distance and dogs howl. Tina's eyes go to the road.

"If I was you," Marley says, "if this was my story, and Billy was my child, I would make sure it had a happy ending. I would do anything I could to protect my family."

The siren grows louder. The maple leaves glow blue in the lights from the road.

Tina says, "Anything?"

Marley turns to the sounds and the lights, watching as Timmons's police cruiser pulls into the front drive. Ava's still wailing from inside the house, but her cries are softer now, like maybe she's given up.

"Yes," Marley says, still facing the road. "*Anything.*"

When she finally turns back to the swing set, Tina is gone, replaced now by Trent, standing in the door that leads to the kitchen. "Mar? Who were you talking to?"

"I was talking to"—Marley's eyes scan the backyard—"to myself."

"Oh," says Trent, clearing his throat. "Okay. Timmons is here. He has some questions about Lorna."

Marley can make no sense of her husband's words, eyes still scanning the shadowy maples. There's a woman standing in the tree line. It might be Tina. It might not. It might be any woman in the world. Marley sees that now. A connection has been made, a bond formed through the labor of their love, a hurt only mothers know.

"Did you hear me?" Trent says. "He's here. We need to . . ."

An impulse minnows its way through Marley's blood: the thought of running to Tina and telling her everything.

Instead, she stuffs her hands into her pockets. She's cold now, a different sort of chill. Almost numb.

"I'm not ready to come inside," Marley says, turning to her husband. "I need a minute, okay?"

"But," Trent stammers, "Ava's awake. She's still crying, and Lorna is—"

"I know." Marley looks away. "I'll only be a moment."

A few seconds pass. Marley can feel Trent's eyes, the way he stares at her some nights in bed, when he thinks she's asleep but she isn't. Trent mutters something Marley can't quite make out. He's so far away from her now. As the back door latches shut, Marley's fingers go tight around the cell phone in her pocket. She doesn't even feel the glass screen against her thumbs, doesn't realize she's dialed the number until she hears the familiar voice.

"Daddy?" Marley whispers, trying hard to ignore the distant cries of Ava, still echoing up from the house. She closes her eyes and lets her father's strong, assured voice wash her worries away until she's a little girl again, caught somewhere between Ava and Lorna.

"No," Marley says and doesn't whisper this time. "Everything's not okay."

Blue lights cascade across the house, illuminating the windows in swirls. Timmons stands beside his cruiser parked in the driveway, the engine still running. His face glows like the windows, blue then black then blue again.

"We'll find her, Coach. Don't you worry," Timmons says. "Got a pretty good idea where she's at already."

Trent feels lost without Marley by his side. There was

a look in her face when he'd found her in the backyard, like her amber eyes had finally burnt out. Standing in the driveway, talking to Sheriff Timmons, Trent can still see the way his wife looked at him, through him. He can still feel the crushed wires of that feather earring, the weight of his daughter's blood.

"Coach?" Timmons says.

"Where?"

"Where what?"

"Where do you think you'll find my daughter?"

Sheriff Timmons yanks at his belt. It slides back beneath the fold of his gut. "Piece a shit Jesse Lowe lives in a trailer out by the river. Reckon that's about the only place Billy's got left to go."

"What about Tina?"

"Tina's like a cockroach. She'll find some hole and bed down for the night." Timmons pauses. Grins. "Don't worry, Coach."

Trent glances over his shoulder. He can barely make out Marley's silhouette through the living room window, holding Ava tight to her chest. Trent watches them in flashes, a reel-to-reel projector warming up as the blue lights spin round and round.

Timmons's voice breaks the spell: "She's a suspect, you know?"

"Who?"

"Tina. And we'll find her too. Bet my life on it."

Trent is still looking through the window at his wife and younger daughter. The baby's eyes are closed and unaware. "You have my cell?" he says.

Timmons taps the breast pocket opposite his badge. A

faint rectangular outline bulges against the fabric. "I'll call you, Coach, soon as I got some good news."

The police cruiser creaks as Timmons squeezes himself inside. Trent expects him to hit the siren, expects the tires to throw rocks, but instead the sheriff simply pulls his squad car out onto the road, nice and easy, the blue lights dimming until they're gone.

"So that's it?"

Trent turns to the familiar voice, finding Marley standing in the doorway, Ava asleep in her arms. "Uh, yeah. Timmons said—"

"Really, Trent?"

"What?"

"You're just going to leave Lorna's safety—her *life*—in the hands of that mouth breather?"

"I-I—"

"No," Marley says, stepping out of the doorway, revealing an overstuffed, rolling-style duffel bag behind her in the hall. "We're not staying here. We're going to find our daughter."

Trent steadies his breath.

"As soon as we find Lorna, we leave. It's as simple as that," Marley says, off the front porch now and into the driveway, bouncing Ava softly with every step. "Now grab this bag and let's go."

"Mar," says Trent. "Come on. We need to talk about this."

Marley is already at the Prius, gently strapping Ava into the car seat. "We already talked about what you did. And maybe, if we wait around, we can see if Timmons wants to talk about it too." Marley's voice is hard and sharp, a stark contrast to the soft movements of her hands. "How's that sound?"

The tips of Trent's fingers tingle, the same numbness he'd felt after the Prius clipped Travis Rodney. He's back there again, dragging the body into the trailer, praying aloud as he scanned the cabinets for a blunt object, a weapon Tina could've used.

"Fine. We'll go," Trent says, praying all over again, recalling, suddenly, the story of Moses, the murderer, the stutterer, who led God's people to the Promised Land. "I just need to go pack my bag."

"No, Trent," Marley says from the backseat of the Prius, buckling herself in next to baby Ava. "I've already packed everything we need."

39.

"Bill Junior," say Jesse. "About time you came out and say hidy to you baby girl."

Hard to remember Jesse as the quarterback. Hard to see anything in them tiny black eyes sunk deep in his head. And the way the rest of him so big, so fat, even the trailer cain't hollow Jesse out. Eat too much, drink too much. Bet he weigh close to three hundred pound.

"That some bullshit," I say.

"Bullshit?"

"You heard me."

"Bill Junior go off, score a few touchdown, find him a fancy little bitch and grow a pair? That what you done? You finally growed a pair?"

I can feel Lorna shaking, like she the one with blood dripping down her arm. She scared now. One thing to have Creesha step at you, whole nother thing to come face-to-face with a bear. She ain't never seen nothing like Jesse Lowe. Don't wanna look at her, but I got to. I got to let her know everything alright. Jesse just talking. Turn my head. The black of her eyes huge, like she looking so hard for the light. I raise my pinky, leave it out there for her. She take it. Hold my little finger tight like Little Brother used to do.

"Ain't like that."

"Naw, course not," say Jesse, moving, stumbling around the trailer. "But I know you kilt Travis. Momma ain't never gone admit it, but I know."

"Don't know what happened to Him."

Creesha huff like she about to say something but Jesse point a finger at her. She don't say nothing. Nobody saying nothing now. Jesse just standing there pointing, but then he turn his head, real slow, back to me and smile, teeth like rotted fence pickets.

"Alright, Bill Junior. If you ain't kilt Travis, what you come to see me for?"

I don't say nothing. Just turn my shoulder so Jesse can see the blood. "Didn't have nowhere else to go."

"Sound about right," Jesse say, like he don't see that hole in my shoulder. "Run out a options."

"Come on, Jess," I say. "You see this—"

"Want you to say it," Jesse say. "Say you need my help. Say you a fuckup, just like the rest a us."

Lorna hand go tight around my finger. My head feel light and fuzzy. "I'm a fuckup."

Jesse slap his leg. "What else?"

"And I need your help."

Jesse bouncing around the trailer now, crunching beer cans. "Course you do. What the hell happened to your shoulder, anyway?"

He come at me, take me in his big, thick paws, and hug me around my neck. Whole left side of my body go tight and start to burn. All that blood I lost. Jesse don't care none. He still got power in his arms. Feel it when he squeeze me then pull back, looking in my eyes. "Good to see you, Bill Junior. Damn good to see you."

Jesse stumble over to the couch. He wave for us to come sit, swiping beer cans onto the floor. "Come on," he say. "Mi casa, su casa. Ain't that what the Messkins say?"

Lorna let go my finger and take a step forward, pointing back at me. "His shoulder. Billy's hurt. We need to get some pressure on that wound. Some antiseptic."

"Some what?" Jesse say, still patting the sofa.

"Mr. Lowe, listen—"

Jesse eyes go wide, staring straight up at Lorna now. "What you call me?"

"He-he's been shot."

"Yeah? What you want me to do about it?"

Lorna look at Creesha real quick before she say, "Antiseptic spray. Antibiotics. Whatever you have—Billy needs it."

"How about some whiskey?" say Jesse and let out a laugh that shake the trailer walls. "For a pretty little thing like you, hell, I'll even break out the good stuff."

Jesse drink thirteen Busch Light in two hours. Counted every one. Don't know how many he drank before we got here. He take the two he got left out the case, set them on the table, and put the box on his head. Tear out little holes for his eyes. Write BAD-MUTHR-FUCKR across the front with a black marker.

I feel drunk, but not the good kind. The kind where you just keep drinking and drinking, and it don't matter none, just don't never feel good. Cree went to work on my shoulder with a bottle of Early Times, pouring it straight on the blood. Burned like shit. Then she start cutting off these long strips of duct tape with some scissors. Put that tape straight down over the hole.

Jesse laughed and drank his beer, pointing like I's getting a tattoo, like that hole in my arm weren't nothing. Creesha went to bed after that. Took Neesy with her but left Little Brother.

Lorna pushing the gray tape down at the edges where it pulling up now. Tiny red drops bubbling up and running down the crook of my elbow. I can feel every drop. Jesse keep trying to get me to drink a beer or take a slug of that whiskey. No way I can drink that shit. Not feeling like I'm feeling now. Lorna know how bad I don't want that poison in me. Like she can feel it. So she take the bottle of cheap-ass whiskey from my brother and turn it up, eyes going tight as she force it down, and Jesse laugh again.

Lorna put her head in my lap, and it feel good. Lay my arm over her shoulder. Keep Jesse from getting any ideas. It like we all know what's coming, but don't nobody wanna say it.

Jesse crack open another beer, lift the box, and drink the whole can in one slurp. He crush the can then throw it at the deer head.

"Fucking Uncle Urshel."

"Uncle Urshel?"

"Uncle *Urshel*—remember him?"

"Nah."

"Probably too young. One a Daddy's brothers. He the dumbass that mounted that deer for me. Look at that damn thing now. Half it face gone."

Jesse's got the beer box pushed up on the back a his head. I study his face as he talk. His cheek fat and pink, not much different than the bad side of Uncle Urshel's mount.

"What was he like?" I say.

"Uncle Urshel piece a shit."

"Talking about Daddy."

"Come on, Bill Junior, you don't remember?"

I don't say nothing. Little Brother sitting beside me, not even playing with nothing, just sitting.

"How you gonna forget a man got the same name as you?"

"Don't nobody call me Bill, except you and Coach."

"Got to make sure you don't forget."

I turn to Jesse. He smile before he slide the beer box back down over his face.

"Forget what?"

"That you ain't no different," say Jesse. "No different than Uncle Urshel, no different than Daddy—just a piece a shit like the rest us."

I watch Jesse eyes as he says it. I can see that they my daddy's eyes. Not mine. Not Little Brother's. All this time I thought maybe my daddy was different, but now I can see that Jesse just like him.

"I ain't nothing like Daddy."

"Keep telling youself that, Bill Junior. Least I know what I am." Jesse start walking his fingers across the sofa toward the bottom a Lorna dress.

"The hell, Jess?" I say and take hold a his arm.

"Love-boy."

It kinda slide out his mouth, a gurgle. He ain't even mad, not yet. But he struggling under my grip, trying to get at what Lorna's got hid under there.

"Cut that shit out," I say, and Lorna jerk up from the sofa, looking half drunk. Then I remember that pledge she said her daddy made her sign, how she ain't never even had a taste of nothing. Not even beer.

Jesse pull free. Little Brother flinch on the sofa, raising his small hands up to his face, mouth open. But Jesse don't go at Lorna. He pointing his hairy finger at me. Hair on every knuckle. "Who the fuck you think you talking to, Bill Junior?"

"Cain't let you touch her."

"You in love now?"

"You heard me."

"Shit," say Jesse, waving his finger. "You sure didn't seem to mind when we was tapping Creesha's bony ass few years back."

"Things different now, Jess." I look to Lorna. She stare back at me and nod, her eyes telling me it's okay, just say it. "Trying to get me a scholarship."

The beer box rattles. Jesse laughing so hard the eyeholes slide down around his neck. "Shit, Billy, thought you'd know better by now."

"He's good enough," Lorna say, first words out her mouth in a minute and it don't matter how bad I'm hurting, they sound good. "My dad says so, too."

"Your daddy?" Jesse say, looking at me now. "Her daddy some kinda scout?"

Mouth tasting more and more like rust, like every word cost me something to get out. "He the new coach," I say, "for the Pirates."

Jesse nod like that tell him everything he need to know. "Sound about right. Same way they did me. You know I got a scholarship? Southern Arkansas University offer me a full ride. The fucking Muleriders. Just couldn't get my grades right."

"Bullshit."

"Ain't lying," say Jesse and raise the beer box up. "And you ain't got it like I had it. No way. Beside, you a running back. Least I was a quarterback."

Lorna cut in again. "What's that supposed to mean?"

"Ain't no white running backs, girl. Not in college. None them coaches gonna care if our daddy got a drop a Black blood in his veins."

"Daddy got more than a drop," I say.

"That what you gone tell them college scouts?"

"Took shit my whole life cause everybody thought Daddy's Black."

"Naw, more Cherokee than anything, way Uncle Urshel told it."

Jesse words eat at me like them bugs eat at the fur on that mounted buck. Lorna looking lost now, like she don't understand a word of what we saying.

"So that why you got to take what life give you," say Jesse. "I know that much. Like when it lay something all nice and clean in front you like this right here." Jesse grin and go again for Lorna's dress, but this time she slap the shit out him, so fast I never saw it coming. Jesse didn't either. Knocked the beer box right off the back a his head. Four red lines from her fingers on his fat pink cheek.

"Well, hello, Miss Lady," Jesse say, grinning, like he liked the way Lorna just popped him. "Now that we having some fun, got something here I wanna show you."

Jesse reach around, trying to get at something in his back pocket.

"Easy, Jess," I say, watching his hand.

"You scared now?" he say, not grinning no more, still digging at his crusty jeans. "What about you, wildcat?"

He talking to Lorna and she know it, but she don't say nothing now.

"Look scared. Both you do. Like you don't know what I got back here."

I stand and almost fall over soon as I do. Cheeks buzzing and numb. Lorna keep sitting there, so close to my drunk-ass brother, I know she can smell him. Little Brother fall back but catch himself with his hand, leaning there, watching. The scissors Creesha used to tape my shoulder sitting on the arm of the sofa. I snatch them up, press the blade against my wrist so cain't nobody see, and now I'm ready—ready for whatever Jesse got coming.

Marlboro Red 100's.

Fucking cigarettes. Same brand Daddy smoked. I remember that. The pack all flat and nasty, look like there ain't a cig left in there. Jesse go to laughing and digging around till he find one. Laughing hard now.

"Should a seen you face," he say. "Both of you. Y'all was *so* scared."

My fingers go loose around the scissors but I don't put them down.

Lorna adjust the bottom of her long dress and say, "I wasn't scared."

"Big talk," Jesse say, picking the beer box back up off the floor and putting it on his head again, cig dangling from his mouth out the bottom. "You got a light?"

Jesse talking to Lorna but it like she ain't never been asked that question before. She just sit there, looking at me still standing there with those scissors in my hand. Cain't tell if she see them or not.

"Billy?" Jesse say. "You got a light?"

"You know I cain't smoke."

"Since when?"

"Football season."

"Shit," say Jesse, cracking another beer, chugging it down. He wipe his mouth then stick the cig back in his lips. "Go fetch me one then. Got a lighter in the drawer under the sink."

I don't say nothing, just head for the kitchen, thankful he only drinking beer.

"Hey, Bill?"

"What?"

"Heard about how you went all psycho at the game the other night. Beat the shit out a some poor kid."

I scrounge around the drawer. All kinda stuff in there.

"Asked Momma what the hell happened," Jesse say. "What made Bill Junior go crazy?"

I bend down, look all the way in the back of the drawer. "Don't see no lighter," I say, and then I smell it.

Smoke curling out around Jesse face, Little Brother in his arms. Lorna eyes wide, looking up at my brothers, both of them. The cigarette tip glow orange, dangling out the corner Jesse mouth.

"Momma said it was a burn that got you all worked up," he say, bouncing Little Brother. The cig bounce right along with them. "But, shit, Billy, a little burn good for a boy every now and then. This one here, especially. You know he ain't even got Daddy's blood?"

"*Jesse*," I say, but then he inhale and the tip glow red.

The beer box hiding everything but his eyes—Daddy's eyes—as the tip of that cigarette creep closer to Little Brother neck. It just about there, about to leave a mark forever, like the one I got, and then it gone.

Lorna slap at Jesse but this time she only hit the cig. It fall to the floor. Small sparks pop and fly. Then she stomping on it, grinding her heel and looking straight at Jesse, like she don't realize the things he could do to her worse than what he's about to do to Little Brother.

Jesse peel the beer box off his head and drop Little Brother on the floor, grinning like this what he been waiting for ever since we walked in the door.

"*Tango*," say Jesse and step over Little Brother. Coming for Lorna. I can see that much. Jesse ain't gonna let a girl like Lorna do him like she done him. Not twice in one night.

Jesse almost there, almost to Lorna, and I'm still standing in the kitchen with them scissors in my hand, when light fill the whole room and Creesha come in screaming from the back, Neesy in her arms. Just standing there screaming. She know better than to touch Jesse when he all worked up. And then, just as the blue lights get real bright, Jesse hear Creesha and say, "What, goddammit—*what*?"

"Fucking cops," say Creesha. "Shit-bag Timmons just pulled up."

Jesse suck his teeth and keep his eyes on Lorna.

"Ain't scared a no cops, specially Timmons," say Jesse and stumble to the window. All that blood pumping, probably sobered him up a little, but he still drunk. He pull at a blanket they got nailed over the window.

I'm still in the kitchen. Everything blurry, hazy, like I the one that drank that case a beer. Lorna still standing there too, caught out in the middle of the trailer. I come around the kitchen counter and start toward her.

"Sit the fuck down, Billy," say Jesse, leaning back and shoving me in my hurt shoulder. I fall straight down on the sofa, the spot his hand touched burning, thumping heat all through my chest. "You the reason we in this shit now."

I ain't looking at him. Studying Lorna, still standing there, toe-to-toe with my big brother. The blue lights close, washing over her face like a bruise.

"Bringing this girl here," say Jesse. "Got a mind to just push y'all both out the door."

"Jesse," I say.

"Lucky I cain't stand Tyler Timmons."

"You have to hide us," Lorna say, and I know she ain't helping none. The way she keep picking at him, like watching a reptile show, when the guy sticks his head in the gator's mouth.

"Alright," Jesse say and raise his hand, fingers touching the spot on his cheek where she slapped him. "I got it figured."

Creesha start hollering from the kitchen, asking Jesse what's the plan. Lorna still got this look like she ain't gonna take her eyes off Jesse, but she still follow him across the trailer to the back door. I don't say nothing cause Jesse my big brother, but Creesha just keep hollering.

"What the fuck?" say Cree. "Where we going?"

"*We* ain't going nowhere," say Jesse, already halfway out the back door.

"Jesse Lowe, don't you leave me here."

"I ain't leaving you, shit," Jesse say. "Me and you, we'll stay back and handle Timmons."

Somebody knocking on the trailer door now. I try to lift my arm and push Lorna out toward the porch, but my arm don't move. I step around her instead, and she follow me out.

Lorna stand there, like she cain't figure out what's changed. Why Jesse gone from trying to stick a cigarette in Little Brother neck to helping us out now. Don't got time to tell her about our blood, lost too much of it already. Besides, there ain't no words to explain the way brothers fight, head-on sometimes, and other times side by side. But when shit hit the fan, I know Jesse gonna have my back. I reach through the door with my good hand, take hold of Lorna wrist, and pull her through.

"*Billy.*" Jesse whispering but it loud cause he drunk. "You know where you got to go?"

I know, and I try to say it, but I cain't. Everything hurting too bad now. Last damn place I wanna go. Don't know how I'm gonna run all the way out there. But I know Jesse's right. Timmons won't never find us at the cave.

"Eden Falls," Jesse say, hunched down behind the sofa, grinning at me like we kids again, about to do something stupid. "I'll come get y'all when the coast is clear."

Three more knocks rattle the door.

I'm watching my brother, watching Cree, standing there with both them babies in her arms as she open the front door. I got Lorna hand in mine now. I can barely feel her fingers. Everything cold.

"*Billy.*"

Lorna breath warm and soft in my ear. I don't wanna move. Don't wanna run. Can barely even hear Cree when she start talking shit to Timmons. Time slow down.

My eyes getting heavy like I'm about to pass out, but then Lorna say, "Let's go." She slip her head under my good arm, put her hand on my back, and then we gone, weaving through pine trees, stumbling over creeks, cutting a path through the woods on our way to Eden Falls Cave.

40.

The sheriff's cruiser descends upon the scraggly trailer, lights flashing, brakes squealing—a welcome party. The siren yips, short and loud. Timmons steps out of the vehicle.

Trent winces and glances up at the rearview mirror, finding Marley in the back beside the car seat where baby Ava sleeps. She does not look at him, eyes scanning the trailer for their missing daughter.

Sheriff Timmons moves toward the front door, adjusting the brim of his hat as he walks. Trent is close enough to hear the crunch of the large man's footsteps, but Timmons doesn't see him. The Prius hums almost silent through the night, full electric under twenty miles per hour. With the lights off, the car is nearly invisible. It's also skinny enough to weave through the loblolly pines surrounding the trailer. Trent works the machine like a scalpel through the grove. He's nearly even with the trailer now, scanning the front and the back. If Lorna's in there, he'll see her.

Timmons knocks three times on the door.

A girl appears, stepping out from the trailer bent against the night, skinny in all the wrong places, knees and elbows hard and protruding like pine knobs. A soft paunch hangs from her midsection—not fat, just loose, stretched-out skin, pushing against the tight fabric of a dingy tank top. She holds two children in her arms.

Trent feels Marley's hand on his shoulder, giving him a firm squeeze at the same time he recognizes the boy child as Billy's younger brother. His heart pounds in his ears. He's close. He cracks the car's window to listen.

"Tyler Timmons," says the gangly mother.

"Creesha," says Timmons, lifting his hat from his head.

"What you want?"

"Well, I's gonna say you looking good, Cree. Youngin's looking good, too."

"Cut the shit," says Creesha, bouncing the babies. "What you want?"

"That Billy's little brother you got there?"

Creesha examines the boy child in her arms but says nothing.

"Let me put it a different way," Timmons says. "Billy here?"

"What you think?"

"But you know why *I'm* here?"

"Know about Travis, if that what you asking."

At the mention of Travis, the blood drains from Trent's face. Marley's fingers dig into his shoulder.

"You know he's dead?" says Timmons.

"Good riddance, you ask me."

"Ain't nobody asked you."

"Then what you out here for?"

"Looking for a girl."

Trent's hand goes to the cup holder in the center console and finds Lorna's earring waiting there.

"You seen any girls around you don't know?" says Timmons. "Or how about I just come on in, take a look around?"

"Got a warrant?"

"Aw, Cree, it's just me. Just old Timmons."

Trent works his thumb over the earring's wire backing, pressing down hard enough it hurts.

"I know all about Tyler Timmons," Creesha says. "You was big-time back in the day. Stud linebacker, number forty-four."

"That's right," Timmons says. "And now I'm the sheriff of Izzard County."

"You ain't got a warrant, then that don't mean shit."

"Maybe not," Timmons says and grins. "But what about you? You want to show me your papers? Show me the deed that says you own this land?"

Creesha cocks her hip but stays quiet.

"Yeah," says Timmons, loud, like he's talking himself into it, strutting toward the trailer now. "How about you show me the papers, Cree."

Creesha shouts, "Fuck you!" and slams the door.

Marley's fingers dig into Trent's shoulder. He lets the earring fall into the cup holder again and watches Timmons bound up the trailer's three front steps, the sheriff already reaching for the knob when it opens. Creesha is gone, replaced now by a towering figure. Trent remembers the story Bradshaw told him about Jesse Lowe—the busted coaches' office, the dismantled cars—all the damage done by this man's bare hands.

"Jesse?" says Timmons. "That a beer box on your head?"

"Yeah, Tyler. It is." Jesse reaches up and touches the cardboard box on the back of his skull, grinning a little. "See what I got wrote up there?"

Trent squints.

"Yeah," Timmons says. "What's that even supposed to mean?"

Even across the darkness, across the night, Trent can hear the worry in the sheriff's voice. But he's worried about the wrong thing. They're out there, Billy and Lorna. Trent nods to the shadows beyond the trailer. Marley pinches his shoulder again.

"You come here looking for my brother," Jesse says, "and expect me to do what—*help* you?"

"This is serious. I'm talking about a murder investigation," Timmons says. "You ain't got no choice."

"That badge don't fool me none, Tyler. You still the same kid you was in high school." Jesse starts to chuckle, pulling the beer box down until his eyes find the two torn away holes. "Same goes for me too."

Timmons waves, like he's fanning a swarm of bees, a signal of his retreat. "I'm gonna go get in that cruiser, and I'm gonna drive up and down these back roads until I find them. I know Billy's out here. He don't got no place else to go."

Jesse's still laughing, Timmons halfway back to his squad car, when the shadows on the back porch turn to form, two bodies tearing through the night, running for the tree line behind the trailer.

Trent is frozen until Marley leans forward, bringing her mouth close to his ear, and whispers, "Follow them."

41.

The whole time we running, I feel like somebody following us. Paranoid. You paranoid, Billy Lowe. Ain't nobody seen y'all take off back there. Black as midnight. Jesse scared the shit out Timmons. Nobody following y'all. Ran a half mile down that logging road, all the way up to the mouth of Eden Falls Cave. Only thing you got to worry about is your shoulder, all that blood you left behind, and Lorna. You got to worry about her too, even if she think she got to worry about you.

"Should we go inside?" Lorna say, her voice far away.

I blink, trying to hold on, wanting to tell her about how the limestone cave go deep and got this creek that run right down the middle. How it ain't easy walking. Even if you know the cave like I do. And how now, in November, in the night, the cave get real cold. I'm cold. Never been so damn cold in my life. I can hear the waterfall back there pushing out that icy spring water, the big room where the water come pouring out the mountain.

"Big room." That's all I can say. Trying to tell Lorna how if somebody start coming down that dirt road, we gonna have to go all the way in, all the way back to the big room.

Lorna sit down on the rock and pat the place beside her. I huddle up against her shoulder. Bet she tired, carrying me all that way.

"The big room?" Lorna say. "Listen, Billy. I have something I need to tell you."

Keep my eyes on the logging road. It crazy to be hoping for Jesse, like we didn't just get done running from him, but now here we are, waiting for my brother to come tell us we safe. Thinking about blood, how Jesse know the power of blood and that why he got us out the trailer as soon as the sheriff showed up. What Lorna talking about, though, the way her voice keep cracking, it sound like she talking about blood too.

"I heard my parents," she say, but I can just barely make out her voice. "That's why I ran to the river. Because I heard Dad say—"

Lorna jerk away from me now and stand up. Had my eyes closed, remembering her busted ear, her foot dangling out over the high bluffs. I try to open my eyes but they heavy. So heavy and sandy, like river bottoms. Then they open, just a crack, and I can see Lorna standing there, kinda bent forward like she looking real hard down that logging road.

Something coming through the dark. Something weird.

The moon skinny and hooked, look like the mark a fingernail make in a bar a soap. Its light catch on the thing weaving down the road. All I hear is the dirt and a few rocks crunching beneath it. Lorna just standing there, staring at the thing creeping through the darkness.

"Lorna," I say. "Looks like a UFO hovering around out there. Like aliens."

"No, Billy. Not aliens," Lorna say, as the little car pull into an opening in the trees and I see exactly what coming for us. "That's my dad."

42.

The opening to the cave hangs dark and exposed like some yawning, putrid mouth. Trent sees them through the windshield, two mangled teeth rising from the rocky gums. Lorna and Billy at the entrance. And then they're gone. Something rises in the back of Trent's throat. He swallows it down and says to Marley, "Did you see that?"

"What did you expect?" His wife's voice, no longer warm or close.

"I-I—" Trent stammers. "I don't know?"

"You said it yourself, Lorna is trying to help him."

"But I thought he . . ." Trent pauses. "I thought Billy took her? The blood? There was blood."

Outside the car windows the world is country dark like Trent can't ever remember seeing in his life. So far from home now. The cave mouth seems sad, barely visible in the dim light of the moon. The thick loblolly pines hang low over the Prius.

"Maybe the blood at the house wasn't Billy's," Marley says, finally. "Did you ever think about that?"

Trent takes hold of the steering wheel with both hands.

"Maybe it was Lorna's blood and Billy was never there. Lorna just hurt herself or something." She pauses, her breath quiet but fast. "Think about it. Where was most of it?"

Trent replays the grisly scene in his mind. "The stairs."

"Exactly. Right where Lorna would've been sitting if, say, she'd come home early from practice and seen the light on in the kitchen. If she were trying to listen . . ."

It takes Trent a moment to realize the full ramifications of what Marley is saying, like the undertow before a wave breaks and crashes to the shore. Trent squeezes the steering wheel white-knuckle tight, fighting to keep his head above water.

"She heard us?" He breathes. "You think she heard what I—"

Marley's back in his ear again, leaned up between the seats before she drops something in his lap. Trent can feel the weight of it, the shape. He's almost sure of what she's given him. He can't imagine where she would've found such a thing, but he won't look down. Not yet.

Trent wants to turn and make sure his wife is really there. Make sure she's not like his memories from the trailer, that look in Travis Rodney's eyes, frozen forever in the headlights. The story has gotten so twisted. As soon as he came home that morning, as soon as Marley started telling him what to say, what to do—Trent did it. He took her coaching without question. He forgot his mistake and moved on. But now, Trent can't remember the truth. Travis Rodney is dead. He's sure of that much. And Lorna—his daughter—she's inside that cave.

"It makes sense, Trent." Marley's voice is cool again. "You and Lorna are so much alike. She's just trying to do what she thinks is right."

Trent sees Lorna in the moonlight, still wet from the river, and again he fights the urge to turn and look in the backseat, afraid if he looks away from the cave mouth, Lorna will be lost forever.

"Trent?" Marley says. "What are you waiting for?"

His arm slides across the passenger-side headrest and he almost turns around, but stops short, eyes still on that dark hole in the ground. "You want me to go in there? And do what?"

"You have to go in that cave and send our daughter back out."

It hits Trent again, another wave.

"If Lorna heard us talking," Marley says, "if she heard *you*, then what's kept her from telling Billy?"

The dismal tide rises and Trent's hands fall free of the wheel, finding what Marley had dropped in his lap. It's not what he was expecting. Not at all. Trent takes the black Maglite flashlight in both hands. A blunt, solid object, heavy enough and strong.

"Look at me, Trent."

His eyes pull away from the cave mouth to the large round rocks and the ice-cold water bubbling through the cracks. The logging road now. The hood. The dash, and finally, Trent turns to face his wife.

The way Marley is holding their youngest daughter, like she hasn't held her in forever, cradled in her arms, Ava's thick dark hair, fanning out in waves—it surprises Trent. He'd almost completely forgotten Ava was in the car.

"Billy is hurt," Marley says.

Trent tries to put words to what his wife is telling him to do, but he can't.

"I want you to hold her before you go in," Marley says, passing their youngest daughter up between the seats.

Ava's breath smells like Marley's down in the basement of her father's house. Like Lorna's did at the river. Ava's heavier than Trent remembers, and long, her body running all the way across the console to the driver-side door. Trent puts his nose into Ava's cheek. So warm. So soft.

"We're a family." Marley's voice tickles Trent's brain. "We're nothing without you, and this is your chance to make it right. All of it."

It hurts Trent to pull away from Ava, but he does, lifting her back over the console. The baby hovers there for a moment, squirming until Trent pulls her into his chest again, away from the waiting hands of her mother. There are no words. Nothing seems real. Trent sets the baby in the passenger seat and opens the door.

43.

Run so hard, so fast, slipping over all that wet limestone, cain't think nothing after a while. Just run. Blood don't matter no more. The pain almost gone. That's all I'm thinking when we finally come to the big room.

The cave just one long tunnel, a skinny crack in Linker Mountain. Got to go in a couple hundred feet before it open back up again. I can feel all that space around me now. Ceiling hanging thirty feet up. Eden Falls hiding back there in the dark. Cain't see the waterfall. Cain't see nothing. I can feel it, though. Feel the little drops sprinkling me. Hear it, too. Sound like the river. Like my whole life rushing out that crack and raining down on me. All of it falling in this big pool out in the middle of the room.

That pool got a ledge where the water only come up to about your hips. When we was kids, Jesse liked to go diving in the deep part and see if he could touch bottom. He'd go out past the ledge, like a dumbass, and dive under. Leave me sitting there in the dark, waiting with a flashlight pointed at the spot where he went down. After a while, he'd break the surface, gulping for air, and I'd ask him if he touched it, if he'd really made it all the way. Jesse answer was always the same: "There ain't no bottom, little brother. It just keep going down."

The big room the end—I know that much—a dead end. Only hope we got's if the water ain't as strong as it sound. Sometimes, in the summer, you can crawl right out the waterfall hole and on up the backside of Linker Mountain.

"Phone," I say but the water so loud. I try to say it again but nothing come out. The pain rushing back now, like the water pouring out that hole in the ceiling, mixing with the blood.

But then Lorna phone light up like maybe she heard me. Small in all that dark, but it's there. If I can just see how much water coming out that waterfall, we might not have to mess with Coach at all. We could climb on through the hole and be gone.

I'm reaching out for Lorna in all that dark, trying to get ahold of her hand, when her cell phone light flash over the roof of the big room, just long enough for me to see water pouring out like the dam broke. I know right then there too much water. The only way out is the way we come in.

I feel a hand in the dark, and then I hear a voice. Lorna voice, whispering, "He's coming, Billy."

A new light in the cave now. This one ain't coming from Lorna.

"You have to hide," she say. "He can't see you in here. I-I'm not sure what he'll do."

It come back to me then, whatever Lorna was trying to say when we was sitting outside the cave. Said she heard something, heard her parents talking.

"What you mean?" I say and just saying that much take something out of me. I bend over from the pain. Shoulder hurting something nasty now.

"You have to hide," Lorna say. "I'll think of something. But you—"

"*Lorna?*"

Coach voice come out ragged from down the tunnel, sharp enough to cut her off. Sound like he out a breath, sound far away, but he ain't.

My teeth rattling. Cold. Too cold. There only one place I can think to hide but it so damn cold, and all that water only gonna make it worse. I move back toward the fall, sliding my feet on the slick limestone, around the deep pool where the water come crashing down. Then I go through it, hiding behind the waterfall now, right when Coach walk in the big room.

44.

The flashlight reveals the cave in splotches, a small circle of white light working its way across the floor, over the creek cut deep in the limestone, on back down the tunnel. The deeper Trent goes the more he remembers, the darker the memories. The beam reveals a dripping point, a stalactite, hanging from the ceiling. The formations remind Trent of a church organ. The ceiling shrinks down around the bend, so low Trent has to crawl, like Travis had been just before the—

Trent's standing again, but still bent. A fear cuts through him, the thought he may never stand tall again. The walls close in on all sides, so close Trent's shoulders scrape as he pushes his way through. He emerges on the other side covered in a film, soft and gooey, like Travis's head when—

Trent pushes the memories down as the walls pull back around him, a great space expanding overhead. A sanctuary. The creek is gone now, but there's still the sound of water rushing everywhere. Trent walks faster, slipping across the limestone. He can feel the size of the cave as he makes a final turn and is washed away by the fall.

Water everywhere, splashing his face, dotting the flashlight lens so the beam is refracted. Trent wipes the glass on his shirt and the room goes dark for a moment. When he points it back to the water, two eyes are revealed in the glow.

"*Lorna*."

She doesn't move. Hands down by her sides. Just standing there. The fall crashes behind her, bubbling in a pool about the size of a large baptismal font. The place where the water goes down.

Trent doesn't think before he says, "Where is he?"

Lorna's eyes burn hot in the light, the whole cave condensed down to a single beam. Her mouth moves, but Trent can't hear her words over the fall. He takes a step closer, and she speaks again:

"Who?"

The flashlight trembles in Trent's hand, shaking the image of Lorna, hair wet and plastered against her scalp. She doesn't seem cold, though, or afraid. Something about how calm she seems sends Trent's mind back down the tunnel, out to the car where Marley waits with Ava, a similarity he'd never noticed before.

Trent says, "*Bill*," and he can tell Lorna doesn't hear him, so he shouts it a second time, his voice bouncing down the cave shaft, echoing across the water.

Lorna flinches in her father's light.

Trent takes a step forward, wanting to hold her the way he held Ava before he'd entered the cave. But she jerks away, hugging herself against the spray.

"Lorna," Trent says, loud enough for her to hear him but without shouting. "Your mother is waiting in the car. I need you to—" He almost doesn't say the rest, fighting against the memory of baby Ava, asleep in his arms. "I need you to tell me where Bill went. I need to talk to him."

Lorna's mouth moves again, but this time she doesn't speak. The words catch and bite. Trent can see her jaw pulsing, just like Marley's, like she's forcing whatever it is she has to say up to the surface, and then, finally, her voice comes rushing out.

Lorna screams, staring straight back into the light, unable to see the man who carries it. She will not think of him as her father. Not anymore.

"I know what you did!"

The light doesn't move. The cave offers no reply.

"I-I heard everything," she says, ashamed of how her voice quivers, breathing the moist, cave air down deep in her lungs. "You did it. You killed—"

The rest is washed away by the fall, leaving only the sound of the water, rushing down into the pool, dipping beneath the limestone, trickling through the creek and out the cave mouth. The light does not move, exposing her, blinding her, but it will not silence her.

"You hit him with the car. And then you brought Billy to stay at our house. That's the worst part. How you tried to cover it up. I heard what you told Mom. I heard—"

When the light leaves Lorna, her world flips upside down. She can see shapes again, textures. The holes where her father's eyes should be, only sunken shadows now. He's holding the flashlight below his chin, a boy telling a ghost story. His mouth moves. Lorna can hear him. She recognizes the sounds, but she cannot make sense of her father's words because of what—*who*—she sees standing behind him.

Billy cast in the shadows of the flashlight's beam, a rock

raised high above her father's head. The light rises up, throwing their shadows against the wall like hieroglyphics.

Lorna tries to scream, but instead whimpers like a puppy in a plastic sack, the cry of Ava or Little Brother against the dark of the night. Hers are the sounds of all the helpless things in the world. What has been started cannot stop. Not until it's over.

45.

What Lorna said—how her daddy killed *Him* and ain't said shit, got me and my momma all tied up in this mess—that's what make me come out from behind the waterfall. Mad enough my shoulder don't hurt no more. Mad enough I can lift that rock over my head. But the way the light shining straight up now, the whole room open around me. The ceiling, where the water coming out, the deep pool that go down forever, and Lorna's face. Her *eyes*. That's what make me stop—the look in Lorna eyes.

But, damn, that rock feel good in my hands. Feel *real*. Like maybe what He felt when He stuck that cigarette in my neck. Like what Daddy must've felt before he ran away. All that's left for me to do now is bring it down, but then Coach start talking again, ain't got a clue I'm standing there behind him.

"It-it was an accident," he say.

Lorna don't say nothing, still staring straight at that rock in my hands.

"I can explain," say Coach. He ain't turned around or nothing. Don't even know how close I am. "Please, Lo, just let me explain what happened to Travis Rodney."

When Coach say His name, my fingers dig in hard against the slick, wet rock.

"Think of the pain that man caused Bill," Coach say. "Think of all the horrible things he'd done to that boy and his brothers. Not to mention their poor mother."

Something change in Lorna's face, and I can feel it changing in mine too.

"What I did—what happened—it was an accident," say Coach, "but it might have been the best thing that ever happened to Bill."

Lorna's mouth move, lips puckering like she about to say my name, but Coach cut her off. "And now I'm here. I'm here because I'm trying to save him. I've been trying to help him all along. You can't imagine the sort of pain Bill has had to endure." He pause and take a deep breath. "But I can."

Coach say that line and something break inside me. Something that been stuck down in there so long finally just let loose and fall away. Coach *know*.

I'm thinking about that when I hear a sound. Ain't no words for a sound like what I'm hearing. Maybe it the sound you make when they drive the last nail through your hand and into the cross. It ain't until I see Coach turn, watch his eyes and that flashlight beam go down to the rock I just dropped, that I know the sound coming from me.

I'm howling, like Little Brother but worse. Everything rushing out—the blood, the tears, all that hate I kept inside—it all falling down the pit that ain't got no bottom. I know I'm about to fall too. Knees wobbly, head spinning, but then Coach drop the flashlight and slide his arms around me. Feel the last of my blood scream, but Coach don't do nothing. He holding me up, hugging me. Feel his warm tears on my cold cheek.

"Lorna, hurry," he say, still holding me tight. "Go get your mother. It's going to take all three of us to carry him out."

The flashlight on the ground now. All I can see is Lorna white shoes. She take one slow step, then another, and now she close. Close enough I can smell her hair. Lorna foot stop right by the rock I dropped. The one I held up high above her daddy head. Cain't see her face, though. Cain't see nothing but one of her white shoes, waiting there by that broken rock, like she taking in the weight of it, and then she walk away.

46.

Every step out of the tunnel, every time she slips and almost falls into the creek, the water calling her back to the big room, everything she left behind—Lorna remembers the rock.

The look in Billy's eye as he held it above her father's head. When she'd shown him Theogenes. When he'd read her Hemingway. The way the water felt that night at the river before they came to the dam. Lorna thought she had changed Billy, but now she isn't sure.

Up ahead, the cave mouth appears, a faint outline, calling to her. She runs out of the darkness and into the light. The night air is crisp on Lorna's face, so different from the cold damp of the cave. Her mother sits in the driver's seat of the Prius. The window rolls down.

"Hurry, Lorna, *hurry*," Marley hisses. "Get in the car."

Standing there, not far removed from the cave mouth, a thought comes to Lorna, a sound. The pop that rock made when it hit the limestone and cracked.

Billy had dropped the rock.

It's enough to get her moving again, turning for the cave, but then she sees movement in the backseat of the car. The realization that Ava—her baby sister, barely two years old—has been brought into the depths of this mess, stops Lorna from going any farther.

"Y-you brought Ava?"

"Lorna, listen—"

"Dad sent me out here to get you. He said it would take all three of us to get Billy out of that cave. He's hurt, Mom. He's . . ."

The Prius clicks on. Marley puts both hands on the wheel and turns her head toward the windshield. "Get in the car, Lorna."

Lorna straightens.

"You, me, and Ava," Marley says, eyes darting down the old logging road. "That's all that matters now. Don't you realize what your father has done?"

Lorna's back in the living room again, sitting high on the stairs, listening to her parents whispering in the kitchen. "It-it was an accident."

"Maybe it was," Marley says, "but do you know what your father's doing now?"

Lorna feels the cave mouth behind her. From a distance, it seems smaller somehow, like it's closing in. "He's helping Billy."

"No," Marley says. "He's saving our family."

The cave mouth opens and swallows Lorna whole. She's down deep in the wet black, sinking beneath the water, feet screaming to run again when a shape forms in the distance, coming their way.

"*Lorna*," Marley snaps, eyeing the man in the road. "Get in the car. *Now*."

The light from the moon doesn't reveal the details of the

shadowy figure, stopped at the edge of the tree line, like he's studying the car and the women.

"*Lorna*. I'm not telling you—"

The back door opens and closes as Lorna slides in, right next to her baby sister, sound asleep with her mouth hanging open.

"Who is it?" Lorna whispers, leaning up between the front seats.

"Do you want to stick around and find out?"

Before Lorna can answer, there are four sharp clicks, the doors locking, and then the Prius jerks forward.

"Stop!" Lorna screams. "Jesus, Mom! *Wait*. We can't just leave—"

Marley slaps the wheel and slams on the brakes, shooting Lorna up over the console. Her forehead smacks the dash. Warm blood runs down between her eyes. Lorna fights to ignore the pain and takes hold of the wheel, turning toward her mother. "I won't let you leave them," she whispers. "I can't."

The man in the distance steps out of the tree line, heading their way again.

"You can and you will," Marley says. "You don't have a choice."

Her mother's words scrape at the walls Lorna has built, the ideals of her youth. She squeezes the steering wheel tighter, holding Marley at bay for a short while longer. She scans her memory—all the books she's read—for the right answer, something she can say that will make sense of this, but there is only the rock left broken on the cold cave floor. Blood drips from Lorna's forehead into her eyes. The world goes cloudy, and finally, she lets go of the wheel.

The fancy woman's words had burned their way into Tina's brain: "*I would do anything I could to protect my family.*" Tina walked away from that two-story house without thinking, her feet leading her back to a place she knew. Across creeks and rocks and through mud puddles. Thrown-away mattresses in brush piles by the road. The farther Tina got from the fancy woman's house, the more it felt like home.

Standing at a crossroads now, Tina realizes her feet have taken her to the river. She's nearly walked all the way to Jesse's trailer instead of her own. The road to the right will take her there, to the place where her oldest son lives. To the left, though, the road leads out to the deep woods. The Ozarks, sprawling and wild. Tina has cousins who live in the hills. She imagines holing up there for a while and letting this ugly mess blow over.

Tina wishes for a sign, something to show her the way. She tries to remember Billy. She can just make out the shape of him, running, breaking through the line, sprinting down the field, all of Denton thundering in his wake. And then the lights appear, faint at first but growing brighter as a car barrels down the road.

47.

Coach don't never let me go. That flashlight still on the ground, pointing over at the fall, throwing shadows from the water against the cave walls. Coach just keep holding me, waiting for Lorna to come back with Mrs. Powers. I cain't move. Probably couldn't even sit up if Coach weren't holding me so tight. His body jerk, real hard, like Little Brother do sometime when he throwing a fit and cain't stop crying.

The rock I dropped sit broken in the light. Like me. Two pieces. The good Billy and the bad. The boy I used to be? He'd a brought that rock down on Coach head before he ever got the chance to explain anything. Coach said he trying to "save" me. Coach don't know it, but them words what saved him.

Cain't see Coach, just feel him, still holding on to me. We out the light, sitting in the cave shadows, waiting. Coach body jerk one more time, hard, and then it like he all done waiting. Standing up now, taking me in his arms. Coach stronger than I thought he was, and now I'm thinking, Why'd he send Lorna to get help when he could carry me on his own?

My brain go fuzzy and the world blur. Don't feel like

nothing at all. Feel like I'm floating. Then Coach say my daddy's name.

"Bill? Can you hear me?"

Cain't talk. Can barely think straight. Try to nod my head, but even that much send a red line down my neck and into my shoulder.

"I want you to know that everything I said," he say, going on talking like it don't matter whether I can hear him or not, "everything I've done—it has all been for you."

The light all over me now, and I start thinking maybe Coach picked the flashlight up and we headed back down the tunnel already—maybe we getting out of here—but then I feel the water.

"When I saw you hit that man, when I saw him fall, I understood exactly what you were doing, Bill. I felt your pain."

The water so cold, and it just keep getting deeper. Feel like I'm outside my body, looking down on the big room as Coach wading into that pool with some boy in his arms, the other Billy, the one I ain't no more.

"I want you to know the truth, Bill."

The water all around my head. Coach arms the only things holding me up.

"I saw Travis crawling in the road. I turned the wheel and I—" Coach voice crack. I feel it in his arms too, and I jerk my hands up, pawing at his shirt, trying to hold on. Coach push my hands away. "I went straight for him, Bill. I saw him but I did not stop. It was the only way."

The waterfall crashing so close it getting in my mouth, my eyes. All I can see is Coach chin, looking up to the ceiling where it all come out, like he trying to look on through to the sky.

"And this, what I'm doing here, this will make it right," Coach say, his voice broken now. "Confess and repent. Turn away from your sins, Bill, and never look back. That's the only way."

Coach slide one hand out from behind my back and my head go under. He catch it with his other hand, holding me by my neck. I don't say nothing, but my heart howling, telling me to run.

"I dragged his body into the trailer. I took your mother's skillet from the cabinet and I—"

His body do that jerking thing again, like he cain't say no more. Hearing what he saying, I don't want him to say no more.

"She was hurting you too, Bill. Your mother, the same way my mother hurt me. She was letting that man do those things to you and Stephen."

I look up past Coach to the ceiling. All the shadows and the shapes up there, they moving, swirling like the water. Cain't even feel my shoulder no more. Too cold. All my blood gone now. Ain't none of the old Billy left in me. That boy gone. Flowed out through the cave and into the hills.

"Then everything went wrong," Coach say. "Horribly wrong. And for the longest time, I thought I'd failed."

I can feel the water rising, his fingers digging in.

"But now that we're here, in this dark place, together, I see that I've forgotten the most important truth of all. I can still *save* you, Bill."

He wait a few more seconds, breathing fast and loud. Almost don't recognize his voice when he say, "I now baptize you in the name of the Father, the Son . . ." and then he push me under.

The water come up around my face like a mouth closing in. It swallow the fall, the sounds, Coach voice, everything but his hands, still holding me under, pushing me down. Can barely see the flashlight beam up through the water, calling me to the surface. My hand move in slow motion, going for Coach arm, but then he let go.

The light falling away from me now. The water getting colder. Close my eyes, trying not to think about what down there. Try to remember Lorna. Try to bring her up through the dark, but all I see's Momma. Don't see Jesus or nothing. No matter what Coach say, Momma the only one I'm gonna see in the end. She swimming down from the light, reaching out for me. Close my eyes and the cold gone now. Feel my back touch the bottom. No more pain. No more light.

Just nothing.

48.

The woods are alive in the headlights, like some sort of signal, a sign, illuminating all that lay before Tina Lowe. For a moment, the road is not quite as dark as it had been. And then the car blows by like a storm.

Brake lights burn through the dust cloud, skidding sideways in the road. From this angle, the vehicle is hidden behind the plume. Tina takes one step toward the car and sees the row of blue lights, the decal emblazoned on the door. She lets herself imagine Billy in the driver's seat, making his great escape, stopping to pick his mother up before he hightails it down to Mexico. Her tears taste like the ocean.

"Tina?" Sheriff Timmons says. "The hell you doing out here?"

Tina takes hold of the police cruiser's side mirror, bracing herself.

"You found him? You got my Billy?"

"Not yet, but I ain't going nowhere till I do."

Tina reaches through the passenger-side window and pops open the door.

"Shit, Tina. Can't give you no ride."

She can see Billy's face again, out on that field where he was stronger and faster than the rest. The way he'd grin when he did something nobody else could do, a quiet, confident look like his father had before the world caught up with him and made him pay his dues.

"You ain't got to worry about Billy no more, Sheriff," Tina says, breathing in deep through her nose before plopping down in the cruiser's passenger seat. "Not after what I'm about to tell you."

49.

Think maybe I'm dreaming, shit, maybe I'm dead. The water cold again but the air feel warm on my face when I break the surface. Try to blink the water away, wanting Coach to see the truth in my eyes. I been down to the bottom and didn't see no great white light—didn't see shit—just more cold, more dark. But the face that looking back at me, it ain't Coach.

"How many times I got to tell you?" Jesse say, hefting me over his shoulder, breathing hard. "There ain't no bottom, Billy. It just keep going down."

Jesse don't even take the flashlight, just leave it there in the big room. He know the dark way. Know every bend and turn of Eden Falls Cave. Can barely keep my eyes open, barely see anything through all that wet and all that cold, but I can see enough. The way the flashlight still pointing at the falls. The way the water pouring out, hard. Maybe even harder now, like a storm blew up outside, or like the cave know what it trying to keep buried—Coach lying there, facedown in the water.

50.

The Prius flies past the GATEWAY TO THE OZARKS sign just outside the Denton city limits, but Lorna doesn't see it. She's sitting in the front seat now, head propped against the window, the gash between her eyes throbbing, reminding her of what she's left behind. The pain grows brighter with distance, every mile adding fuel to the fire inside her, shining light on the cave's damp walls. There's blood in the water. Lorna can feel it on her hands, her fingers rising toward the door handle as her mother's voice fills the cab.

"*Lorna*. Do you hear me? Put your seat belt on . . ."

It's hot inside the car. So damn hot. Lorna can't breathe. She just wants to *breathe* again. The fire rages on as her fingers curl around the handle, giving it a jerk without thinking. The door falls away, replaced by the cracked blue highway rushing past beneath her.

Marley screams.

Ava screams.

The sound of their fear is louder than the highway's roar, but Lorna cannot hear them. The air is cool on her face as she lunges forward, hoping this will be enough to put the fire out, praying like she's never prayed before. The road rises to meet her and Lorna smiles, white teeth shining through the dark, inches above the asphalt, hovering there until a hand wraps tight around her wrist, yanking her up as the Prius skids to a stop.

The world is alive with sounds, each one coming back in time: Ava wailing in the backseat, an alarm buzzing from somewhere inside the dash, and Marley's voice, soft but clear, whispering her oldest daughter's name:

"*Lorna?*"

The way Marley says it sounds like a question, shifting her pitch up at the end. Lorna turns, pulling free of the darkness calling to her outside the still-open door, and stares at her mother straight on. She wants her to see what she saw in the depths of the cave. She wants her to hear the rock hit the limestone and crack. She wants her mother to walk down that long dark tunnel and know there's no light at the end.

There are no answers.

Lorna opens her mouth, ready to try anyway, but Marley reaches across the console and pulls the door shut, all the uncertainty gone from her voice as she punches the child-lock button and says, "Put your seat belt on, Lorna. We still have a long way to go."

51.

A little bell on the door ring when Jesse push it open. Like the kind they got down at the Kum & Go off Main. But this ain't no gas station we walking into.

Been less than a day since I ran my ass out of here and Rome pulled his gun on me. Don't blame him none. Not now. Not after Jesse carried me all the way back to his trailer last night and Creesha got the Early Times out again. Made me drink some. Didn't give me no choice. She pulled the bullet out with fishing pliers, and then I drank some more. Ran a warm bath, poured half a bag of Morton Salt in there, and just left me soaking. Burned like hell. Jesse come in, then Creesha come in—Little Brother and Neesy in her arms—checking on the water. Had to make sure the pink weren't turning too red.

Don't know how long I's in that tub, going in and out, thinking about Coach and the bottom; thinking about Lorna and the way her white shoe stopped by my broken rock, and then she was gone. What'd she see in my eyes? What'd Jesse eyes look like when he done Coach like he done him? Were they Daddy eyes, or mine?

That's what I's thinking when Jesse come in the bathroom and didn't check the water. Just said, "Come on, Bill

Junior. Just got word fuck-tard Timmons picked Momma up last night."

Jesse didn't even ask if I could make it. Didn't look at that hole in my shoulder. Just tossed me a towel and said, "Let's roll."

Whole drive over I kept my forehead pressed up against the car window, watching Denton fly by. The Dollar General where Creesha worked before she got pregnant with Neesy. The chicken houses. The Walmart. All them churches and banks. High school the only good-looking building in the whole damn town. Don't look nothing like the rest of Denton, the stadium lights rising up around the field where everybody know my name.

Close my eyes, and when I open them again we at the Sheriff Department. Right before we get out, Jesse turn to me, wrap his big meaty hands around the back of my neck, and say, "This as good as she could do. You hear me, Billy? Don't say nothing."

Blink, and then we walking through the door, jangling that dumbass bell. Now Jesse standing there, talking to Timmons. Rome sitting at the desk in the lobby like he didn't just shoot my ass the night before.

"You really think it's a good idea," Timmons say when we walk in, "for you two to be coming around here?"

Jesse eyes barely open. The part that shine through the color of spoilt milk. He still hungover as hell and ain't in no mood for talking. "You got something on us, Tyler," Jesse say, "then take us the fuck in."

Timmons suck his teeth and move his head like he gonna look at me, but he don't. Just keep staring at Jesse. "Well, I do got one question."

Jesse take a deep breath, and I cut my eyes at Rome, the Black man with the itchy trigger finger. Rome keep staring at me, probably wishing he was a better shot.

"I got a call from Mr. Bradshaw early this morning," Timmons say. "Said the whole Powers family up and left town last night. You two know anything about that?"

Feel my blood run thick as I turn to Jesse, trying to see it all through his eyes, the look on Coach face when the lights went out. Did Jesse use my broken rock or just hold him under? How far did my brother have to swim to pull me up from the bottom? Jesse don't look at me, though. He just keep staring at Timmons.

"Don said the wife was the one that called. Her daddy's real sick or something." Timmons stop and take hold his belt with both hands. "She weren't sure if Coach Powers would be back in time for the game, but she said he'd try."

"And if he don't make it back," Jesse say, "who gonna coach the Pirates then?"

"Bull's been named interim coach until Powers gets all this sorted out."

"Sound to me," Jesse say and step toward the door that lead to the holding cell, "like the Pirates got the better end of this deal."

"Easy, now, Jesse," Timmons say, stepping between my brother and the door. "That's a violent criminal we got back there."

Jesse give Timmons a look that make the sheriff clear his throat and lift one hand.

"I mean . . ." Timmons say. "Y'all heard, didn't you?"

"Yeah," Jesse say. "We heard."

"She took my phone out my pocket when we was

driving in last night," Timmons say. "Recorded it for me and everything."

"Weren't that nice of her," Jesse say.

Timmons nod. "Since I already got her confession, I *can* let you boys go back there and see her, but you can't go back together. Like I said, that a violent—"

"Heard you the first time, Tyler," Jesse say and give me a soft nudge in the back. "Go on, Bill. She'll wanna see you first."

The door slam shut behind me. The way the lights are down so low, the way they got her locked in that cell, remind me of the cave.

Try to push it away as I come up to the bars. Barely even see her. Don't really look like Momma. The way she sitting there on that concrete bench, eyes down on the floor. Try to remember Momma from before, back in the stands with her bottle of Coke spiked with Southern Comfort, screaming her ass off every time the Pirates scored.

We a long way from that place now.

Momma don't turn to me, she just start talking funny, like she talking to somebody far away. "They don't never tell you what it cost," she say. "How all them pieces of you gonna come together and make something new. How this little person gonna be walking around, on its own, out in the world."

Put both my hands on the bars, trying to make sense of what my momma saying.

"And Lord knows the world ain't no easy place to be walking around in. Ain't that right, Bill?"

"No, Momma," I say. "It ain't easy."

She cock her head, like she really don't see me standing there, like she ain't talking to me at all. "It's tough," she whisper. "That's what it is, and that's what our boys are. Tough, Bill. Now you tell me I ain't done good by you after all these years? Tell me I ain't raised them up right."

Momma stand and I can see her chest rise and fall. She turn to me and there ain't a single tear in her eye, just red lines everywhere, cutting through the white. She press her mouth to the bars and whisper, "*Billy*."

Got my letterman jacket on. My bad arm all folded up in my shirt. "Hey, Momma."

"Bull come by earlier. Said he gonna be head coach for a little while now."

"That right?"

"Yeah, baby. Talking about how the Pirates in the semifinals for the first time since Jesse was out on that field."

I don't say nothing, trying not to think about how bad my shoulder hurts.

"Bull told me something else too," she say. "Some good news."

"Yeah?" I say, trying not to hear the hope in Momma voice, wanting real bad to stop her talking about football and tell her what I know about Coach Powers. What that man did and how he the reason she in this shithole now. But all I can see when I think back on Coach Powers is him lying facedown in that water when Jesse carried me away.

"Said there's gonna be some college coaches at that game on Friday." Momma's voice bring me back up out the water. "Some scouts from Arkansas Tech. Bull said they're coming to watch *you*."

"Alright, Momma."

Momma stand up straight. "After everything I done, that's all you got to say? Now you got a chance, a *real* chance, and you standing there on the other side of them bars, saying, '*Alright*, *Momma*'?"

Every bit of blood and bone in my body wanna slide that jacket off my shoulder and show Momma that hole in my arm, show her there ain't no way I'm getting out on that field, wouldn't matter if the Dallas Cowboys came to watch. But then Momma say, "No way, baby. That ain't my Billy."

And I turn, just a little, so my bad shoulder ain't in the way. Push my arm through the bars—number thirty-five on my sleeve, LOWE stamped just above it—and I take hold of Momma hand. Squeeze it hard, hard enough to make her think everything gonna be okay, hard enough maybe she'll remember it when they take her away.

Want so bad to tell her I'll be out on that field come Friday, want her to know I *know* what she done for me, but then she start pulling me in to her and my bad side touch the bars. Feel her hand working up my arm, past my elbow until it stop on my shoulder. Momma fingers trace the edge of my pain, like she trying to take it from me. She lean in close enough I can feel her breath warm on my neck, not hot, almost back to where all this started, and then she say, "You run that ball for me, baby. Don't never let them catch you."

ACKNOWLEDGMENTS

Huge thanks to Peter Lovesey for somehow connecting with Billy all the way across the pond, and for deciding to host a first-novel contest instead of a party for his fifty-year anniversary celebration. Thanks to Juliet "The Positivity Ninja" Grames for pushing me like a Green Bay Packer in *Pitch Perfect 2*. Thanks to Bronwen, Paul, Steven, Rachel, and the rest of the Soho team. Thanks to Alexa Stark for her keen, persistent eye. And thanks to David Hale Smith, a true believer.

Thanks to Johnny "Wife" Wink for Tuesday nights and Rum Grizzlies and reading everything I've ever written. Thanks to Mike Sutton for always having my back and for the letter that still hangs in my office. Thanks to Alex Taylor for telling me, early on, writing is nothing like fishing. Thanks to Jack Butler for taking me on as an apprentice way back when. Thanks to Ace Atkins for the sage advice and for buying me too many rounds to count. I owe you (more than) one. Thanks to William Boyle for reading and believing in this book when nobody else did (and for finding this contest). Thanks to Jerry Spinelli for *Crash*, *Loser*, *Maniac Magee*, and *Stargirl*. Thanks to Dog Ear Books, the best damn bookstore. Period. Thanks to Debbie Franks and Mary Anne Crews, two teachers who lit the fire early. Thanks to Robin Kirby for the close read and honest feedback. Thanks to the ARWDC: Josh Wilson, John Post, and Travis Simpson. We need to get together soon. Thanks to all the coaches who showed me the way. Thanks to all the boys I coached. Y'all taught me more than I ever taught you.

Thanks to Mom, my biggest fan, who gave me the confidence I needed to stomach the over two hundred rejections it took to get *Don't Know Tough* published (and for letting me read this manuscript aloud to her, *twice*).

Thanks to Dad for teaching me how to see the world.

Thanks to Emmy and Fin for keeping my head out of the clouds and in them at the exact same time.

Most of all, thanks to Mal, who waded into uncharted waters with me all those years ago. You lived this book as much as I did, if not more. Love you. Forever and always.

Continue reading for a preview of

OZARK DOGS

Inmate: 06-2140

Cummins Unit
P.O. Box 500
Highway 65
Grady, AR, 71664

All these letters I keep writing but I still ain't got the guts to send them. All these questions in my head. Did you think about me before you pulled the trigger? Maybe so. Maybe that's why you did what you did.

I'll never know.

I'll never know you, either. Not really. Don't matter how many letters I write, I still got to walk around this town with everybody talking about what you done. I live in the wake of your storm. Can't tell you how many people I heard around █████████ say they would've done the same damn thing. But talking about it's one thing, and pulling the trigger's something different altogether. Them bullets you shot tore a hole in my life too. Ain't a day goes by I don't feel the weight of what you done.

That little red dot's still blinking above the junkyard office door. Sometimes, when I get in real late, I close my eyes and I can see through the lens of that rickety-ass security camera, the kind that swivels side to side but only catches half the story.

I can see what it saw that night.

The tower of cars where you sat and waited, rifle in

your hands, rifle to your shoulder, and then you pulled the trigger. I blink and the camera moves on, creaking as it turns to the north where the bullet found its mark and the boy fell. Eighteen years old. And that other boy, who'd just turned fifteen, ran.

Fast.

The camera don't linger. It don't remember. It just keeps going, pointing toward the jagged gash in the tree line up Highway ■*. All that's left from that night. The twister that tore its way across* ■■■■■■■■*, tossing Baptist churches and redbrick banks aside. Dollhouses in the hands of God. The funnel cloud was headed straight for the junkyard, like God knew what you were about to do, but then it stopped.*

And that's the part I'll never understand. God knew. He knows everything. So why the hell did he turn that twister up Highway ■ *just as the shots rang out and the one boy fell and the other ran?*

Don't answer that.

And don't think about it too much, okay? If I ever decide to send this letter and it makes it past the prison mailroom and they don't black out all the good stuff, then just think on this: that camera's still out there, turning on its tracks, watching me like it watched you.

Jo

1.

The sun sank behind the ruins in ribbons of red, long shadows running the length of the junkyard. Cars stood in towers above the old man. He steered the front loader as two prongs pressed down on the hood of a rusted Crown Vic. A claw emerged and the engine block came out clean. In the distance, a hydraulic slab crunched a Ford truck like ››a beer can.

The last of the day's light caught and gleamed on a small glass bottle in the man's breast pocket. Tucked neatly behind the bottle was an envelope. Sounds of destruction crackled as the man guided the Crown Vic into the crusher atop the flattened Ford. He reached for the pocket, letting his finger slide across the bottle's plastic lid, rough at the edges. He took the envelope instead, black fingerprints on white paper, eyes scanning the words:

Dear Joanna Fitzjurls,
We are delighted to inform you that the Committee on Admissions has admitted you to the University of Arkansas's class of . . .

The letter crumpled in the old man's hands. He stood in the cab, stretched, then exited. His steps stirred small clouds from the dried red dirt. He walked up close to the crusher. Close enough to see the dark splotches marring the giant slabs. In the dying light, the oil stains reminded him of blood. With a flick of his wrist, the letter disappeared inside the deconstructed Crown Vic.

Junkyards were good for that.

Still, the old man knew nothing was ever buried in the junkyard, only lessened, reduced, then stacked high to the sky, pyramids built block by block, secrets hidden deep within their tombs.

The crusher descended again and the old man limped away. He was thick around the waist. More square than round. Thick all the way through, from his ankles to his neck with skin the color of natural leather, pale but tan. The oval nameplate on his Carhartt work shirt read, "Jeremiah."

The sun disappeared over the heap as he made it back to the office, a sheet-metal structure with concrete walls. No windows. A small patch of thorny roses grew up through the cracked earth beside the front door. Jeremiah steadied himself, the bottle quivering in his fingers.

"Drink up, Hattie," he said, pouring the brown liquid around the base of the stems, a ritual he performed every evening.

Jeremiah tucked the bottle back in a pocket of his camouflage cargo pants and opened the door. The office was more than an office but not quite a home. A fireplace. A hearth. Two chairs around a table in what could be considered a kitchen. Cellar shadows shrouded the expanse, darkening a largemouth bass that hung above the doorway. Jeremiah closed the door, tapping at an electronic keypad welded to the wall. A red light, a green light, and then a heavy clunk—the office doors locking behind him.

Music came from the depths of the office house. The trebly tenor out of place. The walls reflected the sound in eerie echoes, the thick concrete erected for protection, not acoustics. Jeremiah tiptoed his way through the living room, glancing toward the melody. In the corner, back behind the threadbare sofa, there stood another door, this one small, barely reaching his shoulders, but thick. Six inches of steel. Jeremiah ducked as he entered the vault.

Inside there were enough guns to start a war, or end one. The room was an armory, the walls lined with friends from his past: sawed-off shotguns, Glocks hanging from their trigger guards, assault rifles with bump stocks, infrared scopes, and banana clips. An M72 LAW, an anti-tank weapon, lay atop a table in the back of the room as if it were a rusty lawnmower blade, some broken part the old man had put off fixing.

Jeremiah dug in his pocket for the bottle, then placed it on a shelf. The handgun went up next. He hung the belt and the holster from a hook up high. Dangling beside the gun was a Bronze Star, a thing Uncle Sam had given Jeremiah once he'd taken everything else away. In rows beside the star stood books, shelves of them: Hemingway, Faulkner, Flannery O'Connor, even some John Grisham and Stephen King. Then there were the ancient tomes, books that held the answers: Plato's *Republic*, a few thicker volumes of Schopenhauer, a skinny paperback edition of the *Tao Te Ching*, and of course, the Bible, its spine loose and bendy—leathery—like the old man's skin. There were more books than guns. Jeremiah learned long ago a book was a weapon, and like always, he'd gone about arming himself.

There was a single picture tacked to the wall: an old man and a child, the sun setting over the tip of a distant Ozark hill. Jeremiah lingered there, eyes falling to the lone rusty rifle in the vault. The rest of the guns were clean, spotless, even the old rocket launcher. Jeremiah closed the door on his way out.

He walked briskly through the house now, free of burden, the music growing louder the deeper he went. He stopped outside the bedroom door, peering through the crack, and watched as his granddaughter mouthed the words to a song he did not know. Her room was dull despite the pinks and paisleys, the only light coming from a fluorescent tube flickering above her head. She wore shorts and a Razorback T-shirt, the University of Arkansas mascot snorting across her chest. A full-length, fancy blue dress hung long and sequined from the closet door. It had cost more than the junkyard brought in over the last two weeks. The dress sparkled as Joanna brushed layer after layer of thick pale powder onto her cheeks.

"Can't hide it, Jo," Jeremiah said, standing outside the door. "You are what you are."

Joanna glanced over her shoulder. "And what's that?"

"My granddaughter."

She smiled.

"Just think you might be overdoing it."

"Go get dressed," Jo said, leaning into the mirror. "You got to be presentable, too."

"You sure about this?"

"Who else is gonna walk me?"

Jo turned and looked at her grandfather, her face a mixture of everything good from both her parents: steel-blue eyes, full lips, high cheek bones, and the cutest little nose that turned up at the tip when she smiled. But try getting the good people of Taggard, Arkansas, to see beyond the girl's history, her father, or worse—her mother. Maybe tonight, Jeremiah thought, lost in those dark-blue eyes. Maybe just for tonight, they'll forget.

"You hear me?" Jo said.

Jeremiah blinked.

"You think we could call him?"

"Already running late."

"Shit, Pop."

To look at her, you'd think Jo was a saint, but the girl already had a mouth on her, and Jeremiah knew right where she'd gotten it.

"Cost an arm and a leg to make that call," Jeremiah said. "Hell, there's no guaranteeing he'll call back."

"*Pop*."

That was all she had to say: that one word, those three letters, and Jeremiah would do just about anything. He produced a blocky flip phone out of his cargo pants. He dialed the number, pressed the ancient device to his ear, and waited. Jo eyed only the phone. There was a silence behind the music. They were closer now, back to where it had all begun. The junkyard felt it too, despite the four-foot thick weatherproof walls, despite the armory in the living room vault. These hallowed grounds had not forgotten the storm.

"Need to leave a message for an inmate," Jeremiah said, breaking the silence. "Yeah, Thomas Fitzjurls. Tell him to call his daughter in the next thirty minutes. She's about to win Homecoming Queen."

Jo beamed and turned back to the mirror. Her hair was woven in tight braids around her head, an attempt to control her thick mane. Jeremiah knew she'd done the braids herself. A girl raised by a grandfather had to learn to do things herself: hair and makeup, cook and clean.

"You heard anything else from Tech?" Jeremiah said, sliding the phone back in his pocket.

"*Tech?*"

"I'd sure like to keep you close."

"You know I'm going to *the* University, Pop. Going up to Fayetteville," she said, pointing at the snarling tusker on her shirt. "They got the best pre-veterinary program in the state."

"I could still use some help around here. And money, we ain't even talked about the money."

He studied her reflection in the mirror. Her eyes gave nothing away, steady and focused. He knew the school would email her—he could only crush so many letters—and then summer would come and she'd be gone.

"Jo?" Jeremiah said, tugging at his lapels. "I's thinking tonight, me and you could climb up Babel and watch the stars."

"But we got the dan—" Jo cut the word short, eyeing her grandfather. "Yeah, Pop. Sure. That sounds good."

Jeremiah grinned.

"But now I got to try and squeeze my ass in that dress."

"Right," Jeremiah said and turned.

"Let me know when Dad calls."

Jeremiah closed the door behind him. He waited until he heard the security chain on the other side slide across the groove, a sturdy, secure sound, and then he limped back down the hall.

It took Jeremiah less than five minutes to shave and change into his suit. His pants were black, the blazer blue. Dangly buttons lined his cuffs like golden cicada shells. Jeremiah was unaware of anything other than his old phone, waiting for something he knew better than to wait for.

"Damn it, Tommy. Call the girl back." The old man's voice hissed against the silent walls. "It's the least you could do."

He tossed the phone up, caught it, then walked back to Jo's room.

Three knocks.

Nothing.

Jeremiah knocked again and then he heard talking, low hushed tones. He knocked twice more before the security chain slid away. Jo stood before him, the dress erasing any misconceptions he'd had of her still being his little girl: tight in the hips, the curves of a woman above and below.

"Talking to somebody?" Jeremiah said.

"Humane Society. They want me to work tomorrow."

"The Saturday after Homecoming?"

"Said it's the least I could do, since you're always crunching up their strays."

Jeremiah nodded, but his eyes were trained only on the phone in her hand. "You didn't call her, did you?"

"Who?"

"You know who."

"Pop, come *on*. I don't even have her number."

Jo held the cell phone at an angle where Jeremiah couldn't see the screen. She'd heard this speech before. She turned to face the mirror, smiling at her reflection as she said, "This'll do."

Jeremiah had never been good with words, especially when Jo and sparkly dresses were involved.

"You hear from Dad?"

Jeremiah considered lying, telling her the prison had called back and said the phones were down, but it was too late. Jo was staring at him now. Jeremiah looked away, down at the nightstand. The stationery he'd gotten her last Christmas—and every Christmas since she'd first learned to read and write—burned holes into the old man's memory. The fountain pen she'd bought herself with the money she'd earned from the Humane Society rested neatly on the stationery, a half-written letter to a man she barely knew.

"I'm sure something came up," Jo said and turned from the mirror, snatching her purse as she started past him. Jeremiah caught her arm before she made it to the door.

"You check your gun?"

Jo flashed him a look.

Jeremiah wasn't letting this one go.

"It's in the nightstand drawer, Pop. Right where it's supposed to be. Safety's on and everything."

"One in the chamber?"

Jo leaned forward on her toes, pecked his cheek, and whispered, "There's always one in the chamber."

And then she was gone, down the hall, halfway across the living room when Jeremiah called out for her.

"Yeah?" she said, already at work unlocking the series of bolts and chains attached to the front door.

"I's thinking maybe tonight you should take The Judge."

Jo stopped and turned to face him, eyes wide because she knew the reverence her grandfather held for his truck: a jacked-up, 1984 Chevy Silverado 4x4 with KC lights, a brush guard, and ribbed mud tires so thick they made short work of the Ozark hills.

"You mean it?"

"Figured you might need something mean to go with that dress."

"What're you gonna drive?"

"Thought maybe we could ride in together."

Jo looked down. "But I'm already late."

"I'm ready," Jeremiah said, lifting his keys from the kitchen table.

"*No*," she said, then caught herself. "I mean . . . All the other girls won't be riding to the game with their parents."

"Neither would you," Jeremiah said, a look on his face like *I'm just Pop*.

"You know what I mean."

Jeremiah tossed the keys across the living room. Jo caught them with one hand.

"But I *will* be the only girl rolling up in a souped-up Chevy."

Jeremiah watched his granddaughter turn and start working the locks again. Beyond that door were bloodlines and violence that ran deeper than the limestone caves burrowing their way through the Ozarks. He'd tried to explain it all to her before, tried to drudge up their history and put what had happened into words, but it never came out right. There were no words for the past.

The old man was so lost in his memories he didn't realize the door was open now, revealing the junkyard and all that came with it. Jo's voice brought him back, though, just like it always did.

"See you at the game, Pop. Don't be late."

2.

Evail Ledford watched his cousin Dime Ray Belly scribble the slogan onto another wrinkled poster board. Dime was a short round man with a scrunched face that gathered near his jowls and puckered like the protruding ass of a monkey. Evail, on the other hand, was wholly unremarkable. Average height. Bald and skinny. Beyond that, he held no identifying marks. No tattoos or scars like so many others who'd done time inside. Evail had stayed away from the skinheads and their homemade tattoo guns. The process was disgusting. The needles were mostly just springs from mechanical pencils, and the ink was melted-down Styrofoam. Tattoos weren't free, either. Everything on the inside had a price. Evail had passed his time at Cummins *thinking*. Hour after hour, day by day, Evail had paced the confines of his cell and plotted his revenge.

The television flickered behind Dime, the reception fuzzy at best, Andy Griffith and Barney Fife talking about Otis, the town drunk, trying to decide what to do with him.

"Can you explain to me," Evail said, "what exactly it is you're doing?"

The marker squawked to a stop. Dime looked up. "Getting ready, man."

"For what?"

"The rally. What you think?"

Evail rocked forward in a shabby recliner, his lithe, clean frame standing in stark contrast to the rest of Dime's singlewide trailer. There was one bathroom, one bedroom, and this room, with the television and the flags covering the windows like curtains. Confederate flags: red, white, and blue, the stars cutting diagonally across the middle like crosshairs slightly askew. Gadsden flags: yellow, with the coiled rattlesnake and DON'T TREAD ON ME printed in loud black letters. So much history crammed into such a small place. So much hate.

"Do you even know what it means?" Evail said.

Dime stared blankly at the TV, lost in Mayberry, awash in the black and mostly white sitcom from days gone past. The signal scrambled just as Barney was about to shoot himself in the foot. Dime laughed anyway.

"What *what* means?" Dime tossed the marker on the table and slapped at the television.

"Those words: 'Blood and Soil.' Do you understand their importance?"

"Sure," Dime said as the screen flickered and Barney reappeared, handing his gun reluctantly over to Andy, a disappointed look on the sheriff's face. "It means what it says. Blood and—"

"*Boden*," Evail snapped, his German coming out a little stiff. "*Blut* and *Boden*, Dime. That is what it means."

"Butt and what?"

"A catchphrase, popularized by Richard Walter Darré.

Hitler liked it so much, he stole it for the Lebensraum program."

Dime turned back to Mayberry, Andy lecturing Barney while Otis burped in the holding cell. "Why're you telling me all this?"

"That slogan," Evail said, at the window now, peeling back the rebel flag and peeking outside, "was a rallying cry for the native Germans. The Aryan race. It spoke to them, to their hearts. Some even say it led to the Holocaust." Evail let go of the flag and turned to Dime. "Are you ready for that? Are you prepared for the ramifications of tonight?"

"Shit," Dime said, standing now too, the remote dangling from his fingers. "I just like the way it sounds. It's kinda badass."

Evail pointed to the remote in his cousin's hand and curled his fingers.

"Let me at least watch it through to the end," Dime pleaded. "This the one where Andy lets Otis stay in the drunk tank and Barney throws a fit."

"If you already know how it's going to end," Evail said, snatching the remote and pointing it at the screen, "then what's the point?"

Dime's eyes tightened. "It's just nice. It's a nice show to watch."

"It's a lie. There is no truth in it."

"You know Andy and Barney was cousins?" Dime said, arching his eyebrows and nodding back to the sheriff and his deputy.

Evail almost pushed the button anyway but hesitated when Opie Taylor entered the scene. Try as he might, Evail couldn't ignore the boy's freckles and curious twinkling eyes.

"Always thought Opie kinda looked like Rud." Dime's voice was quiet across the tiny trailer. "You know, back when he was little."

"Do not," Evail said, pointing the remote at Dime now, "speak of my brother."

The screen went black.

"Come on, man!" Dime wailed. "It was just getting—"

"Your slogan," Evail said, stepping on the poster boards Dime had strewn about the room, "it's perfect."

"Really?"

Evail took another marker from the coffee table, fingers foraging through the cigarette butts, weathered *Hustler* magazines, and folded tracts outlining the steps toward pure white hate. The marker ran smooth and neat across the poster's glossy surface, an almost feminine scrawl. Evail stepped back and surveyed his work.

"Sangre—y—Suelo?" Dime said, sounding it out. "The hell?"

Evail slid the marker into the front pocket of Dime's crusty jeans, his fingers lingering a little on the way down. "Your message was right, cousin. You've just been speaking the wrong language."

Dime's hand went to the marker in his pocket. "I can handle a little German, but now you're talking Mexican?"

"I need you to do something for me," Evail said, turning toward the door.

"I'm all in, cousin. You know that. Me and you, we been working on this since high school, since—"

"I've secured an all-terrain vehicle for tonight," Evail

said, cutting his cousin off. "I simply need you to pick it up."

Dime's hand was still pressed to his thigh. He lifted the marker, holding it carefully, like a loaded gun. "What you need a rig like that for?"

Evail ran a hand across his slick, shaved head, staring back at his tattooed cousin. "I'm going hunting."

"Want me to come with you?"

"Meet me at the rally," Evail said, "after you pick up the ATV."

"My car's got a tow hitch and all, but it ain't no truck," Dime said, his face scrunching up in thought. "I still drive that old Impala."

Evail turned before opening the door, a small grin on his threadbare face.

"Perfecto."

Other Titles in the Soho Crime Series

STEPHANIE BARRON
(Jane Austen's England)
Jane and the Twelve Days of Christmas
Jane and the Waterloo Map
Jane and the Year Without a Summer

F.H. BATACAN
(Philippines)
Smaller and Smaller Circles

JAMES R. BENN
(World War II Europe)
Billy Boyle
The First Wave
Blood Alone
Evil for Evil
Rag & Bone
A Mortal Terror
Death's Door
A Blind Goddess
The Rest Is Silence
The White Ghost
Blue Madonna
The Devouring
Solemn Graves
When Hell Struck Twelve
The Red Horse
Road of Bones
From the Shadows

The Refusal Camp: Stories

CARA BLACK
(Paris, France)
Murder in the Marais
Murder in Belleville
Murder in the Sentier
Murder in the Bastille
Murder in Clichy
Murder in Montmartre
Murder on the Ile Saint-Louis
Murder in the Rue de Paradis
Murder in the Latin Quarter
Murder in the Palais Royal
Murder in Passy
Murder at the Lanterne Rouge
Murder Below Montparnasse
Murder in Pigalle
Murder on the Champ de Mars
Murder on the Quai
Murder in Saint-Germain
Murder on the Left Bank

CARA BLACK CONT.
Murder in Bel-Air
Murder at the Porte de Versailles

Three Hours in Paris
Night Flight to Paris

HENRY CHANG
(Chinatown)
Chinatown Beat
Year of the Dog
Red Jade
Death Money
Lucky

BARBARA CLEVERLY
(England)
The Last Kashmiri Rose
Strange Images of Death
The Blood Royal
Not My Blood
A Spider in the Cup
Enter Pale Death
Diana's Altar

Fall of Angels
Invitation to Die

COLIN COTTERILL
(Laos)
The Coroner's Lunch
Thirty-Three Teeth
Disco for the Departed
Anarchy and Old Dogs
Curse of the Pogo Stick
The Merry Misogynist
Love Songs from a Shallow Grave
Slash and Burn
The Woman Who Wouldn't Die
Six and a Half Deadly Sins
I Shot the Buddha
The Rat Catchers' Olympics
Don't Eat Me
The Second Biggest Nothing
The Delightful Life of a Suicide Pilot

The Motion Picture Teller

ELI CRANOR
(Arkansas)
Don't Know Tough
Ozark Dogs

GARRY DISHER
(Australia)
The Dragon Man
Kittyhawk Down
Snapshot
Chain of Evidence
Blood Moon
Whispering Death
Signal Loss

Wyatt
Port Vila Blues
Fallout

Under the Cold Bright Lights

TERESA DOVALPAGE
(Cuba)
Death Comes in through the Kitchen
Queen of Bones
Death under the Perseids

Death of a Telenovela Star (A Novella)

DAVID DOWNING
(World War II Germany)
Zoo Station
Silesian Station
Stettin Station
Potsdam Station
Lehrter Station
Masaryk Station
Wedding Station

(World War I)
Jack of Spies
One Man's Flag
Lenin's Roller Coaster
The Dark Clouds Shining

Diary of a Dead Man on Leave

RAMONA EMERSON
(Navajo Nation)
Shutter

AGNETE FRIIS
(Denmark)
What My Body Remembers
The Summer of Ellen

TIMOTHY HALLINAN
(Thailand)
The Fear Artist
For the Dead
The Hot Countries
Fools' River
Street Music

(Los Angeles)
Crashed
Little Elvises
The Fame Thief
Herbie's Game
King Maybe
Fields Where They Lay
Nighttown
Rock of Ages

METTE IVIE HARRISON
(Mormon Utah)
The Bishop's Wife
His Right Hand
For Time and All Eternities
Not of This Fold
The Prodigal Daughter

MICK HERRON
(England)
Slow Horses
Dead Lions
The List (A Novella)
Real Tigers
Spook Street
London Rules
The Marylebone Drop (A Novella)
Joe Country
The Catch (A Novella)
Slough House
Bad Actors

Down Cemetery Road
The Last Voice You Hear
Why We Die
Smoke and Whispers

Reconstruction
Nobody Walks
This Is What Happened
Dolphin Junction: Stories

NAOMI HIRAHARA
(Japantown)
Clark and Division

STAN JONES
(Alaska)
White Sky, Black Ice
Shaman Pass
Frozen Sun
Village of the Ghost Bears
Tundra Kill
The Big Empty

STEVEN MACK JONES
(Detroit)
August Snow
Lives Laid Away
Dead of Winter

LENE KAABERBØL & AGNETE FRIIS
(Denmark)
The Boy in the Suitcase
Invisible Murder
Death of a Nightingale
The Considerate Killer

MARTIN LIMÓN
(South Korea)
Jade Lady Burning
Slicky Boys
Buddha's Money
The Door to Bitterness
The Wandering Ghost
G.I. Bones
Mr. Kill
The Joy Brigade
Nightmare Range
The Iron Sickle
The Ville Rat
Ping-Pong Heart
The Nine-Tailed Fox
The Line
GI Confidential
War Women

ED LIN
(Taiwan)
Ghost Month
Incensed
99 Ways to Die
Death Doesn't Forget

PETER LOVESEY
(England)
The Circle
The Headhunters
False Inspector Dew
Rough Cider
On the Edge
The Reaper

PETER LOVESEY CONT.
(Bath, England)
The Last Detective
Diamond Solitaire
The Summons
Bloodhounds
Upon a Dark Night
The Vault
Diamond Dust
The House Sitter
The Secret Hangman
Skeleton Hill
Stagestruck
Cop to Corpse
The Tooth Tattoo
The Stone Wife
Down Among the Dead Men
Another One Goes Tonight
Beau Death
Killing with Confetti
The Finisher
Diamond and the Eye
Showstopper

(London, England)
Wobble to Death
The Detective Wore
Silk Drawers
Abracadaver
Mad Hatter's Holiday
The Tick of Death
A Case of Spirits
Swing, Swing Together
Waxwork

Bertie and the Tinman
Bertie and the Seven Bodies
Bertie and the Crime of Passion

SUJATA MASSEY
(1920s Bombay)
The Widows of Malabar Hill
The Satapur Moonstone
The Bombay Prince

FRANCINE MATHEWS
(Nantucket)
Death in the Off-Season
Death in Rough Water
Death in a Mood Indigo
Death in a Cold Hard Light
Death on Nantucket
Death on Tuckernuck
Death on a Winter Stroll

SEICHŌ MATSUMOTO
(Japan)
Inspector Imanishi Investigates

CHRIS MCKINNEY
(Post Apocalyptic Future)
Midnight, Water City

MAGDALEN NABB
(Italy)
Death of an Englishman
Death of a Dutchman
Death in Springtime
Death in Autumn
The Marshal and the Murderer
The Marshal and the Madwoman
The Marshal's Own Case
The Marshal Makes His Report
The Marshal at the Villa Torrini
Property of Blood
Some Bitter Taste
The Innocent
Vita Nuova
The Monster of Florence

FUMINORI NAKAMURA
(Japan)
The Thief
Evil and the Mask
Last Winter, We Parted
The Kingdom
The Boy in the Earth
Cult X
My Annihilation
The Rope Artist

STUART NEVILLE
(Northern Ireland)
The Ghosts of Belfast
Collusion
Stolen Souls
The Final Silence
Those We Left Behind
So Say the Fallen

The Traveller & Other Stories
House of Ashes

(Dublin)
Ratlines

KWEI QUARTEY
(Ghana)
Murder at Cape Three Points
Gold of Our Fathers
Death by His Grace

KWEI QUARTEY CONT.
The Missing American
Sleep Well, My Lady
Last Seen in Lapaz

QIU XIAOLONG
(China)
Death of a Red Heroine
A Loyal Character Dancer
When Red Is Black

MARCIE R. RENDON
(Minnesota's Red River Valley)
Murder on the Red River
Girl Gone Missing
Sinister Graves

JAMES SALLIS
(New Orleans)
The Long-Legged Fly
Moth
Black Hornet
Eye of the Cricket
Bluebottle
Ghost of a Flea

Sarah Jane

JOHN STRALEY
(Sitka, Alaska)
The Woman Who Married a Bear
The Curious Eat Themselves
The Music of What Happens
Death and the Language of Happiness
The Angels Will Not Care
Cold Water Burning
Baby's First Felony
So Far and Good

(Cold Storage, Alaska)
The Big Both Ways
Cold Storage, Alaska
What Is Time to a Pig?
Blown by the Same Wind

AKIMITSU TAKAGI
(Japan)
The Tattoo Murder Case
Honeymoon to Nowhere
The Informer

CAMILLA TRINCHIERI
(Tuscany)
Murder in Chianti
The Bitter Taste of Murder
Murder on the Vine

HELENE TURSTEN
(Sweden)
Detective Inspector Huss
The Torso
The Glass Devil
Night Rounds
The Golden Calf
The Fire Dance
The Beige Man
The Treacherous Net
Who Watcheth
Protected by the Shadows

Hunting Game
Winter Grave
Snowdrift

An Elderly Lady Is Up to No Good
An Elderly Lady Must Not Be Crossed

ILARIA TUTI
(Italy)
Flowers over the Inferno
The Sleeping Nymph

JANWILLEM VAN DE WETERING
(Holland)
Outsider in Amsterdam
Tumbleweed
The Corpse on the Dike
Death of a Hawker
The Japanese Corpse
The Blond Baboon
The Maine Massacre
The Mind-Murders
The Streetbird
The Rattle-Rat
Hard Rain
Just a Corpse at Twilight
Hollow-Eyed Angel
The Perfidious Parrot
The Sergeant's Cat: Collected Stories

JACQUELINE WINSPEAR
(1920s England)
Maisie Dobbs
Birds of a Feather